She Lived Unknown

By

Mark Moore

Copyright © 2024 Mark Moore

ISBN: 978-1-917129-86-2

"She lived unknown and few could know"

Wordsworth, "Lucy"

Chapter 1

Lorraine was woken up by her radio alarm. Leaving Zoe Ball talking to an empty room, she showered and returned to join Adele in a near perfect bedroom karaoke. A quick breakfast, a scramble around to harvest her keys, iphone and work lanyard, and minutes later Lorraine was on her way to the tube station. The messy red ink on the whiteboard reassured her that there was a good service on the Bakerloo line. As the train shivered itself into life and accelerated away from Elephant and Castle, Lorraine looked around at her fellow passengers. She made the same journey every morning, at roughly the same time, but every day found herself in the company of strangers, as a twist of the kaleidoscope produced a different pattern. At each station the carriages swallowed more people. Lorraine prepared herself for the Piccadilly Circus crush where a rapid high-pitched cry whooshed the doors shut. "This service will not be calling at Marylebone station. Passengers for Marylebone should alight at Baker Street. The next station is Oxford Circus". Not the end of the world, thought Lorraine. It only adds ten minutes to my journey.

An hour earlier, an impatient motorcycle blue-bottled around Dorset Square, then settled in Boston Place. Its rider carefully fed a package under the heavy lid of a wheelie bin parked on the forecourt of Marylebone Station, then sped away. The insect's whine faded on the air; time passed. Then the slightly open mouth of the bin began to exhale wisps of smoke into the sullen sky. The plumes thickened and darkened until tongues of flame licked at the lips. The black shape began to dance, weaving and kinking in involuntary spasms; tears of melting plastic ran down its contorted face. Its pain summoned three wailing fire engines whose strobing lights swept the facade of the station entrance. Unfurled, whipping, hoses inundated the protean creature until, in a hissing welter of steam, it burnt itself out. Time stilled again. The motorcycle nosed its way through the murky gloom. It accelerated hard into Gloucester Place before entering the purgatorial darkness of the Park Road NCP. Its rider climbed the twisting turns of its seven terraces, smoke coughing from the exhaust, and parked in the darkest corner. He took a packet of disinfectant wipes from the storage box and expertly cleaned the seat and handlebars. He peeled off the sticky backed plastic he had used to obscure the number plate and headed for the pedestrian exit.

The Bakerloo line train drew into Baker Street where it remained for a longer time than usual to allow the Marylebone bound passengers to get off. "This train will not be calling at Marylebone. The next stop will be Edgware Road". Lorraine must have heard this announcement a dozen times. The zealous flow of redundant information was the most irritating thing about the disruption to her journey. She waited her turn to shuffle along the crowded platform, then patiently allowed herself to be carried in the throng up the escalator. As Lorraine moved closer to the exit, the rider of the abandoned motorcycle was making his way south along Baker Street. He knew that he would arrive within thirty seconds or so of Lorraine emerging into the thin light of the morning. The exact timing would depend on where in the carriage she had been, how long it took her to move along the platform, the speed of the escalators, and whether the ticket barriers were open. He had allowed for all these variables. He knew which exit would be the most convenient and the most logical for

Lorraine to use, but there was a chance, a small chance, that she would exit on either Marylebone Road or even on Chiltern Street. The drizzle was a complicating factor; unfurled umbrellas would partially obscure her from his view. Lorraine was in the melee working its way through the open ticket barriers and slowly edging her way towards the exit where the human river widened into a delta. Lorraine was able to quicken her pace as she passed through the exit. She had not noticed the man who bumped into her from the side and who was already walking briskly away from her. Lorraine thought nothing more of it other than sensing a brief stinging sensation in her right thigh.

Lorraine began to falter sooner than he had anticipated she would. Perhaps she had lost a little weight or perhaps her heart was beating a little faster than usual. He knew he had prepared exactly the right amount of sedative. But it was only a matter of a few seconds. Anyone watching would have thought Lorraine had caught the heel of her shoe as she dipped and rose again to recover her stride. Another ten paces and she lost her footing again, this time instinctively sticking out her left arm, like a cyclist indicating a left turn. Lorraine sensed a slight blurring at the edges of her vision; cars and buildings in the near distance appeared as if seen through a smeared lens and she felt a slightly pleasant inner warmth. He quickened his pace so that he was only a couple of paces behind her, near enough to be able to catch her when she stumbled again. The drizzle had eased a little but it was still persistent enough to make them both wet: he did not want her to slip through his hands. He had to reel her in. Lorraine realized that she could not sense the ground beneath her feet. The corner of Bell Street and Cosway Street would serve as her Church of the Holy Sepulchre, the site of her third fall. As Lorraine began her slow-motion crumple, he slipped his arm under her and supported her weight. She had not yet lost consciousness and he was able to walk her the remaining few yards to the Honda Jazz which he had parked at five thirty earlier that morning. Holding her with his right arm he opened the door with his left. Lorraine obligingly fell into a perfect, seated position and he secured the seat belt.

Chapter 2

The Honda Jazz negotiated its way through the streets of St John's Wood and out on the A41. The day was light enough now not to need headlights and the drizzle had almost ceased. Slippery, grey roads shimmered in flat light. He drove through the tight streets to the nondescript terraces of flats above shops. He had rented one some time ago and made it ready.

Lorraine Watson came to for the second time that day. She found herself on a large and saggy old sofa. Gradually her eyes cleared of their misty smears. The room was small and apart from the sofa, it contained nothing but a television on a stand in the corner. There was just one small window and as far as she could tell this had been sealed with a painted black board made of wood. No light came in or out from the window and the only light in the room was a single overhead bulb in a dusty lampshade. It was just enough to see by. As she recovered her senses, she looked for her handbag. It was at the side of the sofa. Instinctively she grabbed it and started rummaging through it. No mobile phone; no purse, no bank cards. Oddly, a small bundle of five ten-pound notes remained exactly where she had left it, in the pocket on the inside. She put the bag down again and slowly gathered herself to her feet. Yes, everything seems to work, she thought, and she felt no pain anywhere. She still had all her clothes on, though her coat, she noticed, was hanging from a hook on the back of the door. Rounding the sofa, Lorraine tried the handle of the door; it was securely fastened. She patted down her coat as if it were going through airport security but the pockets were empty. She tried to remember what she had in them; probably just her keys. Lorraine had no idea what time it was and, as there was no natural light in the room, she had no way of guessing. The day had been a dull shade of grey from the moment she left her flat. Her faculties were returning and she tried to make sense of her surroundings. Her professional life had been spent working with people each of whom had, in Auden's memorable phrase, their own nuance of damage. She had known some very disturbed people and had seen the debilitating effects of hydra-headed mania. Because she still felt groggy, she was not, for the moment, frightened by her predicament: her life did not seem immediately in danger. She knew she was alone and in a barely furnished room. She knew she had been given a sedative. She remembered the stinging sensation in her right leg but whatever else had happened to her, she did not seem to have been the victim of an assault. Although Lorraine was breathing deliberately and rhythmically, as she had taught so many of her anxious patients to do, her pulse quickened as she heard footsteps approaching.

****

DCI Paul Wilson had, as usual, started talking before DCI Rob Martin realized he was in the room.

"There is a possible pattern to the banks used to present the stolen cheques. The sequence seems to map to bus routes." Silence. Rob did not look up. Paul jogged his memory.

"The cheque book case? Remember?"
Rob had, in fact, a theory about the case, a theory that there would be an underlying pattern, a "latent geometry" was how he put it.
Paul saw that being right about the underlying pattern was a matter of indifference to Rob. Paul watched a good deal of television and compared Rob's indifference to Sherlock Holmes' detachment. In the face of Rob's

silence, Paul changed the subject. Paul did his best to pretend he was being a bit obtuse. Like Dr. Watson.

"And?"

Rob still hadn't looked up from the papers he was studying.

"I'm going to get some coffee. Want one?"

"Coffee? No thanks I had a skinny"

".....latte on the way here?" Paul knew Rob's morning routine and finished his sentence for him.

"Do you know how we found the latent geometry of the cheque book case?" Rob looked up. Perhaps he wanted to know exactly how he had been right.

"A cashier at Barclays Bank in Finsbury Park suspected a man of trying to cash a stolen cheque. He fled, leaving the cheque behind. We identified the thief from CCTV."

"Excellent", said Rob. "And the source of the stolen cheques will be a left-handed postal depot worker at one of the sorting offices in north London."

Paul was surprised by this new theory.

"I noticed that the cheques were all ripped from their stubs from bottom to top which would suggest a left-handed person holding the cheque books upside down."

"A sort of Jimmy Hendrix of crime?"

Rob stared blankly.

"He played the guitar upside down, left-handed" Paul explained.

"Hendrix? I didn't know that."

Rob took a moment to digest the information, as if trying to recall footage of Hendrix, then continued.

"Of course, the issue here is not so much that our source is left-handed but that he is almost certainly working for someone else for whom the money is being stolen, to order. Maybe I will have another coffee. Skinny latte please."

Paul took that as his cue to leave.

Chapter 3

Lorraine's captor had made sure that the fridge was fully stocked with basics and he was bringing fresh bread and milk. Lorraine instinctively stood up as she heard his approaching steps. She was determined to remain calm. The door swung inwards and like a genie he appeared fully formed in front of her, an implausibly handsome man in a navy suit, his dark hair swept back from his face.

"Good morning, Lorraine. I thought you would be awake by now. Are you hungry?"

This completely matter of fact assumption of domesticity disarmed Lorraine. Her years of experience taught her to stay calm.

"Yes, I am a little hungry." Her years in nursing may well have had one sole purpose, to prepare her for this moment. She told herself to keep breathing, slowly, through her nose, to hold off the adrenaline rush.

"In that case, I have everything we need for brunch. Coffee?"

Lorraine could feel her pulse slowing down.

"Milk, no sugar."

"I know". He behaved as if they knew each other well. Breathe. Breathe, she told herself. And act normal.

"Can I do anything to help?"

"No thanks I have it all under control. Why don't you sit down? There is a television."

"Yes, I know."

"I am so sorry that the flat is so basic. I tried to make it as comfortable as possible." He whisked the eggs with a practised hand. Lorraine did not want to sit down. She did not want to move. She wanted to stand and watch.

"Where did you learn to cook?"

"I have been cooking since I was fifteen."

It was a curiously precise answer in one sense but in another it did not answer the question at all. What she really wanted to know was who he was.

He signalled to her to take one of the two seats at the kitchen table. She was presented with buttered toast made from wholemeal bread, scrambled eggs topped with smoked salmon and pepper, and coffee with warm but not frothed milk. This was very much to her liking. Her chef had the same, except that he took his coffee black. As they sat at right angles to one another and ate in silence Lorraine made sure not to catch his eye. She noticed that his left index finger reached down and pressed against the end of the handle of his fork and that he held his knife as if it were a weapon. The significance of this was not lost on her and as she enjoyed her brunch, she reflected on both his culinary skills and his fine table manners.

Softly, gently, he said,

"You can call me Tom."

"Is that your name?"

He smiled.

"Maybe. But it is what you can call me."

"Tom it is then. You know my name of course."

"Of course."

"More coffee."

"Please: it's very good."

"Italian."

He rose from his seat and turned to the coffee pot in one sinuous movement.

"In a few minutes I shall have to leave you Lorraine. Help yourself to anything you can find. You won't find your mobile phone, and once I have locked the door behind me, you won't be able to leave. I am genuinely sorry about that. The accommodation is somewhat lacking I know but it serves a purpose. Do you mind washing up?" She heard the door thud shut and his light steps fade quickly away. She sat for a moment in silence before doing the washing up.

Paul breezed airily into Rob's office, as he did every day, for their afternoon briefing.

"It feels as if it is beginning to go dark already; the streetlights will be back on in an hour or so." Rob did not look up. He was having little joy with the batch of papers currently lying across his desk.

"Yes, no better than half-light all day; atmospheric though."

"In the way that the smell of damp dog is atmospheric?"
This time Rob looked up. A small victory for Paul, who thought he detected an incipient smile developing.

"I am not really getting anywhere with this case Paul. There is so little to go on. I must be missing something. How is your day going?"

"Quietly. Paddington Green have been on. One of The Nightingale Hospital's senior nurses has gone missing and her line manager is convinced that her disappearance is so out of character that we should classify her as a missing person."

"Don't you have to be missing for at least 24 hours to be classified a missing person?"

"ACPO guidelines allow us to upgrade a person from absent to missing if there is any reason to believe that the person is at risk of harm or if the person's behaviour is completely out of character. Time is not a material consideration anymore."

"Oh. I see."

"People go missing in London every day. But this person, Lorraine Watson, was like a metronome. She kept time. She travelled to work every day at the same time; according to her boss she never missed a day."

"The fact that she is missing is completely out of character?"

"Meaning that she meets the definition of a missing person. Yes she does."

"You think there is more to her disappearance than meets the eye?"

"I think the circumstances are suspicious, yes."

As Lorraine finished cleaning out the coffee pot, resting it gently on the draining board, she felt strangely untroubled. She was being held captive, which ought to be extremely frightening, but her kidnapper, if that was the right word, seemed to bear her no ill will. At least he had not expressed any so far. Lorraine had come across many people who were a threat to the safety of others; Tom did not seem to demonstrate any of the familiar characteristics of psychosis. His slightly distracted air seemed to suggest that he was concentrating on something other than intending her grievous bodily harm and that intrigued her. She had spent less than half a conscious hour in his company and yet she felt she could sense this about him. She hoped she was not mistaken and that he was not about to reappear with all the paraphernalia of rape, death, or both. That would be cinematic, but it just did not seem plausible. In the murky half-light of a day which had never fully revealed itself to her, she considered her options. Lorraine resigned herself to the sofa. She must have fallen asleep because she did not hear Tom come in, but there he was standing in the kitchen area, boiling the kettle.

"Tea?"

"Please."

She was aware that she was not quite fully conscious. Must be the sedative. It will wear off soon. Did Tom have some sort of medical background, she wondered.

"Earl Grey?"

"Lovely."

"I imagine that you have tried the usual means of attracting attention." Again, his tone was matter of fact; it was the same tone with which he enquired whether she preferred milk or lemon with her tea. Lorraine did not reply since it was clearly a rhetorical question.

"The rental agreement described these rooms as fully furnished, which stretches the truth a bit, doesn't it?"

"Is this where you live Tom?"

She knew the answer must be no. She felt like Louis Theroux asking such a faux naive question. But she also knew that a soft and gentle line of questioning worked with her patients and represented her best tactic now. He simply smiled. For the first time Lorraine was unnerved, not because she was suddenly aware of the danger she was in, but for quite the opposite reason: Tom's handsome features were lit up by his smile. She knew how Nick Carraway felt the first time he saw Gatsby. And that unnerved her. Lorraine rifled through the filing cabinets of her mind. Stockholm Syndrome. She remembered the case study. She rehearsed her notes. Originally defined by Ochberg, a clinical psychologist, it described the phenomenon whereby captives mistake a lack of abuse by their captors as evidence of kindness, and as a result feel empathy and sometimes even sympathy for them. She could not remember any of the details but knew it was something to do with a siege in a Swedish bank. They took their tea in silence for a while, a silence broken by Tom.

"The Nightingale Hospital will have reported you missing by now Lorraine."

He made his preparations to leave. As he closed and locked the door behind him, Lorraine told herself to be rational and not to empathize. But desire is not susceptible to reason.

Chapter 4

Paul Wilson was already talking as he came into Rob Martin's office.

"I spoke to the desk sergeant at Paddington Green. No-one in the vicinity of Marylebone station or the Nightingale Hospital has seen Lorraine Watson. She used her Oyster card at Elephant and Castle at seven twenty this morning. And that is the last trace we have of her. No phone calls, no card transactions: nothing since then. She has vanished."

Rob betrayed no obvious sign that he was listening, but Paul continued excitedly.

"The only consequence of the fire was some congestion on routes and services around Marylebone. There were no reports of anyone being injured. It had all died down by about ten am, and traffic flows returned to normal."

Rob remained unmoved.

"Lorraine's disappearance is the only consequence of the fire."

"That would assume there is cause and effect."
Good, so he is listening, thought Paul. Encouraged, he continued.

"Do you have a better explanation?"
Rob thought for a moment.

"It could be a simple case of someone taking a day off and disabling a mobile phone for a bit of peace and quiet."

"On the other hand, it might be quite sinister. At this stage we can't rule that out."

"You may be right. Rule everything out until only the truth remains."

As Holmes would say, thought Paul.

"Well let's start with the things we can find out: where she works, eats, drinks, shops; Facebook, Twitter, Instagram, her friends, family, pets; financial details, bank accounts, bus passes, loyalty cards; holidays, hobbies, interests, leisure activities, inside leg measurement, everything."

"Inside leg measurement?"

"You know what I mean Paul."

"Of course."

Paul breezed out as airily as he had breezed in. In a couple of hours, he would know enough about Lorraine Watson to ghost write her autobiography.

Lorraine stood near the blacked-out window and listened intently to the background noise. She could hear the gentle ebb and hiss of traffic making its way through the evening drizzle and the occasional muffled sounds of conversation. The snatches of conversation that she did hear drifting up from the streets below did not seem to be in any language that she recognized. She thought she might be hearing phrases of Arabic or Turkish. This paradoxically reassured her that she was still in London. She pressed the red button on the remote control and was surprised when the television bloomed into life; she thought that Tom might have disabled it. She greedily scanned the channels looking for anything regional. Sure enough, the regional programme was for London. She felt a sense of achievement in having established that: a small victory. In the absence of anything else to do, she sat down and flicked through a couple of channels until she found something that would pass the time. About an hour later Tom reappeared.

"I have brought you something" he announced as he came through the door.

She saw that he was holding a bottle of Pinot Grigio and its moist surface suggested to her that it was chilled.

He went to the kitchen and in one continuous movement picked two glasses from a cupboard, turned, put them down, twisted open the bottle and splashed out two measures which shone like glow worms in the gloom of the dimly lit room. She took a deep draught of the wine.

"How did you know I like Pinot Grigio? How is it that you know so much about me Tom?"

"Because I am very interested in you." He fixed his gaze on hers. She took another longish draw on her glass.

"I had worked that much out Tom. But why?"

"You are an intelligent person Lorraine, as we both know. You will know, if you don't already. Enjoy the rest of the wine."

As swiftly as he had arrived, he left; the genie is out of the bottle, she thought. She took him at his word and replenished her glass almost to the brim and fell into the embrace of the near silence of the room.

Lorraine lay on the sofa for some time, the television set burbling indistinctly. There was no other sound except the occasional shivering of the ancient fridge. In her solitary confinement she began to wonder if her calm acceptance of her fate was in fact a symptom of delayed shock combined with the after effects of the sedative; sooner or later there would be some kind of adrenaline rush of fear. There must be something I should be doing, she said in an audible whisper, the sound of her own voice in the empty room surprisingly loud. She repeated her survey of the room, as if to find something known and familiar in the unknown. Instead of patting down her coat she removed it from its hook and subjected it to a much more rigorous interrogation. The pockets remained stubbornly empty, devoid of any clues. She lifted free from the collar a long hair, one of her own. She emptied the contents of her handbag and on the kitchen table. She scooped the assorted lipsticks, mints, hair clips, receipts, and other impedimenta back into her handbag and thought again. She began with the door. She ran her hands along the frame trying to see if there was a gap between the door and the frame into which she could insert a kitchen knife. But the door seemed to be an implausibly snug fit. It was entirely smooth over its surface without even so much as a keyhole, though it did have a small handle for opening and closing. Lorraine reached up with both hands and ran them down the sides of the door: just as she found herself standing with her arms apart, as if crucified, she was startled by fast approaching steps nearing the door. She jumped back instinctively. She took two quick steps back but then stopped: if it was Tom, then she wanted to stand face to face to him as he entered. Though she felt fear, she did not think she was afraid of him.

Chapter 5

"Presumably there is CCTV footage from the forecourt of Marylebone station?"

"You can see smoke beginning to drift across shortly after seven thirty, but not much else."

"Can you access the footage from my screen?"

"Should be able to; it's in the Fire Officer's report." Rob beckoned Paul to sit himself in his vacated chair. Within a few moments he had the relevant file on screen. This was grist to Paul's mill, work he excelled in.

"We know that the fire reached an unusually high temperature" offered Paul as they ran through a sequence of unremarkable images.

"There must have been fuel of some kind already in the bin. You can't generate that kind of heat otherwise, can you?" Paul quickly understood the implication.

"We need to look at CCTV footage from much earlier in the morning."

"Yes, but not that much earlier because we know that the bins were emptied by Westminster City council at five am, give or take five minutes."

"Sure. Just give me a few moments to scan back through the images."

"I suspect the Fire Officer did not have time to do this. His priority would have been the immediate cause of the fire and how his team dealt with it."

"He has done that very professionally."

"Here we go. 4.55. Look."

Paul moved through the grainy images and both men lost themselves in the concentrated effort.

"Ok, so here is the wheelie bin being pushed back to the forecourt empty."

"Stop. What's that?"

Paul looked hard at the screen. Sure enough, there was a figure mostly, but not wholly, obscured by the bin lorry. He ran the images one by one. The shadowy figure could be seen walking towards Melcombe Place and out of shot.

"Ok. We need more CCTV footage."

"I can see what other cameras there are in the area." Paul busied himself at the screen and moments later he was looking at the police map of all the CCTV camera locations in London.

"There's one on the corner of Balcombe Street. I will see if I can get hold of the footage."

Returning, Paul walked straight over to Rob's desk.

"Balcombe Street CCTV should be coming up on your screen any second now."

When they had work to do like this, conversation was unnecessary. A file appeared and Paul, a blur of quick fingers typing and tapping, opened it to reveal the grey grainy imagery of a November morning in Marylebone. At precisely 5.07 am a small beaten-up motorcycle passed briefly in front of the camera.

"The number plate has been deliberately covered over so that it reflects the light from the camera. Someone knew what they were doing. Can't make out what he is holding, but how much would you like to bet me that it is a container of fuel?"

"We can identify the make of the motorbike easily enough."

Rob stood up to review the evidence so far.

"At 5.07 am, we see a motorcycle heading in the direction of Marylebone station, stripped of all its identifying features. The rider seems to be carrying something, hidden from the camera, a camera which he clearly knows is there. We may reasonably speculate that this is a container of kerosene or similar that will be poured into the recently emptied bin on the forecourt of

Marylebone station. At 7.40 am the fire brigade were called to an intense blaze. This carefully orchestrated arson ensured the temporary closure of Marylebone station. The only known consequence of that closure is that a psychiatric nurse of normally impeccable punctuality and attendance failed to report for work at a hospital near the station, and that no sight, sound, or echo of her has been detected since. Does that seem to you a reasonable summary of what we know so far Paul?"

"It does. To get to The Nightingale Hospital, Lorraine would have to leave at Baker Street or go on to Edgware Road. I will see if I can spot her at either of those stations."

Paul ran across the corridor back to his office. Rob went back to the pile of slightly discoloured and limp files that had been distracting him for the past few days. Paul had already concluded that of the twenty-four remaining stations on the Bakerloo line, he might as well start with the two nearest to Marylebone. He set to work almost before he sat down. Shortly after five, he heard Rob carefully close his office door and head for his train back to Reading. Paul smiled to himself as he heard Rob go, knowing that Rob's mind would be turning over whichever unsolved case currently preoccupied him.

Paul's team was having some difficulty researching Lorraine Watson. The Nightingale Hospital had supplied her home address and some recent photographs taken at work; from that they had quickly established that Lorraine lived alone and always paid her rent and all her other household bills on time. Her bank account showed a reasonably healthy balance and no unusual pattern of activity; payments at supermarkets, coffee shops, wine bars, restaurants, and some online clothes purchases. She did not have a Facebook profile, nor did she have Instagram or Twitter accounts. She did not hold a UK driving license but she did have a passport. Her mobile phone had stopped working sometime after eight, when Tom had removed the SIM card. Her Oyster card was last used at the southern terminus of the Bakerloo line, as it was every morning, at 7.20. But that was all they were able to establish from the usual electronic sources.

"What do we know of her history?" asked Paul.
His most reliable team member, Sergeant Louise Tindall, had trawled through the appropriate records.

"We know that Lorraine qualified as a nurse at Saint Thomas's hospital in 1992 and then specialized in psychiatric care. She worked in hospitals in and around London. She moved into the private sector eight years ago and had been at the Nightingale for the last five years. That's about it, sir."

"Well, the move to the private sector explains the healthy bank balance" said Paul.

"Pity there isn't a private sector in the Met sir" Louise replied with some feeling.

"Well let me know if you find anything else. Especially her inside leg measurement."

"What?"

But Paul had gone.

As Tom unlocked and opened the door, he was rather surprised to find himself toe to toe with Lorraine. They stood quite still, face to face, as if about to dance. The moment was broken by Tom half turning to close the door carefully behind him. He then moved quickly past Lorraine into the kitchen.

"I know it's a little late but I have brought us something for supper. Are you hungry?"

"Now you come to mention it I am, yes."
The Pinot had taken the edge off her appetite and she wasn't all that hungry, but she wanted to prolong Tom's stay and she wanted to watch him cook, to enjoy his presence. She imagined him at work with the kitchen

knives as if he were her own Edward Scissorhands carving snowflakes from ice. The dreamily romantic notion brought a wry smile to her lips as she watched Tom assemble the ingredients on the small kitchen table.

"I gather that we are somewhere in London" she said, slightly dreamily, as he chopped an onion and a couple of cloves of garlic and slid them into a frying pan of simmering olive oil.

"Yes, somewhere in London", he replied vaguely. "As soon as the police show any sign of coming to the rescue then we will have to react."

"We?"

That was the only word that mattered to Lorraine. With his left hand, Tom put a couple of handfuls of pasta in a saucepan of boiling water; with his right hand he stirred the sizzling sauce in the frying pan. Lorraine wondered if Tom had ever cut a woman's hair.

"You couldn't pour a glass of the Pinot for the chef?"

"Sure." Lorraine went to the fridge and poured them both a glass.

It was a little after nine pm on the same dank, drizzly, November not quite day. Crepuscular and smeary, the damp air moistened Paul Wilson's warm cheeks as he walked home. Paul had already worked for thirteen hours but knew his day was not yet done. Later he would pour himself a warming glass of whiskey and begin the grainy search for Lorraine Watson.

As Paul made his way home through the darkening hotel-lined streets of Victoria, Lorraine chased the last limp elastic bands of pasta across her plate. Tom had made a fine pasta dish, its rich oily texture relieved by the grassy freshness of her wine, a perfect summer's lunch on a drab November night. In many other circumstances, she thought, this would be a wholly pleasurable experience. Tom had done little to unnerve her, but that was exactly what disturbed her.

"I wonder if you would be so good as to wash up?" Tom's fastidiously polite request was in effect an order. But she did not mind. At that point she would have done anything that Tom asked of her. As she ran the hot water Lorraine heard the door close and the double locks click shut. As Tom's steps faded, she felt as she had once felt as a teenager after a first date. This can't be happening she thought. It is merely my response to trauma, to abduction, she reasoned. It is Stockholm Syndrome. It isn't real.

Tom knew that within the next twelve hours, the police would find his carelessly abandoned motorcycle. It was time for his next move.

Chapter 6

The next morning dawned colder and clearer, the white sky higher and more spacious than the low, grey cloud of yesterday. The outlines of buildings were clearly defined and the landscape visible into the middle distance. It was 7.20 am; day's shoulders shrugging off the mantle of night. The diesel engine of the 6.36 from Reading grumbled passed Jaggers' statue of the Unknown Soldier and then rested alongside platform one. Rob Martin observed the patterns created by intermittent shafts of sunlight through the parabolic curves of the roof high above. He was daydreaming and thinking at the same time. Why was a psychiatric nurse, with no unusual habits and an otherwise unremarkable life, the one person to go missing? He did not believe in coincidence. The laws of thermodynamics determined that every action has an equal and opposite reaction. Thus, every effect has a cause. Nothing happens by accident. As Rob applied himself to the immutable laws of physics on this bright wintry morning, two unmarked police cars drew up outside a residential building in Wooler Street, about a hundred metres from the junction with Portland Street.

Lorraine Watson lived in the spacious ground floor flat at number ten, accessed through a porticoed, double doored entrance. The officers from the two cars were interrupting breakfasts, armed with no more than the picture of Lorraine supplied by the Nightingale Hospital HR department. The denizens of Wooler Street knew Lorraine well. They thought she was the salt of the earth. Lovely. Always smiling. A credit to nursing. A Rastafarian, whose plaited dreadlocks twisted and turned into a roomy beret, greeted Sergeant Louise

Tindall at the door of Lorraine's. He thought that the photograph Louise showed to him was a recent one, which was useful, but that he hadn't seen her for a couple of days, which was less useful. He knew Lorraine well: they shared a garden space at the rear of the property and spent many an evening in the summer there, "lazin' and somting." But they had not done that since the clocks went back and the days shortened. In fact, nobody could recollect seeing her yesterday which confirmed that Lorraine had not been back to her flat since she left, almost exactly twenty-four hours earlier. Louise wanted to ask more questions just for the simple pleasure of listening to the unhurried, linctus smooth voice of Lorraine's neighbour. But she had to move on. The owner of Arments Pie and Mash shop remembered seeing Lorraine walk past on her way to the tube station at about this time yesterday morning; she gave him a cheery wave, as she did every morning. It was a wholly normal day. Lorraine's landlord had agreed to meet them at 7.30 and at 7.29 a black Mercedes A class pulled up carefully and parked neatly. Lorraine's landlady was dressed immaculately in a simple black sari fastened by a handsome broach. Mrs. Nair confirmed that Lorraine took great care of all of the fixtures and fittings. She also confirmed that she had brought a set of keys with her and that she would be delighted to show the detectives into Lorraine's flat.

The tinkling of Mrs. Nair's housekeys carried on the light wind of the morning: for a few moments it was the only audible sound in Wooler Street. Mrs. Nair unlocked the door and stood to one side. She beckoned to Sergeant Tindall, who was briefing her team.

"Remember we are here to look for clues, not to turn the place over, so be careful. If you pick something up be sure to put it back exactly where you found it. Be thorough: show me anything you think might be significant." Three policemen, two male and one female, passed by her into Lorraine's empty, silent hallway.

"Do you need me to stay as I do have a busy list this morning and I would like to be punctual?"

"No, you head off Mrs. Nair. Thank you so much for your help."

"I do hope Miss Watson turns up soon. Let me know if you need anything else."

Mrs. Nair walked lightly back to her Mercedes, her mind already rehearsing the first operation on today's schedule, a nephrectomy. She did not know Lorraine Watson well but there is an informal camaraderie between all healthcare workers and she genuinely meant what she had said to Louise Tindall.

Inside Lorraine's flat everything was exactly as she had left it, perfectly set for her imminent return. There was nothing to suggest that she anticipated being away for any length of time. The fridge was full of fresh vegetables and milk comfortably within its "best by" date.

Her wardrobe could barely contain its cargo of clothes; an empty suitcase on top gathered dust. There was laundry in the washing machine, waiting patiently to be washed. Louise Tindall examined some of the clothes, in particular a pair of a nurse's uniform trousers, not least because she thought it would be quite amusing to report back to Paul Lorraine's exact inside leg measurement, but also because she thought that nurses usually left their uniforms at work. She reassured herself that there was no reason why Lorraine shouldn't have brought them home for a wash and that the trousers were probably not a clue as to her whereabouts. As her young colleagues were clearly becoming bored by the sheer ordinariness of the interior of Lorraine's life, she let them return to the cars and took a slow, careful last look around. Her detective's eye was well trained by Paul and she knew the importance of finding the single incongruity that could be significant. As she left, she noticed on the small bookshelf in the hallway an attractive volume entitled "The Castles of County Clare" and next to it a slim volume which took her eye because the title was written in a language she did not recognize. It read 'Coiste Forbartha Gaeltachta Chontae an Chlair."

Paul busied his way into Rob's room shortly before 8.15, his mood as bright as the wintry sun streaking dustily through the narrow gaps in the blinds.
"Coffee?"
"No thanks. I had a latte on the way…"
They had this conversation every morning.
"Groundhog Day", Paul reminded Rob.
"Oh yes. I remember. Any news?"
"Yes. Lorraine exited the Bakerloo line at Baker Street. You can just make out her face in the crush of people: it took me several goes to spot her, but there she is." He handed Rob a print.
"I can get the image up on your screen if you want." Without a word Rob stood up and beckoned to Paul to assume his seat and within seconds a grainy black and white image timed at 8.04am yesterday filled the screen. There she is.
"Are you sure it is her?"
 Rob thought it worth stating the obvious.
"Yes: we have matched it against the recent photo on her hospital security pass and it is as close as you can get to a perfect likeness."
"I agree that it is her. But how does it help?"
"There's more."
"Ah."
"Late last night the duty caretaker of the Park Road NCP called in an abandoned Honda Grom motorcycle.

He was sure he had not seen it in the car park before and he was suspicious."

"And?"

"Insurance write-off, two years ago. The previous registered keeper sold it for scrap to a garage on the A4 in Hounslow."

"Do we know the name of the ga…"

"We do. And I sent a unit there ten minutes ago" Paul interrupted. Rob raised an eyebrow.

"A motorcycle brought back from the dead in Hounslow and then returned to the dead in Marylebone. And the initial condition of a sequence of events leading to Lorraine's disappearance."

"The geometry of chaos" confirmed Rob.

In Finchley, Lorraine stirred from her quiet slumber. For the first few moments of regained consciousness, she had to relearn her surroundings. The disappointment of not being in her flat in Wooler Street was in part compensated for by the comforting sense of relief that she had not, as far as she could tell, suffered any harm. Gradually that sensation gave way to pleasure as she remembered the taste of the Pinot Grigio and the sight of Tom's elegant hands. She rose from the sofa that had given her a surprisingly comfortable night's sleep and went to dress and decent herself. At seven twenty she heard a noise that made her spit out her toothpaste. She glanced into the room she had only moments before left to see the figure of Tom whirling around the room with the expertise of a professional burglar scooping up any items that could be identifiable.

"Good morning, Lorraine." His manner was as charming as always: he moved swiftly past her to the kitchen checking that everything was in order.

"Estimated time of departure is about four minutes. Will you be ready?"

"Why, yes. I have only my coat and bag. You, Tom, have everything of mine that matters."

"Indeed so. Quite. Lorraine I am so sorry to have to ask you this as it seems so impertinent but would you care for a little more sedative before we continue our journey? It would be much better for both of us if I could trust you without having to resort to such a measure, but I do appreciate that the circumstances in which we find ourselves are highly unusual and potentially stressful." Lorraine trawled her memory trying to find where in her mind she had filed her notes on Stockholm Syndrome.

"No that won't be necessary Tom."
She turned back to the basin and finished cleaning her teeth. She heard Tom leave and then heard the swift whirr of a small hand-held electric drill as Tom removed all trace of the additional external lock. By the time Lorraine emerged from the bathroom Tom was standing waiting to help her into her coat.

"How does it look? Do you think anyone would be able to tell that we had been here?"

Lorraine snaked her arm into the left sleeve of her coat and Tom lifted the collar up and around her neck.

'Hail Mary, full of grace' thought Tom.

Lorraine surveyed the room. It was as if they had made no impression. Lorraine found herself being propelled firmly yet easily to the door, wondering just exactly how inclusive the plural pronoun was meant to be.

Chapter 7

Sergeants John Nixon and Dev Singh were on the A315 London Road, between Isleworth overground station and Hounslow Spiritualist church. Dev knew this part of London, its streets littered with garages with names like "Automania" and "Sunny Motors." It felt like stepping back to the 1990s, its landscape having changed little since. It was home to legions of uninsured drivers, MOT failures and other unroadworthy cars: backstreet mechanics kept every one on the move. Number plates were changed frequently. Written off cars were returned to the road. For this reason, Dev thought that DCS Wilson had sent them on a fool's errand.

"Left here", advised Dev, and Nixon threw the Volvo into Bridge Road, heading down to the Worton Hall Industrial Estate. Not many minutes later they were parked outside the garage from which, allegedly, the Honda Grom motorcycle had been purchased some weeks ago.

"Two things" said Nixon, a man of few words and who chose his moments carefully.

"Firstly why is Wilson so interested in a crappy old motorcycle? I mean there are probably a hundred or so similar write offs for sale within five miles of here. And secondly, what are the chances of the garage having any record of who bought it?"

Dev knocked on the steel door of the garage and called through the gap.

"Anyone in?"

A mechanic slid out from under a decidedly knackered looking Vauxhall. His face fell the moment he saw Dev's uniform.

"What now?"

"Just a routine inquiry sir. No need to panic. If you could pop out from under there, we can have a chat." Reluctantly the mechanic pushed himself out from under the engine bay and slowly got to his feet.

"How can I help?"

"I understand that you specialize in selling on Cat S and Cat N marked vehicles?" The mechanic nodded.

"Do you keep records of them?"

"We do. Properly repaired Cat S and N cars."

"Yes, yes. We are not here to give you the runaround. We are trying to trace a particular vehicle, one which we have reason to believe was involved in a crime."

"Oh, I see. Well yes, we do have full records of everything that comes through so if it was bought here, we should have a record of it. What is it?"

"It is a Honda Grom motorcycle. When it was abandoned, it had no plates but it must be at least ten years old."

"To tell you the truth we don't do many motorbikes: they are usually too badly damaged to be Cat N or S. More your Cat B."

Nixon, a stickler for detail, was impressed that the mechanic knew the difference, though suspected that in practice the odd Cat B passed through his greasy hands.

The mechanic, a burly rough-hewn man with a surprisingly cheerful and friendly air, moved through to the office, a space not much bigger than a downstairs cloakroom. He took down a grease-stained folder with the word "Sales" scrawled on the spine. He began to flick through the pages.

Nixon and Singh looked around as they waited; the office was adorned with the usual array of out-of-date calendars, empty cans of oil, discarded, rusted, fused and badly welded parts and scattered worn out tyres.

"Honda Grom you say?"

"Yes."

"Sold on the 17th of October. Job lot together with another Honda, a Jazz. Cash purchase. Name of the purchaser a Mr. Thomas Eliot. No address. But I do have the registration numbers: you can trace them that way, can't you?"

"We can try."
With that the mechanic wrote down the two numbers on a scruffy bit of paper and made his way back to the Vauxhall. Nixon and Singh made their way back to the altogether more comfortable Volvo.

"That was a result, of sorts: I thought we would come away with nothing. At least we have got something."

"True", replied Nixon, as if rationing his words. "Suppose we will be scouring London for the abandoned Jazz next."

"All jazz is abandoned Nixon: it's the point of it." Dev laughed at his own quick wit but Nixon hadn't understood his play on words.

Tom Eliot was at the wheel of the not yet abandoned Honda Jazz.

"I suspect that the radio has long since stopped working." Lorraine leant forward and turned the left dial and was surprised when she was rewarded for her effort by a yellowish glow backlighting a set of numbers. She pushed another clunky switch which brought up the message "Channel Two;" Zoe Ball joined them in the intimate space of this small, neat car. Honda marketed it as "zenshin," meaning new, progressive. Tom had selected it for its bland anonymity. The familiar voice made Lorraine wonder how the last twenty-five hours would be described in a biography of her life. They were heading up the A1, just passing the sign for "Hatfield and the North".

"The Rotters' Club."

"What?"

"Their second album"

"Who?"

"Hatfield and the North. They were a seventies band."

"Never heard of them. Named after a road sign on the A1?"

"Yes. Not particularly imaginative, is it? 'Kilburn and the High Roads' is better."

"And who were they?"

"Ian Dury. Before he became a blockhead and wanted to be hit with a rhythm stick."

"Do we have reasons to be cheerful Tom?" Tom paused for a moment.

"This may be the last journey that we make in this car. How about that?"

"As a reason to be cheerful?"

"Yes. Horrible little thing, isn't it?"

"Is it yours Tom?"

"Sadly, yes. But not for much longer."

"Where are we going?" she floated into the air, like a child.

"Lorraine, today may be a little more exciting than yesterday." Lorraine thought that yesterday had been quite eventful enough. Tom's warning, if that is what it was, induced a falling sensation in her stomach, as if they had gone over a small hump-backed bridge. Tom was as solicitous as ever.

"There's no need to be anxious."

In truth Lorraine was more bemused than anxious. She had been in dangerous situations before. She had been attacked by psychiatric patients and being captive to and captivated by Tom was less stressful. There was no professional burden upon her to bring the situation under control. Why she trusted a man who had sedated her and kept her prisoner in a dingy flat in Finchley she could not for the moment fathom. But he was easy to trust. She looked across at Tom's hands on the steering wheel. He held the wheel in his elegant fingers; she could tell he was a good driver. She had given up trying to resist her sense of pleasure at being in the company of such a handsome man. Not exactly textbook Stockholm she thought. Tom meanwhile was thrashing the Jazz in the slipstream of the BMWs and Audis heading towards the garden cities and new towns of Hertfordshire.

Rob habitually worked in the near silence of a monastic cell. He was studying some sepia tinted pages typed by an old ribbon typewriter, each page headed "Top Secret" and underscored with wonky red double underlining. The pages were spread right across the desk and Rob was examining them with an archaeologist's keen eye.

"I'm sure that we are missing something about Lorraine Watson Rob," interrupted Paul.

"I mean there is nothing of any significance in her history or her flat and that in itself is highly unusual. There is no clue as to why she might have disappeared."

"I am lost for clues too. Every time I read through these documents I feel sure that there is something that I am missing but at the moment I can connect nothing with nothing. I am stuck on Margate sands."

"What?"

"It's a quotation."

"I see" said Paul, though he didn't.

"There is a narrative, a story that I can follow, but it is fractured, broken, in the wrong order."

"Like a Tarantino movie?" offered Paul. "You know, designed to keep you guessing."

"Well in this set of documents there is a chronology, but the links between the events and the people are missing. The truth is hiding in pages that, like the events they describe, seem to get more elusive the more you look at them."

Paul could see that the documents were classified and he felt uneasy even being able to see them stretched out across the table notwithstanding that he had signed the Official Secrets Act. He could see that the documents were from military intelligence files. He kept his own counsel and updated his companion on his own investigations.

"We have another clue in the Marylebone fire case. We have traced the last known keeper of the Honda Grom motorcycle found abandoned in the multi storey. His name is Eliot. Tom Eliot."

Rob smiled, but as Paul hadn't recognized his quotation he let it pass.

"Almost certainly not his real name. But we have an address. And before you ask I have sent Nixon and Singh to check it out. Our Mr. Eliot purchased a Honda Jazz at the same time, so I have put out a search for that."

At that very moment the Honda Jazz in question turned off the A1 heading for Stevenage.

"Stevenage? Why are we going there?" said Lorraine.

"The first New Town, decidedly middle aged now. It has the combined merits of being both regular in construction and at the same time anonymous. Bit like this car. In Stevenage, everywhere looks just like everywhere else. And even better than that, it's designer, or architect, a Mr. Claxton, insisted on creating a town with the fewest possible number of traffic lights. Roundabouts everywhere of course, but if we need to make a swift exit we are not going to be held up by red lights."

"I don't understand. You took me from Baker Street Station, held me in a flat in Finchley and now we are on a day trip to Stevenage?"

"Put like that I admit that it doesn't sound very glamorous. I mean it is not up there with driving an Aston Martin through the night to a remote Scottish baronial hall before the sky falls in, or rather Javier Bardam arrives in a very noisy helicopter. But backstreets in crowded, small towns, in places that attract the least interest, like Stevenage, have their drama too."

"Tom, are you trying to tell me something?"

"Nothing that you don't already know."

Lorraine fell silent.

"By now the police will be on the lookout for this faithful little Honda so we must say farewell to her. Besides we are almost out of petrol and filling the tank would almost double its value."

With that Tom swerved down Kingsway and entered the Multi Storey Car Park. Driving fast for no good reason that Lorraine could see, Tom expertly avoided clipping the sides of the narrow spiraling tunnel until the Jazz spat itself out onto the rooftop. Lorraine was quite exhilarated. Tom parked the Jazz, its tyres still protesting at the way he had pitched and swerved his way up to the top of the car park, in a space overlooking Kingsway.

"Come on. Stevenage awaits."

Lorraine unclipped her seat belt and got out, her mind, like the Jazz's cooling fan, whirring.

Chapter 8

"This is possibly the least exciting day we have had in a long time," complained Dev.

"Why are we being sent to an address in Merton to track down the mad sod who bought two insurance write-offs from a dodgy garage in Hounslow?"

"Dev" replied the lugubrious Nixon, "ours is not to reason why. You heard Wilson say that the bike was used in a crime yesterday and it has got to be something pretty sinister for him to be that interested in it. In fact, it may turn out to be more important than pulling over some smacked-up joyrider on a county line."

"Maybe."

Singh resigned himself into his comfortably fitted sports seat and let Nixon negotiate his way through the tediously slow traffic.

"You know this thing will do 140 plus, don't you? Here we are in one of the most powerful cars the squad has and we are going on an errand to find a bloke who may or may not be the recorded keeper of a couple of crappy Hondas."

"A Mr. Tom Eliot. Strikes me as a bit of a middle-class name for a bloke buying a couple of insurance write offs."

"What were you expecting? Mr. Arthur Daley?" They both laughed. Nixon turned off the Earlsfield Road into Algarve Road.

"What number are we looking for?

"310. Flat 4. Here you go; the one with the "To Let" sign."

"I will ring the Estate Agents. Read me the number."

Dev didn't want to wait in the car. Opposite the flat the houses had been demolished and blue hoarding was struggling to hold back the trees that were reclaiming the ground. Dev noticed that every house on Earlsfield Road had an Estate Agent's board proclaiming the house either sold or to let or for sale.

"They will be here in five" called Nixon from the car.

The Estate Agent's Ford Fiesta appeared minutes later and the agent introduced himself as Carl. He looked no more than nineteen thought Nixon. Introductions completed, Carl opened the door of the flat.

"All yours. Just make sure it's closed when you leave." Carl returned to his Fiesta and left as undemonstratively as he had arrived.

"Probably doesn't want to be late for Geography", said Singh as the Fiesta scrambled away. Nixon and Singh stepped into the flat. Empty. It was essentially a one room kitchen and sitting area with a staircase leading to a bedroom, also empty.

"Wasted journey", said Singh. "Might as well go."

As he moved to the open door his eye was drawn to the kitchen table. On it was a white A4 sized envelope. In immaculate italic script it read "For the Attention of Dr. Robert Martin. Metropolitan Police. Unsolved Historic Crimes Division."

"Blimey."

Nixon and Singh were almost too stunned to speak. Nixon broke the silence.

"Reckon that warrants a blue light all the way back to town?"

"Definitely."

Nixon, who was a little obsessive, checked twice that the door was firmly closed behind him, before joining the waiting Singh in the Volvo and bright lighting the road with flashing blue.

"Stevenage is a paradox. They say John Cooper Clarke wrote "Evidently Chickentown" about

Stevenage. The colour scheme is bloody brown and the bloody view is bloody vile. But Stevenage has its story too. It was the first of Silkin's new towns yet it was mentioned in the Doomsday Book. A hoard of Roman coins was discovered here in 1986 as it lies just off the old Roman Road from St Alban's to Baldock. It has endless roundabouts to slow the traffic and yet it is the birthplace of Lewis Hamilton, the world's fastest driver."

"Do you work for the Tourist Board?" asked Lorraine rather archly. Tom was undeterred.

"It is a town with a Mondrian inspired clock tower that looks as if it was transported here from East Germany, but it is architecturally more shit-house than Bauhaus. But it has a surprising literary heritage, which is a paradox too. Have you heard of Michael Morpurgo?"

"I have seen 'War Horse'. Will that do?"

"Good enough. Morpurgo's mother was Kippe Cammaerts and his uncle was Francis Cammaerts who was Headmaster of Alleyne's Grammar School, here in Stevenage, from 1952-61. But that's not the most interesting thing about him. He was a witness for the defence in the Lady Chatterley Trial in 1959. His evidence was that he had given his Sixth Formers the novel to read and that none had been depraved or corrupted. It was an important contribution."

"I have read Lady Chatterley. Don't understand the fuss. You read far ruder things in Cosmopolitan."

"I know. There are those who argue that it wasn't the sex but the fact that it was Mellors, a horny-handed son of the soil, pleasuring her ladyship in a shed, that caused such offence. It was a class thing."

"Is that what you think Tom?"

"Well, you can be sure that the lawyers and judges had read far more obscene things studying Horace and

Catullus at school. And Cammaerts' evidence proved that the sex scenes did not corrupt anyone. But even that isn't the most interesting thing about Cammaerts. Like so many of his generation he had an extraordinary war."

By now they had walked beyond the North Hertfordshire College and were heading down Briardale.

"Chickentown" agreed Lorraine looking at the dim prospect of terraced houses which, had they been painted green, would have resembled the houses on a Monopoly board: implausibly simple rectangles with no discernible features.

"Chickentown indeed."

Tom produced a key from his pocket and approached the white plastic door of Number 15. The house contained only rudimentary furniture. It was also chilly. Lorraine found herself rubbing her upper arms.

"The boiler is quite efficient: the heating will be up and running in about ten minutes, called Tom from a cupboard at the entrance to the kitchen. I must apologise for the elementary nature of the accommodation Lorraine, but safe houses are chosen as safe houses for very particular reasons. The windows are all made of plexiglass and are permanently locked, as is the back door. The only way in or out is through the front door. Your bedroom is upstairs and mine is right here so if anyone were to try to enter, or indeed leave, which I would strongly hope you would not begin to contemplate, then they would have to step over, or on, me. And I don't like being disturbed in my sleep."

Lorraine considered her predicament. There seemed, as in Finchley, little chance of escape. But she gathered that instead of being double-locked in on her own she would be locked in here with Tom. And that was not an entirely unappealing prospect. Tom was busying himself in the kitchen. Lorraine watched his quick athletic movements as he filled and plugged in the kettle, reached a teapot and cups from an eye-level cupboard and placed two tea bags in the waiting pot.

"Francis Cammaerts."

"Who?"

"The man I was telling you about. One of the great paradoxes of Stevenage. The man whose evidence helped in the Lady Chatterley trial?"

"Oh yes." Lorraine plonked herself down on a small brown two-seater sofa having first given it a cursory brush with the flat of her hand.

"Francis was the son of a Belgian poet who married a successful English actress, the implausibly named Tita Brand. After minor public school and Cambridge, he was recruited to the SOE, the Special Operations Executive. As a fluent French speaker, he was flown into occupied France and made his way to a safe house in Cannes where he pretended to be a teacher recovering from jaundice."

The kettle's shrill whistle interrupted him briefly.

"From Cannes he worked with the French resistance in Vichy France and built up his own network, christened the Jockey network by SOE headquarters. Guess where they were based?"

Lorraine shrugged

"Baker Street."

Lorraine shivered and not just from the cold.

"Cammaerts remained under cover for fifteen months. He was constantly on the move. He rarely spent more than three nights in one place and became the most important SOE agent in South East France. He won the DSO and the Croix de Guerre and Legion d'honneur in France."

"Tea?"

"Please."

"So, here we are in Stevenage paying homage to one of the best under cover British agents sabotaging the German war effort in Vichy France."

"And he ended up a Headmaster in Stevenage?"

"As paradoxes go it's not exactly up there with Schrodinger's cat but Stevenage is a town of paradoxes and Monsieur Cammaerts is one of them."

Lorraine drank a deep draught of warming tea. As she did so she thought of another Stevenage paradox, a psychiatric nurse who should know better, being irresistibly drawn to her captor in circumstances that ought to be far from romantic. Lorraine drank the last of her tea and summoned up the courage to say what was on her mind.

"Tom, you said that this was a safe house. Safe from what? Are we in danger?"

She deliberately chose the plural pronoun because Tom had done so.

"Stevenage has many merits Lorraine", replied Tom, "and one of them is that it is one of the last places anyone would think of looking for someone who has disappeared. One might say that any house in Stevenage might be considered a safe place to hide, but this is a safe house in another sense too."

"What sense is that?" Lorraine wasn't really interested in a semantic game but again felt the best strategy was to play along.

"A safe house is" …Tom stopped. "But you know all about safe houses don't you Lorraine?"

Tom broke into a smile, a smile as charming and enigmatic as Gatsby's. This was the first time Tom had said anything remotely sharp and it felt like a blade held to her ribs.

"And unsafe houses?" he added, still smiling.

She felt the tip of the blade pressing hard against her. She gathered herself.

"Is there any more of that lovely Pinot Grigio?"

"As a matter of fact, there is."

Tom moved quickly over to the fridge, lifted out a bottle, closed the fridge door with his foot, flipped open a cupboard and withdrew two glasses, span around, placed the glasses on the table and unscrewed the bottle all in one sinuous and continuous motion lasting no more than seconds. Lorraine gasped internally, thrilled by the ballet she had just witnessed.

Once the cool wine suffused her mouth, she felt calmer. That night Lorraine was wakeful, despite the Pinot Grigio which would usually send her straight to sleep. She was not exactly agitated but she was more concerned than she had been before this evening's conversation with Tom. The conversation had subtext. There was an edge to it. Tom seemed to know everything about her, even down to her favourite wine, as if he had researched her. She wondered if he had formed an obsessive attachment to her through one of the research groups she had worked on. She had heard of that happening: it was an occupational hazard of working in psychiatry. But she was sure she had never seen him before. She would surely have remembered him; he was as gorgeous as Gatsby.

Chapter 9

Nixon concluded the speedy journey back into central London with a handbrake turn, decelerating rapidly with a couple of deft flicks of his hands and feet. The two friends left the car and sauntered languidly towards the lift that would take them from the underground garage. Suddenly their mission lacked urgency. Exiting the lift, they wandered into DCI Paul Wilson's office and presented him with the envelope. Paul looked at the italic script.

"You don't see handwriting like that much these days, do you? In fact, you don't see much that is handwritten at all. Where did you find this?"

"It was sitting on the kitchen table in the Flat at 310 Algarve Road."

"The address I sent you to?"

"Yes."

"Are you sure?"

"Well, where else do you think we would have picked it up?"

Nixon was hungry and tetchy.

"Fair point. Thanks."

Paul was troubled. Sensing that there was no more to be said, Nixon and Singh turned to leave. Paul sat down at his desk. His quick mind was already running through possible scenarios. He tapped his pencil on his knee as if to regulate his thoughts. Paul felt very uneasy about this development. Whoever this Tom Eliot was, he had set a trail, via the garage in Hounslow where he deliberately left his name, to the address in Earlsfield, where he knew the letter to Dr. Rob Martin awaited certain discovery. The realization was unnerving. He imagined this Tom Eliot watching him, Jason Bourne to his Pam Landy. "Get some rest Paul. You look tired."

Paul was still tapping the pencil against his knee when there was a knock on the door. It was Nick Booth.

"We have found some images of the Honda Jazz."

Paul leapt to his feet and followed PC Booth through to the open plan office where three of the team were gathered around one screen. There was a grainy black and white, or rather grey, image of the Jazz, the exact model, colour and registration as the one purchased by Tom in Hounslow on October 17th.

"This is from CCTV on Cosway Street at about seven am yesterday morning," explained Nick. "Not very far from the NCP where the bike was abandoned. Seventeen minutes' walk, according to Google Maps. He could have abandoned the bike, then walked to the car to get away."

"He could." Paul looked at route marked on the map

"It is not very far from Marylebone or Baker Street either. Is there a route that would go from the Park Road NCP to Cosway street, but via Baker Street?"

"Via Baker Street? Ok, starting point Park Road to Cosway Street via Baker Street. There you go: twenty-six minutes on foot."

They looked at one another.

"Thanks" said Paul who bounded across the narrow corridor back to his office and jumped into his desk chair. He pulled up a map of Marylebone and began to work out the possible routes between the three known points. His fingers worked quickly and he whispered audibly as he thought.

The Fire Brigade received a 999 call from Marylebone Station at 7.40, so let's assume that the arsonist set the fire at about 7.30. Lorraine Watson disappeared from outside Baker Street station at 8.05. He enlarged the map. That would leave about thirty-five minutes for our suspect to ride to the Park Road NCP, clean the bike of prints, and then walk down to Baker Street by 8.05. It is a twenty-six-minute walk. It would take perhaps ten minutes to park and clean the bike. It is very tight but it could be done in thirty-five minutes. The same person could have been responsible both for the fire at Marylebone and Lorraine's disappearance from outside Baker Street station. Paul let his eye wander along the Google map; it fell upon the statue of Sherlock Holmes.

Chapter 10

Shortly after one o'clock an unremarkable Peugeot slinked its feline way along Wooler Street. Slow moving vehicles are not an uncommon sight in this part of London at this time of night: Ubers uncertain of the whereabouts of their pickups; drivers inebriated, or drugged or merely lost; all navigated their various ways along the streets south of the river. This car attracted little attention as its occupants strained their eyes for an exact location.

"There's number twenty" whispered one of the passengers in the rear seats.

"Back up a bit."

The driver wrestled the reluctant gearbox into reverse; after edging backwards for a few feet he pulled on the handbrake and silenced the purring engine. Without a word the other three occupants of the vehicle pulled on their balaclavas and got out of the car leaving the doors slightly open. They moved noiselessly along the pavement and quickly scaled the iron railings to the side of the building. The three figures hunkered down then squat-walked their way to the side window of the flat that usually contains Lorraine Watson. By dumbshow one of the men warned the other two that there was a light on in the flat next door, a light accompanied by the occasional sturdy thump of a bass guitar, and the instruction was to proceed with extreme caution.

The figure in the vanguard of these nocturnal prowlers crowbarred the pliant window open and pulled himself through the gap. He turned and drew the window closed again so that nobody looking at the house would be able to tell that it had been opened. Seconds later his shadow appeared in the frame of the main door and the three were reunited in a huddle in the hallway. Proceeding only by the dimmed light of their mobile phones the three branched out from the trunk of the hallway. They made no sound. One of the three went to the back of the flat where a door from the kitchen led to a communal garden, a garden currently half lit by a reddish glow coming from the flat next door. The door was slightly stuck and the glass pane shook very slightly as the door resisted being opened, even by this nimble hand. There was just enough light to be able to tell that there was nobody in the garden and the retreating figure did not risk trying to reclose the back door for fear of it shivering again. The three reconvened in the hallway; each gave a quick shake of the head confirming their findings. Exiting as quickly as they had entered, but this time by the conventional method, they soft footed it back to the Peugeot. The driver smoothed them away towards the Walworth Road. The front door of the adjacent flat opened and a tall, dreadlocked figure looked on curiously.

Like Lorraine, Rob Martin could not get to sleep. Although Rob arrived at the office, via Costa, at precisely 8.25 every morning, and left equally precisely for the evening train back to Reading, there were no boundaries to Rob's working day. He made no distinction between work time and non-work time; for as long as he remained awake, he would think about the files on his desk. The current files were highly classified military intelligence dossiers from more than forty years ago. They set out highly sensitive security matters for the highest-ranking government ministers, intelligence officers and certain other specified officers, Rob among them. His task was essentially the same as it was when he was a university researcher; he needed to think, to observe, and if possible, to formulate a thesis. He was struggling to formulate a thesis in this case and the cases that Paul brought to him for his advice and consideration were a welcome distraction. On this chilly November night, he mulled over the fact that Lorraine Watson had been missing for over thirty-six hours. That was not so remarkable. People go missing all the time but he was becoming convinced that her disappearance was not a random event, but was like a single fish breaking the surface of the water beneath which swims a teeming shoal. Detecting patterns was his life's work and he was sure that there would be a pattern beneath Lorraine Watson's disappearance.

Louise Tindall's mobile phone shone blue light upwards from her bedside table moments before it began its urgent ring. It was still black outside, long before-dawn dark.

"Sergeant Tindall, Babylon is not the only one looking for Lorraine."

Louise recognized the mellifluous tone and was alert enough to understand its importance.

"Tell me more."

"Lorraine had some visitors."

"What do you mean, visitors?"

"Let themself in."

"Did you see them? Who were they?"

Louise had so many questions.

"I will be with you in about twenty minutes. Thank you so much for calling me."

She reassembled her uniform, ran to the bathroom to clean her teeth and run her hands briefly through her hair. She glanced down at her phone; 2.10 am. She knew that protocol dictated that she could not go on her own; replacing her toothbrush in the mug she put in a call to Nick Booth who was on standby duty, as she was. PC

Booth was awake when she called, a late-night session of Call of Duty had kept him from his bed, and he was more than ready for an exciting excursion into the south London night.

"Meet me there" Louise signed off as she ran down the stairs in her apartment block.

Paul Wilson scrolled aimlessly through the myriad television channels looking for inspiration. Most were taken up with shameless attention seekers exposing themselves to public view with no apparent sense of irony. Occasionally he would find a truffle in the muddy soil: a Buster Keaton retrospective, a documentary about Groucho Marx, a gentle travelogue with Brydon and Coogan. Unfortunately, tonight all that he could find was the sweaty slapstick of Lee Evans and the childish puns of Tim Vine. He wondered how there could be an audience for such things but he understood that for many people comedy was bubble gum and ice cream, not the haunting alter ego of the tragic muse. In the absence of anything to watch he poured himself a smallish single malt and thought again about Lorraine Watson. She had been the target of a very carefully planned and executed abduction. Such expertise usually indicated the involvement one of three groups: the intelligence services, terrorist organizations or crime syndicates. But Lorraine, a nurse, seemed an unlikely target for any of those groups. But it bothered him that, so far, they had found out so little about her. Why was Lorraine so hard to discover? Ordinary people can become caught up in the world of organized crime and it could be that Lorraine, unwittingly or unwisely had done so. It seemed unlikely: she was financially secure and had no addictions. Tomorrow he would make much more extensive enquiries into Lorraine's life: there must be something that identifies her as a potential target for abduction. As Paul Wilson pondered how to broaden his research into her, Lorraine lay in her bed in Stevenage similarly worrying over the problem of Tom.

As soon as he saw in his wing mirror that his Sergeant's car was safely berthed behind his own perfectly parked car, PC Nick Booth leapt out. Inside the main front door, the air was thickly, sweetly scented. Eventually the door opened.

"Come with me."

Lorraine's neighbour, Anthony Taylor, led them back out of the building, down the side, to the still slightly open back door that led into Lorraine's kitchen. PC Booth shone his flashlight around the perimeter of the window to reveal the splinters left by the intruders. PC Booth and Sergeant Tindall went inside through the back door. Anthony lingered politely breathing in the fresh night air. Inside Louise Watson's flat, everything was exactly as they remembered it. Nothing had been disturbed; the laundry was waiting expectantly in the drum of the machine although the fruit in the bowl was a little browner. A light dust had settled on some of the surfaces.

"Not burglars then" offered PC Booth in a stage whisper.

"No. Whoever broke in was looking for her."

They retraced their steps and cross-examined Anthony.

"I heard noises, but by the time I opened the door they were running back to the car."

"Did you get a look at any of them?"

"No. They were wearing balaclavas."

Louise exchanged a look with Nick, a look that confirmed what they had both feared, namely that they were dealing with something quite sinister.

"Well thank very much: you have been very helpful. I doubt that Lorraine will be returning to her flat any time soon but if you do see her, or any sign of her, or sense any other unusual activity in her flat, call me immediately."

"Sure."

With a gentle incline of the head Anthony returned to his flat. As the door opened the muffled thump of John Holt's "Police in Helicopter" wafted its way into the still cool air. The door was open long enough for Nick and Louise to catch the hypnotic refrain. Anthony gently closed the door behind him.

Louise decided to take another look in Lorraine's flat. She still had Mrs. Nair's key. She moved slowly and methodically through each room and after a fruitless half an hour, approached the front door to let herself out. She glanced at the small bookshelf just before the door in the hallway and appreciated the fine picture of Dromoland Castle on the glossy cover of "The Castles of County Clare." She also noticed that the slim foreign language volume that had accompanied it was nowhere to be seen.

Chapter 11

As the 6.30 from Reading burbled its way into Paddington station Rob Martin positioned himself in the doorway of the carriage in order to catch a glimpse of the War Memorial to Great Western Railway employees. Rob found something deeply affecting in it. The way the soldier stood wrapped in his knitted muffler, rapt by the letter he is reading, helmet jauntily angled, his collar half turned up, seemed to Rob to capture the paradoxical dignity of man and the pity of war. It was more poignant, he thought, than the war poems that he studied at GCSE. Every morning, stooping a little to peer through the open window, Rob would see if he could catch the soldier's eye, but those eyes were immortally fixed in the letter's embrace. Elsewhere in the carriage commuters tensed like sprinters in their blocks waiting for the starter's pistol, the loud click that was the release of the mechanical door locks. Busy commuters poured away ignoring Jaggers' statue, as the delicate ship in Breughel's 'Icarus' sails away from the boy falling out of the sky. Rob stepped down from the train and made his way towards the Circle Line. Gazing into the middle distance he ran through the events of just forty-eight hours ago, when half a mile away a wheelie bin doused with kerosene turned from solid to liquid and a woman disappeared. He was convinced that they were linked.

As Rob Martin walked dully along through the thin morning light Lorraine was conscious of the smell of freshly brewed coffee snaking its way up the stairs. It was not often that her sense of smell was the first to be called into action: usually her sense of hearing led her other senses gradually into the day. But Lorraine could not remember anything before her nose was enlivened by a smell of roasted beans. She made her way into the adjacent bathroom. Tom called up to her, "milk, no sugar?"

"Yeth pleathe" replied Lorraine, through the frothing toothpaste that filled her mouth and dribbled down her chin as she tried to form the words. Lorraine was used to quick ablutions in cramped conditions and in less than ten minutes she had completed a rudimentary shower, dressed, and made her way down the brief flight of stairs that led straight to the door of the kitchen on the opposite side of the narrow hall. She pushed open the half-glassed door to see Tom looking as handsome as she had seen him. He was clean shaven, his still wet hair swept back from his forehead. He was wearing a new or very well laundered light blue shirt with a double cuff and navy chinos. She glanced down and noticed a pair of Ferragamo loafers. She was not usually brand conscious but she recognized these shoes because of one of the consultants at the Nightingale wore them. The sight of Tom was both uplifting and dispiriting; uplifting because it stirred the woman in her, but it was dispiriting because she had read 'American Psycho.'

"Some breakfast?"

Tom's question shook her out of her reverie and he beckoned her to take a seat at the Formica- topped table which Tom wiped thoroughly.

"I must have slept very well" said Lorraine, "because I did not hear a thing."

"I took the precaution of popping something in with your last glass of Pinot. I hope you do not mind but I didn't want you disturbed."

As he spoke, Tom turned and placed a plate of scrambled egg on a toasted bagel before Lorraine.

"Coffee's in the pot."

"Thank you."

Lorraine felt the buttery eggs, with just the right amount of salt and pepper, fill her mouth with cloying firmness.

"So, what have you been so busy with Tom?"

"There have been some interesting developments."

"Such as?"

"The Metropolitan Police made an enquiry at a property in Merton." Lorraine stopped eating and stared at Tom in disbelief.

"Sounds like a headline in the local paper. How is that a development?"

"It is quite an important development."

"I'm not with you."

"It means that they are following us."

Lorraine was very much enjoying her breakfast.

"I left a little something for them and they have picked it up." Lorraine swallowed a piece of eggy bagel.

"Does that mean that they are on their way here?"

"Maybe. Did you know that there are more possible moves in a game of chess than there are atoms in the observable universe?"

"What are you on about?"

"Following us here is one of a number of possible moves they might make. They have choices. But not many."

After a fitful sleep that ended prematurely at five, Paul was so alert that he headed in to work. He was at his desk by seven and had been looking through the evidence that his team had gathered about Lorraine Watson. He was convinced that they were all missing something. But what? It was logistically possible that the person who abducted Lorraine had done so after setting the fire at Marylebone. Why would someone go that much trouble? What was it about Lorraine? Not only that but there was the envelope, almost certainly left for them by the owner of the abandoned motorbike. Who were they dealing with? He had looked at it many times, admiring the beautifully crafted script of this unsolicited letter. Who would send such a letter? He remembered Eddie Izzard's sketch about the furious Corinthians' letters back to "moaner" St Paul. Verses one to a million. More letters to follow. It was a pity Izzard had morphed into Jenny Joseph's badly dressed granny, "wearing a red hat which doesn't go" with his dyed blond hair. He looked at the envelope again. At least he had the certainty of knowing that Rob would arrive, as he always did, at 8.25, which was only fifteen minutes from now. Time for a quick coffee; but he was interrupted by the arrival of Sergeant Louise Tindall and PC Nick Booth.

"You're in early."

"Pots and kettles" replied Louise

"We need to debrief you, sir" she continued. "We have had a busy day already."

"Me too" replied Paul. "I hope yours has been more profitable than mine."

"I received a call early this morning from the guy who lives in the flat next to Lorraine Watson. He knows Lorraine well, as a friend rather than a neighbour. He told me they used to spend the summer evenings chatting in the garden."

Paul gave her a look urging her to get to the point.

"He told us that a couple of hours earlier, he had been disturbed by noises in Lorraine's flat. When he went to investigate, he saw three men in balaclavas running from the flat to a waiting car and driving away from the scene. As Nick and I were both on standby we went to the flat. A window next to the back door of Lorraine's flat had been prised open. But here is the strange thing sir. As far as we could tell, not a single thing had been disturbed: the flat was exactly as it was when Mrs. Nair let us in yesterday."

"Balaclavas he said. Was he sure? Did he say anything else?"

"Not really. The balaclavas were the only thing that he was sure about."

"Not routine burglars, then?" Paul was thinking aloud.

"Obviously not sir. And nothing had been touched."

"Which would suggest that they were looking for Lorraine?"

"It would seem so sir, yes."

"There is something about Lorraine Watson that we are missing."

"Could it be connected to her work, sir?"

"It might be."

"We need to know the details of the teams that she worked in and, if possible, the names all of the clinicians and all of the patients too. Might give us something to go on."

"You mean you think that she has been abducted by someone who knew her through her work?"

"Possibly. Possibly not. But it is an avenue worth traipsing down to have a look at the view."

Paul waved them off with the back of his hand and watched them go excitedly out of his office. He was not convinced that this line of enquiry would lead anywhere. But the science of detection required ruling everything out until only the truth remains. As he reflected on Holmes' dictum, his own Sherlock, in the form of Rob Martin, was silhouetted against the wall of the corridor.

Paul waited just long enough to sense that Rob was comfortably at his desk before making his short way across the corridor. He was too excited to go through the usual 'Groundhog Day' routine.

"You remember yesterday I told you that I had sent Nixon and Singh to an address in Earlsfield, the address of the registered keeper of the Honda Grom motorcycle found abandoned in the NCP?"

Rob nodded.

"And you will also remember that the same Tom Eliot also purchased a Honda Jazz at the same time?"

More nodding.

"We have picked it up on CCTV parked in Cosway Street, close to Baker Street station shortly before the fire at Marylebone station."

Rob leaned forward.

"What is more, it is a comfortable twenty-five-minute walk from the North Road NCP to Baker Street station. So, if we assume that he abandoned the motorbike at around 7.40, he would arrive at Baker Street at exactly 8.05, the exact time that Lorraine Watson exited the station and apparently vanished into thin air."

"Are you sure?"

"Nick worked it out on Google maps. It takes twenty-six minutes in fact."

"Then the arsonist and the kidnapper are one and the same person?"

"More than that."

"What do you mean?"

"Cause and effect. He set the fire at Marylebone in order to kidnap Lorraine from Baker Street. There's more."

"Go on."

"You remember I sent a car to the registered keeper's address? When Nixon and Singh went into the flat at the address, they found it empty. They found nothing else just this white envelope on the kitchen table"

Paul put it on Rob's desk between his mouse and his computer screen. Rob scanned it quickly.

"It's addressed to me."

"But it is addressed to you in a very specific way"

"Unsolved historic crimes division."

"So not just addressed to you but using the formal title of your department. Not only that but it uses your academic title, Dr. rather than your police rank. It suggests a degree of familiarity. And few people know that we have a department of historic unsolved crimes. It isn't on the website."

"Someone could guess that such a department exists."

"Maybe, but your correspondent must have known that we would trace the registered keeper to the flat in Earlsfield and that he could confidently leave the envelope there."

"That assumes that he would know, or has gambled, on Lorraine's disappearance being investigated by someone who would pass the envelope on to me."

"It isn't that much of a gamble. I mean a suspicious urgent Missing Persons case would come through to my investigation unit, wouldn't it? He only needed to get the envelope into the building assuming that an envelope left at that address would be hand delivered to you."

"Do you think we are dealing with someone with inside knowledge?"

"I know we are."

"In which case this is becoming a very interesting case." Rob looked at the envelope.

"What was the name of that film with Dennis Hopper as a disgruntled ex-cop?"

Paul was slightly surprised to find Rob reaching into the world of popular culture, which was normally his domain.

"Speed. Had a lousy sequel imaginatively called Speed 2"

"Yes, that's the one. Do you think it is something like that? Someone who knows police procedure and operational systems and who is also capable of arson and kidnap? Someone with a grudge?"

"It is a plausible theory. It would mean that Lorraine was taken as a random hostage. An accident of time and place, like Sandra Bullock on the bus."

"She could be an ex-girlfriend or ex-wife?"

"Nothing in her profile of that nature: no recent boyfriends and she has never been married. No, my sense is that there is something specific about Lorraine. She was targeted."

Paul knew that at some point Rob would ask a question for which he did not have a watertight answer. But he had one more card to play.

"At about two am this morning Sergeant Tindall took a call from the man in the flat next to Lorraine's on Wooler Street. He said he had been disturbed by noises coming from Lorraine's flat and saw three men in balaclavas fleeing from the scene and driving away. When Tindall and Booth went to investigate, they found nothing in the flat had been touched. Someone was looking for Lorraine."

The two men sat in silence for a moment. Paul had played his trump card.

"Better open the envelope then" said Rob, breaking the silence.

Chapter 12

A short distance away in Southwark, Anthony Taylor was easing his way along Portman Street. Anthony's grace was inherited from his mother. She was known across Lambeth for her ability to stand on the lower deck of the AEC Routemaster, her ticket machine over her left shoulder resting on her right hip, her cash bag across her right shoulder resting on her left hip, the straps crossing just below the top button of her uniform. As the bus lurched its way from every stop she simply and imperceptibly adjusted her weight like a snowboarder, and, unlike the passengers who were trying to make their faltering way down the bus, she was untroubled by the jerks of the clunky gear changes. Anthony had also inherited from his mother a sharp eye and as he turned from Portland Street into Wooler Street, he recognized the Peugeot making its slow, clumsy way over a sleeping policeman. It climbed up and over the raised tarmac like a rocking horse. It was the same Peugeot that had discharged its cargo of balaclaved men hours earlier. Anthony could make out a driver and two passengers inside. He guessed that the fourth would already be at Lorraine's flat and made a noiseless approach. Coolly the fourth man said a quiet "good morning" and went on his way, but not before Anthony had registered his accent and committed each contour of his face to memory.

Lorraine licked the last bubbles of aero-like brown froth from her lips. When, if ever, this ordeal was over, she would certainly miss Tom's coffee. As she sat alone at the rudimentary kitchen table, she rehearsed what she knew about him. He was beguilingly handsome; he was a dab hand in the kitchen; he was attentive and had only once been terse or short with her. He made her feel that she was being looked after, and yet this was the man who had kidnapped her; he had held her captive in a dismal flat then brought her to a safe house in Stevenage. Tom seemed to think it would be safer here. As she washed up the breakfast things, she felt Tom's presence at her side.

"Come on, it's time for a wander around Chickentown."

Rob and Paul stared at the envelope for a few seconds before Rob reached for his paperknife, slit open the top of the envelope and peered inside. He looked quizzically at Paul. He reached into the envelope and pulled out a single piece of paper and rested it on the opened envelope on the table. In the middle of the paper, in the same italic script as the writing on the envelope, were just seven characters. Q885601. Paul picked up the paper and turned it over as if expecting to see more. But there was nothing, just empty white space. He put it down again and looked at Rob. Paul tried to lighten the mood.

"Shall I phone a friend?"

"Hmm?"

"Who wants to be a Millionaire? It's a game show. If a contestant doesn't know the answer to the question, then one of the options available to them is to phone a friend and ask them."

"Why?"

"Perhaps the producers of the show think that it adds drama."

Sometimes Paul regretted introducing these moments of levity into their conversations.

"But there isn't a question here."

"No. I didn't mean it literally. If it is not a question, what do you think that it is?"

"It's clearly a code of some sort."

"Good; that's a start at least. What sort of a code?"

"Not sure yet. But it is interesting, isn't it?"

Paul could not deny that. Just then there was a knock at the open door.

"Sorry to bother you sirs, but we have some leads on the Honda Jazz."

Paul pushed himself up and followed PC Booth back to the busy office on the other side of the corridor. It was best to leave Rob alone for a while so that he could decipher the code. Paul was confident that Rob could crack the code: he just needed time and space. The code must mean something to Rob: after all the envelope was addressed to him. Paul meanwhile could busy himself with some routine detective work tracking down a car. Both the code and the car might be pieces in the same jigsaw puzzle, he reasoned.

"Sir, did you know that there are now 691 thousand CCTV cameras in London, one for every thirteen people?"

"Unlucky for some. No, I did not know that it was as many as that. Your point Nick?"

"Well sir, it would be almost impossible to trawl through 691 thousand of them looking for a Honda Jazz, even one whose registration number we knew. They are quite common."

"We know that this particular car was last seen somewhere in Marylebone."

"Yes sir, Cosway Street. I narrowed the search down to all of CCTV cameras within a mile of Marylebone and then to the main arterial routes leading North and West from Marylebone."

"But how do you know the driver didn't head East or South?"

"I didn't know that sir, but I had to start somewhere. I gambled. And got lucky. Look at this."

Nick started tapping in co-ordinates. The sequence of images that he showed to Paul came from cameras on the A41; they mapped the journey Tom had taken with Lorraine all the way to Finchley.

"Is that as much as we have?"

"No sir, there's more. We think that they must have stayed the night somewhere near Finchley because the following day the car was seen heading north on the A1."

"That means that they could be anywhere between London and Durham by now."

"Not quite sir. Look at this: Junction 8 on the A1(M). See that?" There was an image of the Honda Jazz filtering left at Junction 8 in the direction of Stevenage.

"It is even better than that sir. Stevenage has CCTV cameras everywhere. We have tracked the Honda all the way to a multi-storey car park on Kingsway. It was almost too easy."

Nick stood up from his desk with a satisfied stretch of the arms.

"He made little effort to avoid the cameras. It is almost as if he wanted us to find him."

"You may well be right Nick."

Paul was thinking about the envelope on his colleague's desk. He made it easy for us to find the envelope. And now he had made it obvious where he was.

Chapter 13

The chestnut-coloured Peugeot 504, first registered in 1974, retained its roomy air of cold war glamour as it made its stately way north on the Kilburn High Road. A cargo of crowbars, jimmies, and drills was safely cached in its capacious boot. It had been specifically chosen for its soft suspension which made light of London's many potholes, kerbs and raised pavings. A light tap on the accelerator swung the car across the A5, passing Kilburn High Road station on the right, left into Kilburn Vale and over the cobbled mosaic pavement of Hermit Place. Hermit Place was only yards from the grand houses of Priory Road, but stubbornly retained the squalour of semi-dereliction in a forgotten spot behind The Priory Tavern. The accommodation was fit for a hermit too, spartan and dark, but that did not trouble its four occupants. They gathered themselves in the main room: one of them casually tossed the bag of balaclavas into the corner where four or five Royal Mail bags gave it a soft landing.

"How much money do we have left?" asked Fin.

One of his colleagues, Conor, opened the fridge in the kitchen and took out two large sealed Tupperware containers.

"Plenty" he replied. "I reckon about twenty-five thousand. Enough for a while yet."

"How many cheque books are left?"

"About fifty. Do we need more?"

"No. We can manage with what we have."

Conor returned the Tupperware to the fridge.

"There is a meeting tonight. Usual place."

The other three nodded their understanding.

"I need make a few calls first."

"What are we to do about the woman?"

The speaker was new to the conversation; the youngest of the four, with dark hair and a surly manner.

"And are we sure, for sure I mean, that it is her?"

"I am sure" replied Fin.

He pulled from his jacket pocket a slim volume and placed it carefully face upwards on the table so that they could all see the title.

'Coiste Forbartha Gaeltachta Chontae an Chlair."

"I picked this up from the bookshelf right by the door of her flat." The four men looked at each other.

"Ok" said Conor. "She is the one we are looking for. But we can't find her, can we? There was no sign of her at home."

"Something will come up Conor. It always does. Thomas, will you make us all a cup of tea?"

"Sure." The surly young man went to the kitchen to do as he was told. The other three sat back on the two identical sofas to contemplate their next move.

"We need to find her, before anyone else does."
Conor was a dog with a bone.

"May be that fella who lives next door to her knows something."

"Perhaps we should pay him a visit" called the younger man from the kitchen where he was vigorously stirring the tea.

"Well, it can't be me. He got a too good look at me today. I just didn't see or hear him and then there he was, right in my face. I am sure he would recognize me. If we are going to talk to him, it needs to be one of you because if he sees me, he will smell a rat."

"I'll do it" volunteered Thomas, bringing the teas in.

"Agreed?"
The other two instinctively raised their hands as if supporting a motion to go out on strike.

"I'll go right now, as soon as I have had my tea. Meet you in the Campbell at 6."

"Be careful how you go Thomas. Don't be drawing attention to yourself."

Paul was in Rob's office rehearsing everything that Nick Booth had told him.

"Why is he making it so easy for us Rob?"

"The code isn't proving that easy."

"Oh."

Paul was surprised that Rob had made little progress.

"But why has he made it so easy for us to follow him?"

"He might be playing with us. Do you play chess Paul?"

"I played at school."

"Then you will be familiar with the Queen's Gambit?"

"That's an opening move, yes?"

"In one in eight games, yes. White offers queen's pawn sacrifice in order to control the centre of the board. It's very obvious. Black can accept or decline."

"You think he has played Queen's Gambit?"

"Moving his Honda in such a transparent way could be classic Queen's Gambit."

"What's our next move then?"

"We could accept and go to Stevenage. But that runs the risk that when we get there all we find is an abandoned car."

"And if we decline?"

"We would need a good countergambit."

"Have we got one?"

"Not until I can fathom the code. I don't think we have another move until I do."

"We take the pawn being offered then?"

"Queen's Gambit Accepted is plausible, yes."

"Ok. In that case, it is a job for Nixon and Singh."

"Good idea" replied Rob.

Paul thought that it might be a bit risky sending Nixon and Singh on their own; after all, as their commanding officer he was responsible for their welfare and he was worried that they were all a move behind. Louise Tindall and Nick Booth would follow in an unmarked car. Nixon and Singh could give the Volvo a run up the A1.

Rob returned to the faded papers that had been on his desk for some time now. He was reading through the accounts of a meeting on the twelfth of December, 1974, in Smith's Hotel in a small town in Clare called An Fhiacail, or Feakle in English. The village was the meeting place for secret talks between representatives of the main Protestant denominations in Northern Ireland, leading Sinn Fein politicians and senior figures in the IRA. During the meeting word came through that the Hotel was about to be raided. When the gardai arrived, they found only the clergymen and the Sinn Fein delegates: the IRA members had vanished. Rob was determined to understand two things. Firstly, how did Special Branch learn of the meeting? Secondly, how had the IRA members made their escape? He was reading through the account of the MI6 officer responsible for brokering the meeting in line with the British Government's then covert policy of developing a dialogue with the Provisional IRA. He looked again at the briefing note he had read many times before but this time something jumped out at him. It was a code; R585881. It was the Irish grid reference for Feakle. Seven digits: a letter and six numbers. He searched under the file of papers for the sheet of paper that he had taken from its envelope earlier. There it was in careful italics, Q885601. Could it be a grid reference? He entered the code into a grid reference finder. Nothing. Not recognized. He thought again. Maybe they use a different system in Ireland? He looked up Irish grid references and read that Ireland is mapped alphabetically by squares measuring 100 kilometers by 100 kilometers. Each reference has a letter of the alphabet followed by a six-digit number. He typed the code into an Irish grid reference finder; Q885601 was the grid reference for the coastal village of Kilkee. Rob sank back in his chair. Kilkee. Why Kilkee? He googled a map of County Clare. Why has he sent me the grid reference for a remote Irish fishing village? And as he thought about it, he felt his stomach turn over in the same way as Paul, who had christened it his "Pam Landy" moment. The person who had sent this code, who may or not be called Tom Eliot, did so in the expectation that he would recognize an Irish grid reference. That meant that "Tom" must have assumed that Rob was familiar with Irish grid references. And if he knew that Rob would recognize something as obscure as a grid reference in County Clare, was it because he knew which unsolved cases he was currently working on? Could "Tom" know which files lay open on his desk? But that was impossible. These files are Classified. Only a handful of people had the required level of security clearance. But Rob did not believe in co-incidence. He believed in patterns, hidden though they may be. And, at the moment, the pattern was hidden from him. Still, the game of chess had taken an altogether more intriguing turn.

Chapter 14

"We could be behind the old Iron Curtain, couldn't we?" asked Tom as he and Lorraine stood looking up at the Clock Tower in Stevenage's Town Square.

"The planners wanted to create the first pedestrian-only town centre in England. For some reason they modeled it on Rotterdam, though it is far from any water. The best they could do was that raised pool and fountain. It doesn't look anything like Rotterdam, does it?"

"I don't know. I have never been there."

"There are those who think that concrete brutalism has its appeal, but I can't see the attraction."

"It is ugly."

"And a difficult place to live in. Let's go and take a look at Alleyn's school in the Old Town."

"There's an older part of Stevenage?"

"Not really; it all merges into one. But the school was founded in 1558 and is still on the same site, so to that extent the area around it could be classified as the Old Town. Not so brutalist."

They set off along the High Street with its dreary prospect: Wetherspoon's, Mecca Bingo, Johnson's cleaners, Vision Express and JD Sports. The school also proved to be an architectural disappointment. Now an Academy, it was for the most part a collection of unremarkable brown buildings. However, there was one building that had survived from the reign of the first Queen Elizabeth, a half-timbered, half-brick construction with buckled walls and a blue plaque on the side indicating that this was The Old Schoolroom, circa 1562. Lorraine conceded that it was quite impressive.

"Another one of Stevenage's paradoxes?" she suggested as they turned to retrace their steps in the fading light.

"You are getting the measure of it" confirmed Tom.

"It is hard to imagine that such a distinguished war hero as Cammaerts should spend so many years of his life as the Head Master of this unremarkable school."

"He may not have seen it that way. He was probably a very good Head Master."

"I'm sure he was, though he did let the boys read DH Lawrence."

"Is that such a bad thing?"

They walked briskly back through the centre of Stevenage.

Paul Wilson was still bothered by the fact that there were no significant leads on Lorraine. There was nothing to explain why she might have been snatched from a crowded Baker Street in the morning rush hour. She was not in debt. She had neither boyfriend or girlfriend. She was not in trouble. Those whom they had interviewed at the Nightingale Hospital talked of her professionalism, her experience, her intelligence, and her general good humour. Perhaps, after all, she really was the random hostage. Paul's team, led by Louise Tindall, had contacted the clinicians who had led research projects that Lorraine had worked on. There were no obvious clues there either and Paul was at the point where he could confidently rule out any connection; Lorraine's abduction was unlikely to be related to any. But there must be something, thought Paul: there always is. Could there be something more at her flat? Something we missed. A diary perhaps? Or a squiggled note on a piece of paper hidden by a fridge magnet or discarded in a waste paper bin? Perhaps he should make a further search of the flat, just in case Tindall had, unusually, missed something? Paul needed something to do. In the absence of anything else until the others returned from Stevenage, Paul decided that he would take a trip to Wooler Street and see for himself. Without a word to anyone he quietly slipped out of the office and flagged down the first available taxi.

"Any preferred route sir?"

"Chelsea Bridge then Elephant and Castle" shouted Paul over the rising clatter of the diesel engine.

The driver nodded his approval at Paul's choice as if to confirm it was the way he would have chosen as well. A couple of miles away, a brown Peugeot 504 ambled down Kilburn High Road, through Maida Vale: it was also en route for Wooler Street. It was two forty on a cold, nearly dark wintry afternoon.

As soon as the Volvo cleared Junction 4 on the A1(M) the traffic thinned out, as it always did, and PC Nixon pushed gently down with his right foot. PC Booth reacted quickly, flooring the throttle of the unmarked car, but he could only watch as the distance between the two cars stretched.

"Good job we are not in a hurry" quipped Sergeant Tindall as the speedometer crept agonizingly up to seventy, as if in homage to Dennis Weaver's creeping, shaking, dial in "Duel." Shortly, mercifully, the exit for Stevenage loomed into view; Nixon slowed the Volvo on the approach to allow his colleagues to catch up so that, as agreed, they could enter Stevenage in convoy. At 2.40 pm Tom caught sight of the Volvo slaloming around the A602: Nick Booth followed closely, too closely. Tom and Lorraine were no more than a hundred yards away when Tom saw the two cars scurrying towards the Kingsway Car Park.

"D takes c4. Queen's gambit accepted" Tom mused aloud.

Interesting move, thought Tom. He looked at his phone: eighteen minutes to three.

"I think that the Metropolitan Police have arrived in Stevenage. It is the obvious move."

Lorraine, who had seen the fully liveried Volvo, acknowledged that its array of lights marked it out as a colourful rooster in this drab chicken-town.

"Did you notice how closely the second car was following?"

"I didn't notice a second police car."

"When the kleptocrats speed their way through the empty night time streets of Eastern European cities, their security detail follows so closely behind that the front passenger could easily climb onto the boot of the car in front. It's a standard security arrangement for those who need to be protected. The police do something similar. Your eye is drawn to the lead car: you are not supposed to notice the unmarked back-up car."

Tom seemed to know so much: the overflowing fountain of his knowledge sustained her and she drank deep from it.

Paul's taxi turned right to head down Brandon Street. The Peugeot made its way east along the A2 sweeping left from Stead Street such that Thomas' Peugeot joined the traffic immediately behind Paul's taxi. Innocent of their shared interest in meeting Anthony Taylor, the two cars took little notice of each other until Paul's driver glanced into his rearview mirror.

"You don't see many of those around these days do you, guv?"

To make sure that Paul understood that he was referring to the car behind, he made an elaborate dumb show of pointing backwards over his left shoulder with his left thumb. Paul looked around at the wide mouthed grille and square eyes of the ancient 504.

"No, you don't see many of those around these days".

Paul remembered that this was coincidentally the punchline of a Billy Connolly joke about a wide-mouthed frog, a joke that had rendered an adoring Michael Parkinson helpless. It placed Connolly in the pantheon of the gods of television comedy but Paul was agnostic on Connolly. Paul thought his act to be all style and no content, the art of making a little material go a long way. Unlike his heroes Lenny Bruce and Bill Hicks, Billy Connolly had nothing much to say. Or so Paul thought. As Paul daydreamed his mini lecture, his driver had embarked on a shouty riff about Peugeots. Both monologues were brought to an abrupt halt by their arrival in Wooler Street. Paul responded to the hefty clunk of the released door locks by liberating a single mauve, twenty-pound note from his wallet; he didn't wait to be offered any change and the taxi pulled away, its animated driver still harping on Peugeots. Thomas steered the Peugeot to a gentle rest but remained in his seat. He was watching the man from the taxi who was now standing on the pavement. From the way he was looking up and down the unfamiliar street Thomas guessed he was not a local resident. And that made him suspicious. Paul surveyed the prospect of the neatly terraced houses, each with a pair of green and blue recycling bins on sentry duty at the railings, and headed in the direction of Portland Street. He knew which building he was looking for because he had checked on Streetview before he set off. Paul entered under the portico and spoke into the entry phone. Thomas eased himself out of the car. By the time he reached the building that housed Lorraine and Anthony's flats, the other man had disappeared; presumably he had been admitted inside. Thomas was sure that he was a policeman and did not want to risk being seen. He decided to return to the warm Peugeot. He would watch and wait.

Paul knocked on the door of Anthony's flat. The door inched slowly open liberating a scent of earthy woodfire and lemongrass. In the background Paul could hear Mr. Boombastic, which he recognized not because he had an encyclopedic knowledge of reggae music, but because he had an encyclopedic knowledge of Mr. Bean. Anthony seemed to pass through the barely open door like a spirit and joined Paul on the swirly patterned carpet of the vestibule.

Paul reached into his pocket to show Anthony his ID and introduced himself as Sergeant Tindall's superior officer. Paul ran through some questions about Lorraine's movements. Most of these Anthony answered with a simple yes or no. As they talked, Paul turned over the key to Lorraine's flat in his coat pocket. It was the key Mrs. Nair had left with Sergeant Tindall. Paul was tempted to use it. He thanked Anthony for his time and handed him his card. Once he was sure that Anthony had returned to the gravelly voiced Shaggy, he crossed to the door of Lorraine's flat. Furtively checking that there was no-one about, he turned the key in the lock and let himself in. Back inside his flat, Anthony took in the name on the card he had just received. DCI Paul Wilson. It was the name he had been expecting to see.

Nixon pulled the Volvo up to the barrier at the entrance to the Kingsway car park and pressed the intercom. The voice at the other end spoke through a fog of white noise and crackling: Nixon could not make out a single word. Frustrated he strained through the Volvo's open window and leaned in to the raised silver sieve. Holding down the button he said as slowly and as clearly as he could, "Police. Raise the barrier now. Please." As he was leaning to the right, he inadvertently pressed the accelerator and drowned out his own words with the Volvo engine's throaty sentence. Dev Singh began to giggle. The disembodied voice at the other end came on again but was still incomprehensible. Nixon swore. Singh giggled uncontrollably now. Behind them, PC Nick Booth wondered what the problem was. Sergeant Tindall leaned out of the passenger side window.

"Just take a ticket, Nixon!"
They were humbled into entering the car park just as any member of the public would.

"Do we know where this fucking car is parked?" Nixon's anger was fully expressed in the unnecessary expletive.

"It is bound to be parked on the roof. Any vehicle that the police are looking for is always on the roof of the car park. You must have seen enough movies to know that."

PC Singh's tongue wasn't entirely in his cheek. Nixon used the Volvo's prodigious grip to swirl up the crumbling concrete slabs of the cheaply built car park's driveway. PC Booth twice kerbed his tyres trying to keep up, earning him a disapproving look from Louise Tindall. Both cars were going too fast. When they came to the point where the gloomy covered damp of Level 5 gave way to the bright sunlight of the Upper Deck, both had to brake hard. A middle-aged lady wrestling some reluctant bags of shopping into the back of her orange Seat Ibiza stopped and shook her weary head. Sergeant Tindall gave her a reassuring smile.

"There it is, far right corner, second bay along. Park a few bays away."

"Why? Why not park right next to it? Save the walk."

"Might be a trap. Might blow up."

"You have been watching way too many movies."
Nevertheless, Nixon did as he was told and the two cars parked three and four bays away from the Honda Jazz and approached it on foot. The men held back, deferring

to their superior. Sergeant Tindall peered in through the passenger window. On the seat was a white A4 envelope. The immaculate handwritten italic script read,

"For the attention of Dr. Robert Martin. Metropolitan Police. Unsolved Historic Crimes Division."

Tindall beckoned Nixon and Singh to take a look.

"Blimey, another one."

"What do you mean, another one?" enquired Sergeant Tindall. PC Singh described their visit to the flat in Earlsfield.

"When we went in the flat was empty, unoccupied. But there was an envelope just like this one."

"What did you do with it?" asked Louise.

"Gave it to Sarge Wilson"

"You mean DCI Wilson" admonished Louise.

"And now there is another one" offered Nixon, unnecessarily.

"What should we do?"

"Whoever left the car here intended us to find it and with it, the envelope. I suggest that we do as you did before and take it to DCI Wilson."

"He is using us as his own delivery service" complained Dev.

"Like Hermes?"

"Or DPD or…"

"Yes, I get the point, Nixon."

"Did you know that Hermes was the Greek messenger of the gods?" They all turned and looked at Nick Booth.

"Really? I didn't know that" said Nixon. "Doesn't make it any better: we are still being used." Nixon was still angry from his slight at the ticket barrier.

"Better get the letter then." Sergeant Tindall nodded to Nixon, who went to open the passenger door.

"Wait. What if is a trap? What if there is a suspect device?" chipped in PC Singh.

"Why do you keep going on about that Dev?"

"Yes, but maybe he's right. I mean it could be" agreed Nick Booth.

"Remember the owner of this car is also the owner of the motorcycle used in an arson attack at Marylebone Station. He could have booby-trapped this car."

PC Booth was warming to his theme. Nixon looked nonplussed.

"Actually Nick, that is a good point." Louise came to Nick's rescue.

"If we are dealing with someone capable of arson then booby-trapping a car could be within his capability too?"

"Yes, but why would he do that?" replied Nixon looking rather exasperated. "I mean why booby-trap the car and leave the envelope inside on clear view? Presumably he wants us to find the envelope, so why would he prevent us from getting at it? Doesn't make sense."

Sergeant Tindall pulled at the cuffs of her leather gloves, bringing them tight to her wrists as if making clear that she was taking command of the situation.

"Check all around the car for any signs of tampering. Loose bits of upholstery, anything hanging down. Use your flashlights."

Nick Booth went to his car, reached into the back seat and then pulled on his hi-vis jacket. Singh dived into the back of the Volvo and did the same. Nixon looked at them stupefied. Louise was enjoying this. A moment ago, she was merely on the top deck of a car park, a piece of post war concrete in Stevenage, on a dull, cold and uninspiring day. Now she was dealing with a potential bomb threat in the form of a car of a suspected arsonist. And then there was the mystery of the envelopes. This was the most exciting day's policing she had experienced in a while. Singh and Booth busied themselves around the car, their yellow hi-vis jackets bobbing up and down as they shone flashlights in through the windows. Booth dropped to his knees to shine his light under the car.

"Can't see anything unusual" called Booth from underneath the rear end, "though it smells a bit of petrol down here."

"Knackered old car: bound to be leaking petrol and oil from somewhere" he said standing tall.

They concluded their search and Louise Tindall gave the all clear to Nixon who went, for the second time, to open the door. Sceptic though he was, he approached the task a good deal more gingerly than he had done fifteen minutes ago. The door dropped slightly on its hinges as it opened. Nixon reached in and passed the envelope back to Sergeant Tindall. She unfurled a clear plastic bag and placed the envelope in the evidence wallet as delicately as a cotton-gloved curator at the British Museum handles rare manuscript.

"Arrange for the car to be recovered by tow-truck: we need to let forensics examine it for prints."

PC Booth was already leaning into the walkie-talkie that was strategically attached to his left lapel.

"Blues and twos back home ma'am?" inquired Nixon optimistically as they returned to their cars.

"Once we are on the A1, yes" came the considered reply.

PC Booth was determined to keep up with the Volvo. It would be a good test of the skills he had recently acquired on the Advanced Driving course. The convoy helter-skeltered its way back down the ramp of the car park, nose to tail.

The reason why Nick Booth could smell petrol under the Honda was because Tom had disconnected the fuel pump to allow the remaining fuel to seep out. He had also hidden a motion sensor in the driver's side door pocket, buried amongst some ancient and still greasy McDonalds' napkins, where it was safely hidden from the prying flashlights of PCs Booth and Singh. When Nixon opened the passenger door, the motion sensor had activated the timer on a small explosive device on the exhaust, held in place by a magnet. As the two-car convoy made its way out of the car park, Tom's modest device clicked into life. It made no more noise than a stray banger on firework night. Its magnesium core sizzled and fizzed, spraying sparks onto the spilt fuel underneath. As Nixon guided the Volvo away from the car-park, he glanced into his rear-view mirror. It filled with a bright, orange glow. Beautiful sunset, he thought, and made for the A1. Twenty minutes later, the purging flames had cremated Tom's Honda. Ashen, charred, blistered, twisted metal now stood in its place. An acrid stink clung to the heavy air.

Chapter 15

Paul quietly closed the door of Lorraine's flat. It was a satisfyingly solid door; he felt it ease into place and click firmly shut. He stood for a moment. He felt uncomfortable being here. He shouldn't really be here. Louise ought to have returned Mrs. Nair keys. It felt wrong. He had no paperwork to justify being here and had told no-one that he was here. He felt as guilty as he had felt as a boy when he was caught scrumping in a nearby orchard. It was not that he did not want to understand every facet of Lorraine's life, but not this way, not by intruding like this. He could not work out why he felt so uneasy. After all he had searched hundreds of properties, residential and commercial, luxurious and squalid. He had fastidiously examined the scenes of crimes of passion, crimes of violence, crimes of blackmail, crimes of unimaginable cruelty and scenes of unintended fatal misadventure. But this was not a crime scene: it was Lorraine's home. In a crime scene, doors would be wide open; yellow and white tape would signify the boundary of the area. Colleagues in full PPE would be dabbing and dusting fingerprints: others would be easing tiny flecks of blood from carpets, curtains, baths and sofas; everything would be catalogued in numbered sealed bags. Journalists would be assembling patiently, waiting for a briefing. It was a science. But here he was standing in unviolated, intimate space. It was if Lorraine had just popped out for some milk or a newspaper. He was not usually emotionally compromised. So why did he feel like this today? He had the perfect psychological constitution for detective work. Even in the most appalling circumstances, he could detach himself. He had stared into the abyss, into the unfathomably dark regions of the human soul and he had not flinched. It was not that he was without compassion. It was not that he did not feel the pain and anguish of the victims, of their relatives and families. But like many mired in the murkiest aspects of police work, he had learned to compartmentalize. He had done his time trawling the dark web for child traffickers, molesters, and pornographers; he had seen images that most people could not conceive existed. He understood the human condition in all its depravity. But this was the first time that he had found himself emotionally drawn in. It was not as if he knew Lorraine. What's Hecuba to him, or he to Hecuba, that he should weep for her? Why could he not be like Rob? For Rob, detection was a question of solving puzzles; it was a purely intellectual endeavour. As Rob had reminded him many times, Sir Arthur Conan Doyle was a doctor, and the science of detection was diagnostic. There was no room for emotion. Paul understood that. But something about Lorraine was bothering him; standing here in her flat he was struggling to remain dispassionate. Perhaps it was because he had no way of knowing whether she was still alive. The longer she was missing, the chances of her being found alive diminished: that was a given in missing persons cases. Perhaps it was because the flat was still so obviously full of her presence. There was something about the undisturbed ordinariness of her flat that made him feel that she was still here, or at least might be here at any moment. But perhaps what unnerved Paul most was not knowing enough about Lorraine, not knowing why she had been taken. And that made him feel, for the first time in his professional life, that he did not know what he was doing. Lorraine had been taken by someone who seemed to be drawing them in, toying with them. He felt powerless because he was not the author of this drama; he was, like Hamlet's player, merely an actor in it. He felt like a contestant in a game whose rules he did not know. And that was a sensation he most definitely did not like. As he stood looking vaguely into the kitchen, he felt the vibration of his mobile phone in his left pocket. It came as a relief. Fishing it out, he saw that it was Sergeant Tindall calling. He gladly pressed green to accept the call.

"Louise. Where are you?"

"Heading back down on the A1. Eta London about 45 minutes."

"Good. How was it?"

"The car, the Honda Jazz, was in the multi-storey car park. It hadn't moved from the last CCTV image we had."

"Almost certainly abandoned."

"Yes, but here's the funny thing. The doors had been left unlocked and the only item inside the car was a large A4 envelope on the passenger seat."

"Addressed to Rob Martin?"

"Yes. Dev tells me it is exactly like the one in the flat."

Paul felt his stomach drop.

"What about the car?"

"We have arranged for it to be towed to the forensics lab."

"Good. It's worth a try, but if it is anything like the motorbike it will have been wiped clear of prints and we will be none the wiser. I will see you back at the office."

It would take him forty-five minutes to get back to the office at this time of day, so he had better leave immediately. Paul was in fact desperate to leave and easily convinced himself that he had to go now. If Mrs. Nair knew that he had used her key to enter her property without her permission and without a warrant, she could justifiably make a complaint. Paul let himself out as quietly as he had let himself in and re-crossed the swirly patterned carpet to the main door. As he left the building, he sensed a slight increase in the volume of the reggae music. Anthony must have opened his door. Paul was relieved that Louise had called him when she did.

Thomas had been driving slowly around the neighbouring streets. He knew that people generally tend not to take much notice of moving cars, whereas they will often notice a parked car, especially if there is somebody in it. As he drove by for the third time, he glanced down Wooler Street; he glimpsed DCI Wilson's arched back disappearing into the back of a taxi. If his quarry was, as he suspected, a policeman, then he should follow him. He would abandon the plan to speak to Lorraine's neighbour. He had brought along a wad of notes in case he needed encouraging, but how much would he know anyway? Whether she put her bins out regularly? This new development was likely to yield more useful information. If Thomas could confirm that it was the police who were looking for Lorraine, then that was a better outcome than gleaning next to nothing from her neighbour. His mind was made up, and he eased the Peugeot into the traffic not far behind the taxi. He followed discreetly. As he hoped, on Victoria Embankment the taxi pulled over and discharged its lone passenger right outside New Scotland Yard. Thomas drifted past to get a good look at Wilson, then drove blithely on. He had accomplished more on his little outing than Fin would have thought possible.

"Earl Grey, or an Earl Grey and Afternoon tea mix?" Lorraine replied that she felt in the mood for a mixed brew. About twenty minutes after Tom had pointed out the two police cars making their way to the Kingsway car park, the urgent wail of fire engines made the same journey, interrupting their tea ceremony.

"There are several reasons why cars are parked on the roof of a multi-storey car park" explained Tom as he added the boiling water to the plain white teapot. "It isn't much use if you are going to need the car again in a hurry, but if you might be abandoning it, for example, it is easily the best option. It buys you time, since anyone who is following you will be inconvenienced by the twisting climb. Secondly, fire engines can only access the roof area by means of cherry pickers and ladders."

Tom poured Lorraine's tea and brought it over to the kitchen table where they sat like Cezanne's card players huddled over the board.

"But why did you set fire to the car? asked Lorraine who was genuinely interested to know.

"Once the police had picked up the paperwork that I had left for them on the passenger seat, then the work of the Honda was done."

They sat in near silence for a while taking in the faint bergamot perfume of their tea. Suddenly Tom leapt to his feet.

"I think it is time to leave Stevenage. We have exhausted its attractions."

Lorraine was feeling weary and did not relish heading out into the grim, dark streets. But she had suspected that they would have to move on. Tom sensed her dismay and sought to console her.

"Our next port of call is altogether more congenial. Help me wash up and tidy around. Someone will take care of the beds but we must leave everything else exactly as we found it."

There was so much that Lorraine wanted to ask Tom but she had resolved to keep her counsel.

Rob had spent most of the afternoon thinking about his Pam Landy moment, his unwelcome epiphany. Someone, somehow, knew that he was working on the classified files documenting the events that took place on December the twelfth,1974. By giving him the grid reference for Kilkee, his correspondent was either trying to draw his attention to something he had not yet understood in the papers, or he was trying to lead him astray with a red herring. He faced a binary choice. Kilkee was a coastal resort in County Clare approximately eighty kilometres south west of Feakle; it had no obvious relevance that he could fathom. So, if it is a red herring, why? What is he trying to distract me from? What does he not want me to find? Rob was determined to find a coherent narrative for the events of that night nearly fifty years ago. Rob knew that the meeting in Feakle had been government sanctioned. As Mrs. Thatcher famously remarked, she didn't talk to terrorists, but others did. If the names of all of those who took part in those talks were ever revealed, it would be very difficult for all of those involved, both at the time and in the years since. Was someone trying to silence him? The faded, badly typed documents he pored over glowed dimly. There had to be something in the darkness, he felt sure. But the scientific method of trial and error led him nowhere. I need to construct a hypothetical narrative, he thought, as Holmes would do, and interrogate it. As if to endorse this idea, his Dr Watson, in the shape of Paul Wilson, burst clumsily and noisily into the room.

Chapter 16

Thomas fidgeted in the Peugeot's mottled, fraying leather front seat as he waited for the garage door to inch itself up just high enough to drive in. He waited impatiently for the door to inch its slow way back down again. The reassuring 'click' as the lock fell into place was the signal that the warm Peugeot could be left to tick itself cool. He headed off and made quick work of the short journey to the Campbell. He found himself pulling on the brass handles to ease open its heavy double doors. Thomas felt the hot draft of fuggy air warm as a dog's breath on his chilly face. He breathed in the stale air, his nostrils warmed by the beery fumes drifting aimlessly from the all-day drinkers who supped carefully, their smeared empties littered across the bar. At this time of day, the air was partly flushed and cleansed by the repeated opening and closing of the doors bringing in the evening crowd: thirsty men from building sites and betting shops, girls and women from offices. The Campbell regulars kept faith with the traditional gender divisions of working-class London. New arrivals broadcast loudly as they entered, breaking the bored silence of the dying hours of the afternoon. The hollow cheeked men with rough hands and consumptive coughs, looked up briefly and nodded in recognition at the incoming tide. One or two might have stolen a glance at the clock, surprised that it was that time already. The landlady beamed smiles of welcome. With one hand she guided the pump downwards; with the other she swayed the brimming glass from side to side to settle a creamy quarter inch on top of the dark black malt beneath. In a matter of minutes, the varnished, sticky bar heaved with Murphy's. White wines, spritzers, vodka and tonics, lagers and the occasional red wine huddled on the miniature round tables that invariably proved too small for their cargoes. Conversation levels rose and Thomas found himself having to shout his order across the melee, then resort to sign language, gesturing as he leaned into the low glass screen that ran along the bar. Next to him one of the all-day men simply nodded his order to a familiar bartender and was served silently, promptly; a perfect mime. Thomas lifted his glass over the head of his neighbour, who neither flinched nor spoke. Turning sharp right at the end of the long bar, edging his way courteously through the tables, he entered the oblong space between the back wall of the pub and the carved Victorian screen that separated it from the busy passage to the toilets. Here was sanctuary; celebrants and worshippers could hear and be heard, but their conversational murmur melted into the thick folds of the yellowing wallpaper. Along the screen, at waist height, was a makeshift bookstand. Here readerly types could peruse copies of "An Phoblact", the "Morning Star", "The Irish Examiner" and "The Clare Echo", whilst others could avail themselves of sets of dominoes. On the lower shelves the determined seeker could find copies of "The Gaeltacht Act." Beneath them were half a dozen remaining copies of 'Coiste Forbartha Gaeltachta Chontae an Chlair." In the quiet air of this committee room a dozen or so men and women, in groups of three or four were in earnest conversation. Thomas attached himself to the huddle containing two of his colleagues from Hermit Place. In another age and in another time, one could almost imagine someone reading softly, mournfully, 'The Death of Parnell, 1891.'

"Ah Thomas, come and join us" offered his colleague.

"You know Michael, don't you?"

Thomas recognized Michael, who was still wearing his Royal Mail uniform and cradling his pint in his left hand.

"Michael was just telling us the latest news from the depot."

"Yes. There are four reliable men in there just now. We tell them what we need and they see us right. But I have stood them down for the time being."

"Why is that?"

"One of the runners cashing the cheques says he was followed. Probably means the police have the serial numbers. Best throw them out" said Michael, as if he were remarking on some weary salad leaves that had turned limp and damp.

"OK. We've still plenty of fresh cash in the fridge" replied Fin as if subconsciously confirming the analogy. Michael, who was responsible for requisitions and supplies, nodded appreciatively.

"Ok. Let's go talk to Gerry and Joe."
Michael moved them towards a group of men in labourers' clothes. Two Hi-Viz yellow jackets lay clumsily across the back of their chairs. As the men knew each other there was no need for introductions. After a brief exchange affirming the fine quality of the Murphy's tonight, Gerry lent forward.

"We've everything we need. We've detonators and dynamite, batteries, fertilizer, nails, and screws of all sorts. Joe can put 'em together. We can lift piping from the building site: the contractors ordered more than they could ever need. It has taken months of careful planning but things are coming together."

He drank deep from his glass.

"They tell me you are a fine driver, Thomas?"

"That I am sir."

"Well, that's good because London needs careful drivers."

They laughed, easily; to everyone else in the pub the scene appeared entirely ordinary and natural. Noticing that glasses were running low Thomas motioned to go to the bar.

"Come and sit by me Fin."
Gerry motioned to the leader of the Hermit Place four. Fin took his place next to Gerry. Michael sat opposite them, his back to the bar, effectively using his large frame to shield all three of them from sight.

Fin was urbane and intelligent. He had a Doctorate on the history of the Irish Free State: there was not much about the Fenian cause that he did not know. Michael, on the other hand, was a big-boned, hardy man of ways and means. Gerry was a man without fear. Together, their skills were complementary. And they were bound by both history and geography, born within the same county. Joe took their arrival as his cue to leave the table to the three wise men.

"Everything good at Hermit Place, Fin?"
"Yes, fine."
"Thomas?"
"He's reliable. No doubts about him."
"No doubting Thomas, eh?"
Gerry smiled at his own joke.
As if to prove his worth Thomas arrived with three pints which he deposited carefully and wordlessly in front of them: he knew he was not required to speak and he retired gracefully.

"See what I mean?" said Fin.
The three men settled into their pints. Michael voiced what was on all their minds.

"So, what do we do about the woman?"
"We went to her flat. She hasn't been back for a couple of days. She's not been at work either."
"Are you sure it was the right place?"

Fin reached into his pocket and pulled out a pamphlet. It bore the same Gaelic title as those half a dozen others on the lower shelves to the left of their knees.

"I found this on her bookcase, on top of a fine book, 'The Castles of County Clare.' Must have come from here."

Gerry considered it carefully.

"I don't believe in co-incidence, Gerry. And neither do you" said Fin with some steeliness.

"So, it is definitely her" added Michael rather pointlessly, but more for his own satisfaction. He wanted to press on and feared any delay.

"Where else would she have picked that up?" asked Fin after a short silence.

"True that, Fin."

"But that doesn't mean she knows anything does it?" offered Gerry more in hope than expectation.

"She may not. But why has she gone missing? The fact that she has gone missing suggests that she, or someone else, knows something."

"That's true" agreed Michael.

"Maureen, who works nights at the Nightingale, recognized her as the woman that she had seen here in the Campbell a couple of nights ago. She obviously took that pamphlet back to her flat. And then disappeared."

The length of his sentence seemed to make Fin thirsty; the cream from his stout etched an incongruous clown's smile at the edges of his mouth. He wiped it away with the rough sleeve of his left arm.

"Her name is Lorraine Watson; hardly a Fenian name now, is it?"

"So, what do we do about her?"

"That very much depends upon who she is and what she was doing here in the Campbell. Until we know that, we can't be sure. That's what worries me. As I see it, we have three options. One, we get clearance to go ahead.

Two, we go after her, just to be sure we know who she is, and who she might be working for. Three, we do both."

"Do we have the resources for that Michael?" asked Gerry

"For two simultaneous operations? Yes."

"Then" said Fin, "I vote that we recommend option three."

Gerry swallowed the last mouthfuls of his pint and tapped it on the table twice. Michael did the same. Fin nodded. They were unanimous.

"I will make the call."

He glanced over to Thomas who, despite being deep in conversation with Joe and Maureen, immediately got up and went to the bar.

As Tom led Lorraine through the barrier at Stevenage station, he caught her lightly by the elbow and pointed up at the yellow text of the electronic departures board. He knew exactly which train they were due to take and that it departed from Platform 4 in precisely two minutes, but his intention was to make sure that by lingering here the security cameras would capture a very clear image of Lorraine. Tom wanted her image to be installed on every police computer because he needed the police to understand that she was alive, well, and about to depart Stevenage. Tom stood at the perfect angle to make sure that only the back of his head was visible to the camera and then hurried them both to the obligingly open barrier. Lorraine felt the urgency of Tom's movements and demurred. She digested the information scrolling above her.

"Are we going to Cambridge Tom? I used to work at Addenbrooke's."

"I know."

It was a wintry evening and her breath trailed upwards and away like a wisp of steam. It seemed a metaphor for the way she felt: light, airy, powerless. She had given up any thought of trying to summon attention or escape. Try as she might she could not help herself: she was compelled by Tom's presence, a presence that stirred feelings that she was finding harder and harder to set aside. She knew that Stockholm Syndrome was a contested illness but she was beginning to feel that she could vouch for its legitimacy.

The drab flat land of north Hertfordshire slipped by: there was little of interest outside the window. Black embankments alternated with open fields. The land and the sky were as one. She preferred to gaze idly on Tom, who sat opposite her. Their knees occasionally greeted one another under the table. He was busy shuffling three different telephones from pocket to pocket. Lorraine recognized one of the devices as the latest Apple iPhone, a neat, slim rectangle with three cameras pointing directly towards her. Another she thought might be a Blackberry. The third she did not recognize at all and it was this third that currently held Tom's attention. The train lurched as the driver throttled back to begin their approach to Royston. Tom slipped his third phone into the side pocket of his coat.

"Royston is on the Greenwich Meridien, well near enough."

"Really?" said Lorraine bravely venturing a little sarcasm.

"It's actually one minute and twenty-seven seconds to the west. Shall I tell you something else interesting?"

"Thrill me."

"There was an episode of 'Thunderbirds' entitled 'The Duchess Assignment.' The Duchess concerned was called Deborah, Duchess of Royston. Almost certainly a joke on Gerry Anderson's part: his mother was called Deborah."

The train slowed into Royston whose bleary dim lights were barely powerful enough to light the station platform. Bleakly cold air smacked at their ankles as it burst through the opening doors.

Soon the engine shivered and lumbered its arthritic way out of the chaise longue of the station. Tom felt one of his phones communicating with him. His hands moved as swiftly as a magician's, thought Lorraine, as she watched admiringly. The same dexterous hands that had cooked for her and given her wine were now employed in manipulating the two phones simultaneously. Tom read the message, which was from Anthony.

"Wilson was here." Just that. But it was enough. He pocketed the phone and looked across at Lorraine.

Chapter 17

Paul's skittering entrance into Rob's office brought Tindall, Booth, Nixon and Singh in its wake. Paul looked at Rob self-consciously, surveying the five of them.

"Groucho, Zeppo, Harpo, Chico and Gummo?" Paul offered somewhat plaintively.

"No-one remembers Gummo do they? So-called because he always wore rubber boots."

Nixon, Singh and Booth looked perplexed. Their cultural range of references did not extend to the Marx Brothers. They waited patiently for the conversation to turn. Nick Booth scanned the bookshelves behind Rob's desk. There were books at every angle, filling every inch of space. Some looked as if they were about to fall onto the floor. They were piled horizontally, diagonally, and vertically. More piles grew in twists like stalagmites from the floor. Nick had never seen so many books, not even in the library of the Police College.

Rob gestured to them all to find a seat. That was not especially easy as the chairs were deep in files. The three young policemen carefully removed the files to the floor, doing everything possible to make sure that no papers came out of the files and that the piles remained in the same geometric form that they had taken on the chairs. Paul, as usual, perched on the side of Rob's desk. Once they were all seated, they formed a tableau vivant.

"Louise, please bring Rob up to speed."

Louise began a very thorough description of the trip to Stevenage. As she reached the end of her narrative her phone rang: she looked up at Paul for permission to answer it. He nodded. The message was brief and dispiriting: Louise pressed the button to end the call and sat for a moment.

"I can't believe it. The Honda Jazz has been destroyed by a fire on the roof of the Kingsway multi-storey. How could that have happened?"

"It did smell of petrol" offered Nixon. "But we were careful."

"I don't imagine it was anything you did Nixon. Any of you."

"Thank goodness for that." A relieved Nick Booth was genuinely anxious.

"But that means that we have lost any evidence that might have led us to the car's owner. And the owner of the car could be the same person responsible for Lorraine Watson's disappearance."

"Quite so, Nick. But I very much doubt that forensics would have found anything" said Paul. "You remember that our perpetrator is almost certainly responsible for the fire at Marylebone Station" continued Paul. "It is very likely that he has some considerable expertise in the art of setting things on fire."

"But that means he must have been in or around Stevenage when we were there."

It was the first time Singh had spoken. He was alarmed at the prospect. Remembering his Pam Landy moment with an internal shiver, Paul turned to Singh,

"It is more than possible that he was watching you all the time and set the fire as soon as you left." Paul thought that although the first part of this was very likely, he doubted the second part.

"But the only person we saw in the car park was a lady loading her shopping into a car."

"That's right."

Louise was determined to reassure Paul that that her operation had not been cack-handed. Paul obliged with the reassurance she needed.

"Don't worry Louise. None of you did anything wrong. Not for a minute. And you have the envelope, which is the most important piece of evidence. Now, if Dev is right, then our perpetrator was still in Stevenage this afternoon."

"Which means CCTV."

Nick Booth was following Paul's train of thought carefully.

"So, start work on footage from any of the main points in and out of Stevenage, that's to the say the A1 and the station first."

Paul made a shoo-ing gesture towards the door. Ever one for protocol, Louise Tindall leapt to the aid of her team,

"Nixon and Singh are at the end of their shift sir, but Booth and I can make a start."

Nixon and Singh looked grateful: Booth was first to his feet. As they left the room for Nixon and Singh to begin their respective journeys home and for Booth and Tindall to begin to trawl through hours of CCTV footage, Louise reached over and carefully placed the envelope on Rob's desk.

"Thanks" said Paul, "and well done."

Once they were all out of earshot Paul and Rob exchanged knowing glances.

"You don't really think that our arsonist went back to the Jazz to set it on fire, do you?"

"Of course not: almost certainly used a remote device. But I do think he might still be in or around Stevenage."

"We can't be sure" replied Rob. "But what we do know for sure is that he wants us to have this envelope."

Rob and Paul had not had a chance to meet to discuss the contents of the first one, a point that each of them acknowledged as they looked at the latest, identically addressed, white rectangle.

"Bring over a chair Paul."

Rob rummaged through the various documents on his desk and pulled out the first envelope.

Paul looked at it again. Empty white space with just the one inscription.

"Q885601."

"This is the point we had reached, Paul."

"Yes, but if I know you Rob, since then you will have developed a theory."

"Better than that Paul. I have developed an answer."

"And?"

"It's a map reference."

"Where?"

"Kilkee, County Clare, Eire."

Paul took a few moments to absorb the information.

"How did you work it out?"

"I was re-reading some documents and came across a similar six-digit number."

"And?"

"Well, all grid references on the island of Ireland are prefaced with a letter of the alphabet, with the exception of the letter i. So, twenty-five grids, each of a hundred square kilometres."

"And what is the significance of Kilkee?"

"I haven't got that far yet. But here's the thing." He picked up a heavy lever arch file from his desk so that Paul could see the title.

"This is one of many files of all the extant government and secret service papers concerning a meeting that took place in Feakle, County Clare, on the twelfth of December 1974. When the Gardai broke up the meeting, the IRA members had all vanished. The mystery is how the IRA members knew to make themselves scarce. There is nothing to suggest that the Irish government had anything to gain from the Gardai breaking up the meeting. So why did they? And who tipped off the IRA?"

"Are these white envelopes something to do it?"

"I have to assume so."

"Geography is not my special subject, but isn't Kilkee on the coast?"

"Yes, and about eighty kilometres away from Feakle. But perhaps someone is trying to tell me that it is an important clue."

"Or they could be trying to put you off."

"That had occurred to me too Paul."

"What if it's a co-incidence?"

As soon as Paul uttered these words, he knew how they would be met.

"Come on. You don't believe in co-incidence any more than I do. Only a handful of people know that I have been asked to work on this case. Apart from the Prime Minister, the Foreign and Home Secretaries, the members of COBRA, some very senior civil servants and the Commissioner herself, and you, no-one else knows. Or at least no-one else is supposed to know."

"Which means....."

"This isn't an arcane piece of ancient history. And it is different from Bloody Sunday. We know pretty much exactly what happened on Bloody Sunday: the various protracted inquiries have only ever been a question of how much blame could be apportioned to whom and when. And that is largely a political matter. This is quantitatively different."

"Why is that?"

"What do you remember about 1974?"

"Watergate? Abba winning the Eurovision Song Contest? The Netherlands losing the World Cup Final when they were by far the best team?"

"Closer to home."

"Harold Wilson?"

"The bloodiest IRA bombing campaign ever mounted on the mainland."

Chapter 18

As the train trundled its careful way along the arrow straight track stretching north-east out towards Fen Ditton, Lorraine could just make out the gloomy lights of the platform of Cambridge station. Arriving in this impossibly beautiful city by rail could not be more underwhelming. Indeed, she had witnessed many a tourist looking entirely baffled by its ordinariness: they had been expecting the Victorian Gothic drama of a Bristol Temple Meads or a St. Pancras. The architectural purity of the low porte-cochere of the long classical façade of the station, on the prosaically named Station Road, cannot be seen from the track; all that is visible on the approach is the abrupt, white, right angle of the platform roof, a roof that seemed to Lorraine to be oppressively, broodingly low. But, she reflected, Temple Meads is the prophet of a false dawn; it is much the grandest building in Bristol and it gives no sense of the city centre's charmless, pitiless post war brutality. Conversely, Cambridge's functional station, not much more than a halt, provides no clue that it is the gateway to a city of unmatched beauty. The station is unfussy, restrained and a little austere. The squealing brakes stopped the four carriages more abruptly than Lorraine was expecting. By the time she had regained her balance Tom was gently urging her onto the platform, through the open barriers, and out into Station Road. He immediately summoned a taxi.

"St Mary's College please."

Lorraine had not been back to Cambridge since she spent a year working at the old Addenbrooke's Hospital, but as they sped past Parker's Piece, it felt so familiar. She was looking forward to seeing the colleges in the daylight but her reverie was interrupted by Tom accidentally digging his elbow into her side, retrieving his buzzing phone.

"I am so sorry Lorraine. I didn't mean…"

"It's fine" she said cutting off his apology.

Tom scrolled to the latest message. It was from Anthony.

"Brown Peugeot. Reg K147 OUP"

DCI Paul Wilson's hunch had been right; Anthony had indeed opened his door to check that Paul had left the building. But what he had not realized was that Anthony had followed him out into Wooler Street. Anthony watched as Wilson poured himself slightly gingerly into the taxi. Then Anthony's eye fell upon the brown Peugeot. Anthony saw that its driver was also closely watching Wilson. As Thomas set the Peugeot in motion, evidently tailing the taxi, Anthony logged the registration number as securely as he had catalogued the face, and the accent, of Conor earlier that afternoon.

As soon as Tom had deleted Anthony's message and pocketed the phone, he pressed one of his other phones to his ear. Lorraine could hear its faint ring.

"Carl. Yes, very well thanks. Listen, I have another job for you. A vehicle trace. A brown Peugeot: registration Kilo147 Oscar Uniform Papa."

A slight pause, then,

"Yes, yes, all of the usual details. Everything. Thanks. Bye."

The taxi drew up outside the Porter's Lodge of St Mary's. The studded wooden doors, rising to an arch about fifteen feet high, were firmly closed. Tom clicked the latch of the handle of the smaller door set within the larger doors, and stooped to enter through its narrow portal.

Inside, a Porter stood with his arms placed on the counter like a shopkeeper. He was dressed very differently from a shopkeeper, in a black frock coat, pinstripe trousers, white shirt and grey tie. Lorraine saw the Porter's face light up as he recognized Tom. Withdrawing his arms, he stood upright, possibly even to attention. Lorraine knew that the Porters of Cambridge were often ex-military men, men who knew how to be discrete, and this one seemed no exception as he drew himself up to his full height.

"Good evening, sir. Very good to see you again." The light in the Porter's Lodge was pleasingly low, as if it were imitating the orange candlelight that would once have been the only means of lighting this enclosed space marking the separation of the world outside and the inner sanctum of the College. Behind the Porter Lorraine saw the rows of pigeon-holes and wondered why they were still needed.

"It is very good to see you too Ron. Everything well?"

"Yes, sir, very well. Professor Needham is expecting you in his rooms at seven."

"Splendid."

"In the mean-time, shall I accompany you to your rooms?"

"Yes, that would be very kind of you Ron." Ron had already made his way to the end of the counter and raised its hinged end to vertical. He stepped through the narrow opening to join them.

"This way sir. This way madam." Ron opened a second small wooden door, only just large enough to allow for one at a time to pass through, and which led to First Court. Lorraine looked around with a kind of hushed wonder. There were lights on in every window, as Michaelmas Term still had a week to go, but it was still quite dark beneath their feet and Lorraine had to pick her way carefully across the cobbles.

"Are the young behaving as badly as ever Ron?"

"It is very different from your day sir. They all seem to work so hard now. No time for high jinks. It has all become rather serious if you ask me sir."

They crossed the First Court diagonally and ducked through a small opening in the far corner, an opening which Lorraine had not even noticed. This led them into a much grander space, Second Court. Here the buildings were three rather than two storeys high, and on the left-hand side Lorraine could see the illuminated dark blue and red of stained-glass windows. Ron led them to a staircase about half way along on the right-hand side. Tom stopped to look at the names of the resident undergraduates on this staircase. They were written in black script on a white background. The ground floor bore the inscription "Guest Rooms."

"You remember where to find Professor Needham's rooms sir?"

"How could I forget?"

"In which case I will bid you both a very good night."

"Thank you."

Ron pressed a set of keys into Tom's hands and turned back into the Court: the click-clack of his heels against the cobbles quietened to a ghostly echo.

"I will explain in a moment" said Tom, sensing Lorraine's bewilderment. He opened the outer door of the guest rooms and ushered Lorraine inside.

"My old college."

"I gathered that."

There were two bedrooms, each with a rudimentary bathroom, and a shared sitting room.

"These would have been undergraduate rooms once. Known as shared sets. In these days of jealousy guarded privacy and personal space you can see why they are not so popular with the young men and women. But they were great fun, though not ideal in your final year as they were places where little work was ever done. Which room do you want?"

"Either."

"I am afraid I shall be locking the outer door when I pop round to see the Professor."

"I understand."

Lorraine was thoroughly used to Tom's guardianship by now and made no protest. She was cold and weary and the prospect of an evening in her own company was welcome and necessary.

"By the way" added Tom, "in case you were wondering, the college is named after the other Mary, not the BVM, but Mary of Magdala. The Apostle of the apostles."

Lorraine hadn't been wondering, but was struck by Tom's use of the abbreviation BVM, from the Latin "Beata Maria Virgo." It was an abbreviation familiar to her but she had not heard it for some time.

In Hermit Place an open bottle of Jameson's stood proud and alone on the low coffee table, the upturned red cap to its side. Fin was rehearsing his conversation with Gerry and Michael in the Campbell earlier that evening. The four huddled together cradling their dimpled tumblers. Fin was mid narrative.

"A couple of days later Maudy was watching the news and there was an item about a missing person, a nurse from the Nightingale Hospital, who had not been seen for a while. Maureen recognized her as the same woman who had come into the Campbell a couple of nights before. Maureen had a contact at the hospital and was able to find the nurse's address."

"The address we went to in Wooler Street earlier" confirmed Conor, without averting his concentrated gaze from the diminishing amber puddle at the bottom of his glass.

"But as you know, we found no-one at home when we went there. But I did find this." Fin pulled the pamphlet from his pocket and placed it on the light brown knee-high table. The back page had soggy edges, a little spilt Murphy's from the damp pub table. The others recognized it as one of the pamphlets from the library in the Campbell.

"Now, when we went back in daylight there was still no sign of her. All we could do was keep on watching the flat. This afternoon, as you know, we sent young Thomas alone. Now this is the new part." Conor and Jo sat forward as if to confirm their concentration.

"When Thomas went there, he saw a man that he suspected was plain-clothes and probably pretty senior, going into the building. Thomas waited in the car until he came out again and followed him back across the Thames. Sure enough, he got out of his taxi and went into New Scotland Yard."

"What does that mean?" asked Conor. Fin shuffled forward on his seat.

"It means that if a senior officer from the Met is making enquiries, the police don't know where she is. And they are looking for her. Now it could be a routine missing persons enquiry. It may turn out that she is a regular nurse who simply fancied a drink or a holiday on the west coast of Ireland, and that is what brought her to the Campbell. But Maudy has a sixth sense and she thought she was being evasive when she spoke to her. And she is missing."

"What happens now then, Fin?"

"We sit tight until we receive instructions. We are operationally ready, but we have to be sure that we are not being watched. All of us need to be very careful because it could any one of us that's being watched.

That's why Michael has called a halt, for the time being, to his fundraising campaign at the sorting office."

"Is he worried someone is on to him?"

"I don't think so. Michael works through middlemen who use delivery boys from drug gangs and so on. They don't know who they are working for and they don't care so long as they get paid. That's all they want. For them it's just another service they provide. So even if the police were on to the missing cheques, they would struggle to trace them back to Michael. But we can't be too careful."

There was a thoughtful silence as each digested the significance of the potential threat posed by a nurse whose appearance in the Campbell and disappearance immediately afterwards, were equally problematic.

Chapter 19

Paul had not meant to be flippant and he felt a bit foolish. He should have known Rob meant 'The Troubles'.

"The mainland campaign ranged from targeted strikes on selected individuals …."

"McWhirter, 'The Guinness Book of Records' man" interrupted Paul excitedly. "I remember because I used to watch 'Record Breakers' with Roy Castle. He was non-smoker who died of lung cancer. How unlucky is that?"

"That was in 1975 Paul, and we know that Mr. McWhirter was assassinated by the Balcombe Street gang each of whom received multiple life sentences. My focus is on the events of 1974."

Rob wanted to put the ball into Paul's court.

"Have you seen 'In the Name of the Father'?"

"Daniel Day-Lewis. One of the few films for which he did not win an Oscar."

"Then you will know the story of the wrongful convictions of The Guildford Four. Equally egregiously, the Maguire Seven were wrongfully convicted of the Birmingham pub bombings."

"All their convictions were overturned, weren't they?"

"They were, but the scars have yet to heal. The sense of outrage at the injustices of the British judicial system, hardly surprisingly, is hard baked into Republicanism, as is the memory of Bloody Sunday. There have been so many enquiries but for the Republicans the only fact that matters is the body count, 'Paras thirteen, the walls said, Bogside nil.'"

"Ouch. Who said that?"

"Seamus Heaney. In a poem called 'Casualty'. But the wounds run deep elsewhere not least in the victims' families' campaigns to re-open the Inquiry into the Guildford Pub bombings."

"Nobody else has ever been prosecuted for either the Guildford or the Birmingham pub bombings, have they?"

"At their trial the Balcombe Street gang claimed responsibility, but no-one really believed them. At least two of the them arrived in London on October the tenth, after the bombings. The lawyers for the Crown reasonably assumed that they were trying to take one for the team. But why is it that no-one else has ever been brought to trial?"

Paul understood the implication.

"The obvious answer is that nobody knows who was responsible."

"That is the obvious answer Paul, but it also very obviously the wrong answer."

"Why?"

"Put the question another way. How could we not know?"

"How?"

"Well think about who could have known. How could IRA High Command not have known? They must have known. They gave the orders. And if High Command knew, then what of the Mi6 agents who were working with them, and who brokered the meeting in Feakle in the December after the bombings in order to negotiate a ceasefire? Might they not have known? And what of those present in Feakle? Might not those who gave the orders have been there? Or possibly the bombers themselves?"

"So why don't we bring those people to trial?"

"Because we can't."

"Why?"

"Because most of them have died. But going after those who are still alive is impossible. It would be seen as a betrayal of the peace process and it would jeopardize everything that we have achieved to bring about peace. Especially the Northern Ireland Agreement."

"But surely justice must be done? If we can find out, if we can know who was responsible, we owe it to the victims and their families."

"Impossible. Too much at stake. Far better for everyone to look the other way, as it were."

Rob and Paul entered their own silence. Paul wanted to make sure that he had followed the argument.

"Let me check that I am following this correctly Rob. Are you saying that there are those on both sides who are concealing what they know and, in some cases, may have known for fifty years?"

"Well, it wouldn't be the first time, would it? The intelligence services knew all along that Anthony Blunt was the fourth man. But he was allowed to become Keeper of the Queen's Collections. And they knew Philby was going to defect to Moscow in 1963 and made only a half-hearted attempt to stop him."

"I see what you mean."

"And the envelopes have something to do with all this?"

"Ah yes, the envelopes."

Paul's mind had been working so fast to keep up with Rob that he had almost forgotten the pressing matter of the second envelope. It was resting on a precarious pile of papers, exactly where Louise Tindall had left it.

"Another code perhaps?"

"Hmmm."

Both fell silent. As usual, Paul broke the silence

"Do you know what really, really bothers me, Rob?"

"That Lenny Bruce died young?"

Paul was taken aback. This off-hand remark brought into question one of his core beliefs about Rob. He believed that Rob took no notice of his many babbling references to popular culture, partly because he knew that Rob did not own a television but mainly because he thought that Rob thought it was beneath him. But this piercing shaft of sunlight cast new light on the landscape of their relationship. Perhaps, all along, Rob had been listening. Perhaps all along Rob had taken notice. Perhaps he had even followed them up? After all he had, just moments ago, referred him to a Daniel Day Lewis film. Earlier he had clearly understood his rather feeble Marx brothers' joke. Maybe Paul had misread Rob all along? Maybe there was more to Rob Martin, dry, intellectual, distant, shut-in Rob Martin, than he thought.

"Not just Lenny Bruce. Bill Hicks too. And yes, both of their deaths bother me. But not right now."

"I know. It was my revenge for Abba and Harold Wilson."

Paul understood two things from this, one of which he already knew. He knew that Rob was cross with him for seeming to make light of his question about 1974. But what he did not know was the Rob knew how to tease him. He did not think he mattered that much to him. You only tease people you like. And he did not think Rob liked him enough for that. Paul had thought that real friendship between them was not possible because Rob held him at arm's length. Paul was the blundering Watson to Rob's brilliant Holmes. In "The Sign of the Four" Holmes tells Watson that he could never marry because "whatever is emotional is opposed to the true cold reason which I place above all things." And Paul had always thought that Rob was the same. But here was evidence to the contrary. If not quite an epiphany, it was a realization that he had underestimated Rob. This was an axis tilting moment. But he couldn't let it show.

"You mean something bothers you about these envelopes?"

"Yes. I have been thinking about them. It is very Conan Doyle. 'The strange case of the white envelopes'."

"Conan Doyle would surely have come up with a much better title than that, but go on."

Paul was enjoying this new version of Rob, the Rob who could be playful.

"The story goes like this.…The hapless detectives, you and I, have called in on Baker Street to seek Holmes' help because all our usual methods for finding a missing person have failed."

"A typical opening, I agree."

"We explain to Holmes that we were able to trace the owner of a motorbike, one that was used by the Marylebone arsonist, to an address in Hounslow. The property contained nothing but an envelope, addressed to you, containing the map reference of an Irish fishing village. But we also discovered that the owner of the motorbike was also the owner of a Honda car that was seen parked in Cosway street on the morning of Lorraine Watson's disappearance from Baker Street. We deduce that it is possible that the arsonist is also responsible for Lorraine's disappearance, by the simple fact of the proximal locations of the two vehicles at the time of both events. Two days later, the Honda Jazz was found parked, almost certainly abandoned, on the rooftop of a multi-storey car park in Stevenage. In it there is a second envelope, exactly as the first. Within an hour the Jazz is engulfed in flames and destroyed."

"It does sound like a case for Holmes when you rehearse it like that."

"What would Holmes deduce from all this? He would surely conclude that a person, or persons, unknown has set a trail for us to follow and is watching us every step of the way to make sure that we are following it."

"We are being led by the nose, as asses are" said Rob.

Paul didn't recognize the allusion.

"If I could put it another way Rob, we are being led by Jason Bourne."

He wasn't sure if Rob knew the Jason Bourne films but he thought it was worth a chance. Rob looked thoughtful.

"To uncover Treadstone?"

So, he did know. Another revelation.

"Or more to the point to make sure that you don't discover the existence of Treadstone?"

"A rogue secret service hiding within the secret service? Surely the stuff of fiction?"

"You would have thought so. But we can't rule it out."

Rob knew that Paul was right. He had not realized that Paul understood the predicament he was in. Damned if he uncovered the truth and damned if he didn't. He was stuck between a rock and a hard place. But he was uplifted by his sense their relationship was moving to another level.

"There is a further complication" Paul continued.

"Early this morning, Lorraine's neighbour reported a break-in at Lorraine's flat. Louise and Nick went to the flat. Nothing had been taken or even disturbed. The break-in had all the hallmarks of a professional job. No prints. Nothing."

"Someone was looking for her?"

"Yes, but it is slightly more complicated than that. At a bit of a loose end this afternoon I decided to go and see for myself. I introduced myself to Lorraine's neighbour. He seemed to be expecting me. He looked right through me. He gave me nothing to go on, as if he were just watching for my reaction. When I left, I was sure that I was followed back to the office. We are being watched."

They exchanged nervous glances until Paul lightened the mood.

"Better open the envelope then."

Rob reached for his paperknife and slit the envelope open.

Paul and Rob stared at the paper. It was exactly as they were expecting, blank but for a single line of code in the middle. This time it read R574568.

"May I?" asked Paul pointing at the computer screen.

Rob silently got up and stood to the side so that he could watch Paul's fingers tap noisily over the keys.

"R574568 is the Irish grid reference for…..Limerick."

"Limerick. How far is that from Kilkee?"

More tapping.

"Ninety-one kilometers by road."

"But I am not sure that this is about the distance. There will be something that connects the places in some way, maybe historically. Or perhaps both Limerick and Kilkee connect to a third as yet unknown place or event."

"Only connect."

"What?"

"If you bought a television, you could watch a programme called 'Only Connect'."

"How would that help?"

"It is a quiz show. In the second round of questions contestants have to work out what comes fourth in a sequence. They are given up to a maximum of three clues with a diminishing number of points available after each clue."

"And?"

"Perhaps your correspondent is playing a game of 'Only Connect'."

Chapter 20

Tom locked the door of the guestroom, pocketed the key, walked backwards out of the arched doorway, turned, and headed for the dark green grass of Second Court whose yellow lights suffused the air with a murky, ethereal glow not quite sufficient to light the way. He paused to allow his eyes to adjust as he remembered many a late-night undergraduate trip-up on these uneven cobbles and did not want that piece of history to repeat itself. He made his way to the back of Second Court, rounding the Henry Moore sculpture whose hollows contained only darkness, and made his way through to Chadwick Court. Professor Needham's rooms were on L staircase. He climbed the stone steps and knocked on the heavy oak door at exactly seven o'clock.

"Come."

As apprehensive as he had been as an eighteen-year-old coming for his first supervision, Tom peered around the door to see the Professor busy at his drinks cabinet.

"Ah dear boy! Perfectly on time. Do come."

Tom ventured his way into the roomy study and took in the familiar landscape. As far as he could tell it had not changed in the slightest from the detailed image etched into his memory. It was a Madeleine cake moment, a remembrance of times past, and it was so vivid that he could not tell if it were happening now or if he had somehow been transported back in time. Time past and time present were contained in the instant. The brown leather armchair in which he used to sit to read out his essays whilst the Professor wandered off into the kitchen to fill the kettle, ("carry on, dear boy, I am listening") was in the same place. It sat at about forty-five degrees to the threadbare armchair where the Professor would return with his filled kettle and plug in to an extension lead at his feet. As Tom read, the steam would rise from the boiling kettle as from a Genie's lamp, until it reached the Professor's eye-line, whereupon he would, with apparent surprise at the kettle's urgent demand for attention, reach down to top up his coffee mug. The whole pantomime could take at least two sides of an essay. But Tom knew that the cross examination that would follow would more than demonstrate that the Professor was listening, precisely, carefully, in the general and the particular. Tom imagined that he could see that stained coffee mug now, raised and lowered in time with the Professor's perfectly weighted sentences. Over by the windows the baby grand piano was covered in sheet music; the bookshelves that lined all four walls groaned under the weight of the library of the Professor's mind. There were piles of postcards on almost every available surface except for the generously stocked bar of the cabinet where the Professor was pouring chilled Moet and Chandon Imperial into a flute containing a browning sugar cube dissolving itself in half an inch of Cognac. The Professor handed Tom his glass, his hand perfectly steady, his skin clear and almost gleaming in the faint light.

"The College"

"The College"

"Well, welcome, welcome, welcome. Do have a seat."

"Thank you."

Neither man had made any attempt at a handshake or any other gesture of recognition. It was as if none were needed. Tom resumed his place in the armchair that had received his imprint every week for three years: the Professor adjourned to the ample sofa opposite, as if to indicate that he was not in inquisitorial mode. Tom knew that the Professor was sixty-five now but apart from his greying temples and eyebrows, time had been unusually kind. Twenty years ago, Tom encountered a man on the cusp of middle age, whose youthful handsomeness still cloaked him with more than a passing resemblance to Jeremy Irons; today he encountered him as a man of established middle age, but still tall, still elegant, still strikingly handsome.

"One hopes that it is always going to be a pleasure to meet one's former pupils but I fear that it isn't always so, if you will allow me the candour of speaking openly. Of course, by and large they are utterly charming and gracious but I find some of them a little underwhelming. But that, dear boy, could not possibly be said of you."

Tom knew that the Professor called everyone, including his female pupils, "dear boy." It saved him from having to remember their names. It had never been a problem until recently when a female undergraduate made a complaint and the Professor was asked to attend a seminar on unconscious gender bias. He had not enjoyed it, and it made no difference since he punctuated every sentence with the expression as what had once been affectation had long established itself as a verbal habit, as natural as breathing.

"You are more than kind. But I suspect that some of those whom you describe as underwhelming are successful and prosperous?"

"Quite so dear boy, quite so. And the College is always very grateful to them for their immense generosity. You will have seen the new library? It was paid for entirely by old boys and girls."

"It looks magnificent."

"Oh, it is, it is. Marvelous. It is very gratifying to be in a college that puts scholarship and learning first. Some colleges are more interested in conference facilities and revenue streams."

Professor Needham, or Dr. Needham as he was when Tom was an undergraduate, was known for his enthusiasm for intellectual mavericks. Each year he admitted the most diverse group of undergraduates in the college. He turned away those whom he suspected of being "information processors" however accomplished they might be in terms of exam grades and schooling. The proof was in the pudding and many of his pupils gravitated to the top of the class lists in university exams, though there were casualties along the way. Waggish colleagues nicknamed History "the department of firsts and thirds." Needham would not have it any other way. It was probably something of a relief to the College when Dr. Needham was elevated to Regius Professor and handed the department on.

"I am ashamed to say that I have not donated."

The Professor waved his hand airily.

"Think nothing of it, dear boy; you have contributed in other ways."

He moved briskly and easily across the room to refresh their glasses, beckoning Tom to follow. Tom placed his empty glass on the cabinet which was rumoured to be an invaluable masterpiece, for the Professor to replenish it. The champagne cracked the sugar cubes and swirled up the glasses.

"I was delighted to receive your message. I presume this is both a courtesy call and a matter of pressing business?"

"Indeed so."

Tom returned to his armchair and the Professor moved to his armchair the better to conduct such business.

"I would be most grateful to know everything that you can tell me about Robert Martin."

"Ah. Yes. Well, Robert was a very interesting young man. Four years younger than you I think: you just missed one another. He came up to read Natural

Sciences, from a state school in Reading. Specialised in Psychology. His tutor was Dr Reynolds. Do you remember Dr Reynolds?"

"I do. I had rooms on the same staircase in my second year. Poor man. There were eight of us on that staircase and we must have been awful neighbours. Do you remember Jolyon Martineau?"

"How could one not remember him? I have to say that he does write brilliantly; but then he always did. His column is the only thing that makes 'The Times' worth reading these days. Dr Reynolds once told me that Jolyon took his claret by the pint, from a milk jug. How very eighteenth century!"

"Claret, and the rest. He was as unruly a presence on the staircase as any undergraduate could be."

"A disciple of Dionysus" observed the Professor.

"He still is. He holds court in a bar in St James, a bar packed with government people. Much of the gossip that swirls around him could never be printed in 'The Times' and some of it not even in 'Private Eye'. But he has impeccable sources and he has always been great friends with the Home Secretary."

"They both made significant donations to the new library."

"Jo would have enjoyed the irony of that; he never set foot in the old one."

The Professor laughed easily.

"I am sure Dr Reynolds enjoyed it all otherwise he would have moved rooms."

The shimmering cobwebs of twenty years of shared history were laced across the medieval beams, untouched by any hand. The Professor brought them back to the present.

"Dr Reynolds thought that Martin was particularly bright. He was shy and found the atmosphere difficult. But he excelled in the Tripos and won prizes for topping

a couple of papers. Dr Reynolds tried to persuade him to stay on for his doctorate. His real interest was in neuroscience and so he went to UCL. They led the way in research in neuroscience at the time so it was an entirely logical decision. His post-doctoral research was on whether chemical changes in the brain are the cause of personality disorders, or whether the personality disorders cause the chemical changes."
Tom marveled at the Professor's command of detail.

"We maintained great interest in him, not just as an alumnus of the College you understand."

"Of course. I understand."

"He developed something of a reputation after his research into the likelihood of someone developing psychotic episodes. He found that personality disorders of the kind that lead people to commit murder, for example, can be detected chemically."

"And that's how he was seconded to the Met?"

"Yes, psychological profiling at that time was largely a matter of sociology and circumstantial evidence, building a picture of a suspect that way. But Robert's research brought scientific rigour to the process. It made it a matter of scientific fact. Of the chemistry of the brain."

"Is there anything else that you know about Robert that would help me?"

The Professor had relayed this information with such enthusiasm that he had forgotten to say "dear boy" at any point, an omission he self-consciously corrected.

"Well, dear boy, I'm told he still lives with his mother in Reading in the house that he grew up in and in many ways has never left. He has, as far as we know, neither girlfriend nor boyfriend. His life is his work."

The Professor suddenly stood and raced over towards the door.

"We must go down to dinner. There are some very clever Fellows at the College nowadays and you will enjoy their conversation."

He lifted his ancient black gown from its hook on the back of the door, thrust his arms through the sleeve holes, and without waiting to check that the door had closed, or that his gown was on properly, flew down the stairs, with Tom trailing, laughing, in his wake. Plus ca change……thought Tom.

Chapter 21

Not long after Professor Needham had launched himself fearlessly across the cobbles of Chadwick Court, Fin was treading his more cautious way down Hermit Place before turning left into Belsize Road. Nestled deep in the pocket of his dark blue woollen jacket was a pay as you go phone that he would use only once. Michael and Gerry were equipped with the same disposable burner phones. Each would receive one third of a coded text message. The division of the message across three separate phones offered protection from reconstruction. Whichever one of the three possible courses of action High Command ordered, Fin would have no argument. But Fin knew that they could not ignore the potential risk that a security breach would represent. The disappearance of Lorraine Watson, an unknown interloper in their closely guarded world, may be something and nothing thought Fin, but they could not ignore it. Just in case. They had to be cautious. The political weather had changed: it was easier to make the argument for a united Ireland; Unionists looked increasingly like a minority interest group; Sinn Fein were now the majority party in Northern Ireland; there was widespread support for the promotion of the Gaelic language; it fitted in with the zeitgeist of identity politics. The times seemed to be propitious: fundraising campaigns, of the kind not really seen since the 1980s, had been re-started in certain London boroughs. But there remained the intractable problem of history, of The Troubles, and the danger represented by the reopened Inquiry into the Guildford pub bombings. Fin was determined that the British government must not be allowed to derail the achievements of the last fifty years.

For some time now Michael had been masterminding a gradual stockpiling of resources, the establishment of safe houses and the potential for the deployment of Active Service Units. Fin had worked assiduously for the cause; for him a united Ireland was an article of faith. But Lorraine's brief sojourn into their world was a potential setback. Would they be ordered to stand down? Somehow he doubted it. He was nearing their meeting place, the building site where Gerry worked. Gerry had left the padlock undone but the chain remained looped through the gates so that from the road it looked as if the site had been secured for the night. Firstly Michael, then shortly afterwards Fin, slid through the gap and joined Gerry in one of the on-site Portakabins. Gerry reached into a filing cabinet and liberated a bottle of Bushmills. He sloshed some approximate measures into the plastic cups on the table and looked up at the clock on the wall. It was 8.55. They had five minutes. They placed the silent phones side by side and waited. The three phones began a synchronized display as the choreographed incoming messages lit up the Portakabin. As quickly as they had trilled themselves awake the three phones fell asleep again. Each man tapped in his unlock code to reveal the incoming text and placed his phone back on the table. Together they read across the backlit displays. The first phone read "Action," the second "Option Three" and the third "Immediately." Then, in unison, each man removed the sim card from his phone and Gerry put them through the shredder. They stamped on the handsets, which splintered beneath their feet.

"They'll go in the crusher as soon as it starts in the morning, just to be sure. Well gentlemen, let's go to work."

Gerry threw his head back to drain the last of his Bushmills. Michael left first; Fin about five minutes later. Gerry locked the Portakabin, walked across the site and re-padlocked the gates behind him. Fin was so deep in thought he barely noticed the walk back along the Kilburn High Road and almost bumped into Michael at their agreed meeting point.

"It's a confident call" began Michael. "It means both Active Service Units will be deployed at the same time, which carries a greater risk of course."

"Sure it does" replied Fin. "But we should take it as a vote of confidence in us. Can you put me in touch with the fellers we need to talk to?"

"I have been thinking about that Fin. The people we use are hackers. Brilliant, don't get me wrong, and they can find out anything you want, usually, for a price. Addresses, phone numbers, credit cards, bank details. But they are kids. I think this is out of their league. This needs grown-ups."

He was aware of the sceptical expression on Fin's face.

"We don't have much time, Fin. The Russians have always supported the armed struggle. They will help us."

As Tom negotiated his way back across Second Court, he felt his phone vibrating in his pocket.

"Carl, hi, I will call you back in five, ok?"
Tom knew the way that sound echoed around the amphitheatre of the college buildings and he did not want to be overheard. He hastened his step but then as if the very air resisted him, he slowed again; the Court's mathematically exact proportions, its angles, its colours, its light, its beauty demanded his attention. He could only stroll and then, mesmerized, he stood for a moment, as he had done many times before as an undergraduate, watching his exhalations drift away on the cold Cambridge air. Back in the guestroom he found Lorraine fast asleep on the sofa. He slid into the bathroom, sat on

the edge of the bath, and opened the taps before calling Carl's number from the speed dial menu.

"Carl?"

"Where are you, Tom? It sounds as if you under a waterfall."

"Not quite. What have you got for me?"

"The Peugeot. It is fully taxed, has MoT and insurance. It is registered to a Thomas Mooney at an address in Kilburn. Just a sec. I looked it up. Hermit place. A flat above a garage."

"Anything else?"

"Seen driving along The Broadway this afternoon. Didn't stop though."

"What sort of time?"

"About 5.45 pm."

"Anything on Thomas Mooney?"

"Irish passport. Been in London for three years. Works on a building site."

"Thanks Carl."

Tom stood up and shut off the taps and plunged his hand into his jacket pocket for one of his other phones. He hurriedly scrolled through to Anthony's message. He looked again at the text, "Wilson was here" and checked the time. 5.25. If that was five minutes or so after Anthony had seen the Peugeot in Wooler Street then it was entirely plausible that it could have been on The Broadway twenty-five minutes later. He pressed dial.

"Anthony?"

Tom could hear Bob Marley, but not yet Anthony.

He listened, "Emancipate yourselves from mental slavery, none but ourselves can free our minds. Have no fear for…" but Anthony had obviously turned the music down.

After a few seconds Anthony's familiar voice came through.

"Yeah?"

"Anthony. The Peugeot. Did you manage to get a good look at the driver?"

"Too far away. But I met one of them at the door of the building."

"And?"

"Irish."

"Sure?"

"Accents are one of my special subjects."

"Sorry. And you'd recognize him again?"

"Yes. Faces too."

"Has anyone else been to the flat?"

"All quiet as the grave."

"I think things are about to liven up."

Tom returned to the shared living room where Lorraine was stirring.

"I don't know why I am so tired" she yawned. The sofa was surprisingly comfortable.

Chapter 22

At four twenty in the morning the wintry air was unnervingly still. An unremarkable white transit van made its way along Lincoln's Inn Fields. In bright red letters on either flank it bore the legend "Bread of Heaven" accompanied by a picture of a baker's hand slicing through a malty brown loaf; the parted slices fell either side of the knife like the waves of the Red Sea. The van was so unremarkable that any passerby would readily assume that it was one of the many similar vans supplying the numerous coffee shops and delicatessens that serviced the hungry hordes of Holborn and Chancery Lane. One could easily imagine that behind the doors lay eight trays of warm loaves, of different patterns and types, fresh from the bakery, their rich moist smell contrasting with the chill of the before-dawn morning. Unlike the streets a little to the east where the market traders were in full cry, the elegant green spaces between Kingsway and Fetter Lane were still sleepy. Gerry parked obliquely across the marked bay, as if to indicate that the driver would be back very soon, and made his way down Newman's Row. In less than ten minutes he was in the back of a black Toyota Prius heading towards Fitzrovia. Like the transit, the Prius had been chosen deliberately, to blend in with the fleet of Ubers matrixing their way across London. The cameras would see nothing unusual.

At four thirty-nine the air in Lincoln's Inn Fields was stilled and hushed, a reverent audience awaiting the opening notes of a concerto. In the deep silence, the transit van burst into a billion, jagged fragments. Metal rained down on the buildings like the sudden onset of a monsoon. In a micro-second the landscape was transformed. Discordant car alarms vied for attention with the shrill bursts from the buildings' security systems. Flying shards of glass wedged themselves into the trees and bushes; fragments of paper and litter swarmed the air like locusts on a dying breeze; an airborne car smashed into the public lavatory caving in its green doors. Bits of rubber and metal were held in the moving air before being strewn all over the ground like broadcast wheat. The air was thick with dirty brick dust. Debris arranged itself in artless forms as pieces of masonry, roof tiles and clumps of rendered chimney stacks fell to earth. The scene gradually stilled as a child's Christmas snow-shaker stills. Pungent smoke hung in the air. The wailing banshees of sirens heralded the van Gogh blue lights of the bold red fire engines and the yellow ambulances, whose regular shapes formed splashes of primary colour in the dark.

Tom was up early and walking along the towpath of the Cam. He was watching the news on his iPhone. Aerial shots of the dust shrouded Lincoln's Inn Fields cut to the face of a female BBC news presenter blandly painting a picture of destruction. She was no Orla Guerin keening poetic words from the ruins of the hot gates. Tom felt sorry for her, a "Good Day" presenter who had had greatness thrust upon her. The Deputy Commissioner of the Met was on hand to state the obvious, that it was a major incident. He was not prepared to confirm whether it was a bomb blast at this early stage and was confident that London remained safe. The explosion had occurred at about four forty this morning and although there was some considerable damage to buildings and vehicles there were no reports of any casualties so far, which, in the circumstances was remarkable. The BBC presenter was not satisfied with his answers and pressed him further.

"Do you think that this is a terrorist attack at the heart of London?"

"It is far too early to tell" came his predictably circumspect reply.

The presenter turned back to the studio where another presenter promised viewers that they would be kept up to date with any developments on this breaking story. But urgent news about a minor royal who was having a baby was competing for airtime. Tom slid his thumb across the screen to close the App. It has started then, he thought. A symbolic attack, targeting the institutions of the British criminal justice system, on the law courts, on the barristers' chambers, and on the solicitors' offices grouped around Lincoln's Inn Fields; it had all the hallmarks of a known and familiar foe. It was as Tom had expected. He quickened his step as he returned to St Mary's and to Lorraine. In a couple of hours, thought Tom, Rob Martin would be at his desk and would open the envelope that he had posted from Stevenage yesterday evening. Only connect Rob, he whispered to himself, only connect.

Paul Wilson had arrived in his office shortly after six that morning. He had been able to sleep only in short bursts. All night he had been framing a question. He imagined Victoria Coren-Mitchell asking, what would you expect to see fourth in this sequence? And the two-image sequence revealed so far is: Kilkee, Limerick. The contestants confer: places in Ireland, within a ninety-kilometre radius. Anything else? I don't know. Shall we ask for the third? Next please. But Paul could not see what came next. When he was not trying to solve that puzzle, he was thinking about another one: the abduction of an unremarkable nurse. Why was she taken? He imagined Liam Neeson's gruff, capitalised anger, Why was she taken? Think laterally Paul ordered himself.

Think vertically. Think geometrically. Think any way. Just think. He let his eyes drift in and out of focus. When you can't find what you are looking for, he thought, stop digging and look in a different place, dig a different hole. He tried some different holes until, shortly before five thirty, he struck the spade of his thought into soft, yielding ground. According to her passport she was born in 1969, which made her fifty-one. She studied in London between 1989 and 1992. That meant that she was twenty. But we know nothing about her before she was twenty. Did Lorraine Watson arrive into the world, or at least London, fully formed at the age of twenty? How could that be? Once he had processed the implications of that thought, he leapt from his bed, showered, dressed, and summoned an Uber.

When he arrived on Broadway, he found that although the sky was still murky, the office was busier than in the middle of the day. People swarmed around. There were reporters clambering up onto a makeshift football terrace of scaffolding planks that was, precariously, being assembled underneath them. Opposite the entrance there were TV vans whose satellite dishes seemed like sunflowers searching for the light. At the revolving door of the entrance, the Deputy Commissioner was answering more questions: the media strategy team, whom Paul despaired of, lingered just inside the doorway, nodding approval at the non-committal answers. There was activity everywhere and yet it was strangely quiet: conversations were sotto voce, whispered and secretive. When there was a lull in the proceedings, Paul made his way into the building and found the roomy atrium swirling with people. Police personnel and civil servants mingled together. He recognized a colleague from the counter-terrorist division and sidled over for a chat.

"What's all the fuss about, Dave?"

"Bomb blast. Lincoln's Inn Fields. About an hour and a half ago. Big one. Lots of damage."

"Responsibility?"

"Definitely not Sharia4UK or al-Muhajiroun. We listen to them 24/7. Not their MO either: no martyrs."

"What's the official story?"

"That it is too early to say."

"Unofficially?"

"This kind of stunt is way too difficult for the Jihadis to pull off. For one, you need specialist equipment; two, you need military level explosives expertise. And three, you need to be fucking good. It is the sort of thing Mossad might do, if this were the middle east" added Dave a bit pointlessly.

"Well given that we are not in the middle east?"

"Only one possibility as far as I can see. IRA. Continuity or Real. Take your pick."

"Shit." A long pause. "Shit."

The gravity of the situation registered with Paul as a thrown stone falls to the bottom of a pool.

"But that would mean the there is an Active Service Unit on the mainland."

"That's why the PM called an urgent meeting of COBRA at six this morning. The Commissioner is on her way back from Downing Street now. We are debriefing in about ten minutes. Must go. Catch you later Paul."

Paul walked thoughtfully over to the lift and pressed the concave button bearing the number for his floor. After the swift ride upwards Paul had to exit the lift sideways to avoid the rattling trolley of the cleaners. Given the scramble in the atrium, the silence and emptiness of his floor was slightly surreal. He went over to Nick Booth's desk and fired up the computer. He saw that Nick had logged out at eleven pm. He was impressed. Paul scrolled around the screen to see what files were open. He found a new, unopened Dropbox file. He clicked on it and found that it was from the office of the station manager in Stevenage. Paul entered his own security clearance details to open a file that contained the CCTV footage that Nick had requested shortly before he left for home. Paul slid the cursor along the time line at the bottom until it rested over four forty-five and then worked frame by frame through the surprisingly clear images. There, almost luminous under the bright light, was a black and white image of a middle-aged woman looking up at the rectangular noticeboard. Paul could clearly make out the information: "Next Train…17.04 to Cambridge" and beneath in smaller letters, "On time". Paul froze the image and opened the "Missing Persons" database and entered Lorraine's details. The image taken from her Nightingale hospital security pass flooded the screen. He moved this to the right-hand side of the screen and clicked back to the image that had just arrived from the CCTV in Stevenage. This one he cropped and placed on the left-hand side of the screen so that the two images were face to face.

Two images of Lorraine. Two identical faces. But whose? Who is she? He leaned back in Nick Booth's chair and rocked it soothingly from side to side as he contemplated the possibilities. Euclid, Rob would say. Rule everything else out so that only the truth remains.

Chapter 23

Thomas backed the Peugeot out of the garage in Hermit Place. The engine ticked over reassuringly and quietly as he made his way through the streets of Kilburn. There were quite a few people about though it was still dark and only just after six. People idly scrolled through phones while waiting at bus stops. Shopkeepers clattered shutters open and fumbled keys in locks. Alongside Thomas, Fin, like Tom Eliot in Cambridge, was watching the news on his phone. Fin knew that there was a very small window of opportunity between four and five in the morning when Lincoln's Inn Fields would be as empty of people as possible. This was the hour before the waste disposers moved in, but long after the hardest working lawyers had left for the night. Of course, collateral damage was always possible and he was braced for bad news. But people were not his target: he was taking aim at the institutions responsible for miscarriages of justice against his people.

"It looks as if Gerry's boys have done a grand job and so far there are no reports of any casualties."

"None at all?"

"None. There has been too much blood shed already Thomas. We can bomb our way to the negotiating table without spilling a drop more."

Thomas was struck by the coolness with which Fin made this observation. Fin could justify bombs but not bloodshed. Thomas didn't have such scruples.

"Aren't you forgetting Bloody Sunday, Fin?"

"It's a long time ago Thomas. The political process is what matters now and we cannot allow the British government to betray that political process, to betray the Good Friday Agreement. The bomb is a purely political act, a warning to the British not to go back on their word."

"I'm not sure that they will see it as pure, Fin."

"Maybe not. But my conscience is clear."

"So, what happens after we pick up Michael?" Thomas was not much given to reflection.

"Michael will take us to a meeting."

"Where? With who?"

"Whom. Probably best not to ask Thomas."

"What do you mean by that?"

"They could be dangerous."

There was a long pause. Thomas nodded towards the locked glovebox where he kept his cache of pistols. Fin understood but said nothing. Generally, he abhorred violence and he feared that it was increasingly likely that it would be difficult to avoid. Michael was waiting for them outside the Hilal Butchers opposite Vapehut. Thomas drew the Peugeot alongside to allow Michael to let himself in, glanced into the rearview mirror to make sure that Michael was comfortably stowed, then rejoined the morning traffic.

"You will have seen the news, Fin?" Michael levered himself forward with his arm hooked around Fin's headrest.

"I have indeed, Michael."

Michael reached into his pocket and pulled out a piece of scruffy paper and handed it to Thomas.

"That's where we go."

Thomas studied the paper briefly, nodded to confirm that he knew how to get to the address and returned the piece of paper to Michael. Using his left hand, Michael tore the paper from bottom to top, folded the torn pieces together and tore them again. He did this four times before putting them into the voluminous ash-tray the French manufacturers had deemed necessary for their passengers' comfort. He took out a cigarette lighter; the torn paper burned briefly, and then he dabbed at the flames with his moistened fingers.

"Who are we meeting exactly Michael?"

"People who know people, Thomas."

Fin turned and gave Michael a look.

"Not so cryptic eh Michael?"

Michael relented.

"We are heading for a meeting with two men from Kyrgyzstan. Cultural attaches. You understand?"

"Michael means spies" explained Fin for the benefit of Thomas.

"They will take us to a meeting with some Russian spies."

"Is it safe? asked Fin."

"Nothing is ever safe, Fin. There is the risk that they will betray us. There is the risk that they might be double agents. I have lived with the fear of betrayal for twenty years. But we have to take risks."

"If you don't mind me making the point" said Thomas, "it is an awful lot of risk to be taking on account of a missing nurse."

"If she is a missing nurse, Tom. She disappeared immediately after Maudy saw her in the Campbell. We need to know why she was there, and why she has disappeared."

"Perhaps she was just having a drink. And people disappear all the time" Thomas reasoned.

"I hope you are right Thomas, but we do need to know" said Michael gravely before sinking back into the Peugeot's sun-cracked, peeling, red leather bench seat. For the time being this was sufficient for Thomas who drove on through the traffic, most of which was coming towards them.

"Good morning, Lorraine. How did you sleep?"

"Well, thank you" called Lorraine from behind the slightly open door of her room.

"Professor Needham has very kindly offered us the use of his house. It is not far from here. But first, would you like your eggs scrambled or poached?"

"Scrambled please" she replied opening the door of her bedroom to the communal area of the shared set.

"Thought so." In fact, Tom had already broken the eggs into a measuring jug and was whisking the dark yellow yolks.

"Never add milk. It ruins the flavour and makes them more likely to separate. Help yourself."

As his hands were occupied Tom used his left leg to point in the direction of the coffee pot on the low table. Next to it was a green jug of foamy milk. Lorraine had indeed slept well but as Tom dined with Professor Needham, she had had plenty of time for reflection as well as rest. For many years she had lived a perfectly enjoyable life in London, a life not exactly crowded with incident, but that was just the way she preferred it. In her late twenties and thirties, she had enjoyed all that London had to offer a single girl with a reasonable level of income; in her forties she had acquainted herself with London's abundance of museums, galleries, theatres and concert halls, many of which were in easy reach of her flat. She enjoyed classical music concerts, great plays from the canon of English Literature, and slow walks around galleries. She was comfortable in her own company and had never felt inclined to get married. She had had plenty of boyfriends and enjoyed a number of romances, two of which lasted for several years before custom bedimmed their lustre. Neither break-up was a matter of pain or regret: they were good relationships but they reached natural conclusions. Her professional life was fulfilling. Her work was both varied and challenging: the research projects she worked on ranged from routine but necessary pilot studies, such as a trial for new a drug for the management of ADHD, to more demanding clinical studies, such as the most recent one of the dopamine receptor gene family and its relationship to neuropsychiatric disorders. That had been especially interesting. She had been long settled in Wooler Street and especially enjoyed the summers. As the year darkened and dimmed, she missed the long summer's evenings spent with Anthony in their shared garden. Lorraine put these reflections together and concluded that her adult life had been fine, really just fine. But lately she had a sense that there was something missing. She tried to convince herself that it was a symptom, not exactly of a mid-life crisis but of a mid-life revaluation, a stocktaking exercise many women undertake at her age. She had no children to worry over and her parents were long gone. She was free from the ties that bind. Free in a way that many might envy. She knew so many hard-working consultants and doctors, like Mrs. Nair, who were, at the same age as her, sandwiched between teenage children and elderly parents. Their lives must be like those plate spinning acts you used to see on variety shows, she told herself, only in real life the occasional plate fell to the floor: it could be a parent recently diagnosed with dementia, or a distraught, inconsolable daughter who had not been offered a place at her preferred university. None of these vicissitudes could visit themselves upon her and she was grateful for that. But lately she had sensed that something was missing in her life. She felt disconnected, not perhaps from the world, but from herself. There were so many things that she had forgotten; there were things that had been exiled to the hidden recesses, stuffed into boxes and lifted into the attic of her memory. They were things that she had voluntarily allowed to cloud over. At the very moment in her life when these unsettling thoughts had crept up on her, she had been kidnapped. Was that some kind of metaphor, she thought? Kidnapped by a man who was at once familiar and strange. Where had he come from? What did he signify? Was this what she had been missing? Was this a manifestation of her petit-crise?

As Lorraine looked inward into her soul, Paul was studying her outward image on Nick's computer. Hearing familiar footsteps in the corridor, he pushed against the floor with his right leg so that the chair swiveled through one hundred and eighty degrees, then pressed down with both feet to propel himself to the door.

"Rob?"

He followed him into his office.

"You're in early."

"Pots and kettles."

"I couldn't sleep. Awake all night trying to solve puzzles. How about you?"

"I had a call from the Home Office shortly after five. They asked me to come in. Had to catch the 5.36. I have a meeting in Marsham Street at seven but needed to pick up some files first."

"I presume this has everything to do with the bomb blast in Lincoln's Inn fields?"

"Everything, yes."

"IRA?"

"That seems to be the working hypothesis. There is no other plausible explanation. Consider the evidence." Rob searched for the files in one of the geometric shapes Louise had so carefully handled earlier.

"There is about to be a major government inquiry into the Guildford Pub bombings. The inquiry is to start hearing evidence very soon. The Home Office is also considering the case for a further inquiry into the

Birmingham pub bombings. With respect to Guildford, the victims' families' lawyers have already appealed the coroner's decision that the inquiry cannot and will not address the issue of finding those responsible. As you know Paul there is no such thing as a coincidence. This morning's bomb was a warning. Aha. Here we go." Rob waved the papers at Paul before placing them into an open document case.

"The matter of who knew which IRA Army Council members were at the meeting in Feakle just a few weeks after the bombings has suddenly become an urgent matter. Their lives may be at risk, to say nothing of the embarrassment that the revelation of the truth might cause."

"That is a complication" agreed Paul.

"At the very moment when the British judicial system is turning its considerable resources and attention to the IRA's activities in 1974, a bomb is placed at the heart of that judicial system. It can only be the IRA. I will see you later."

Rob was almost out of the door by the time he said "later." It lingered in the silent room; it echoed around in Paul's mind. He knew Rob was right. There is no such thing as a coincidence. And it was no coincidence that Lorraine Watson had disappeared. But what had she to do with any of this?

Chapter 24

Thomas pulled up outside a five-storey brown-fronted building in Marylebone. The only distinguishing feature of the drab townhouse was the red flag that dangled limply in the light breeze, emblazoned with what Thomas took to be a fiery baseball. Michael reached for his phone and made a call. Moments later the front door opened and a smartly suited man walked briskly over to the burbling car, opened the front and rear doors, and beckoned Fin and Michael to follow him in through the open front door of the building. Thomas took this as his cue to take the Peugeot to the Euro car park at the top of Balcombe Street where he would wait for Fin to call. Fin and Michael found themselves in a dimly lit narrow hallway at the end of which was a lift.

'Please' instructed their host beckoning them with an outstretched arm. The space inside was barely large enough for Fin and Michael, let alone all three. They found themselves forced into unexpected physical intimacy. At no stage did their welcomer make any attempt at conversation but Fin and Michael were experienced enough to know that conversation was both unnecessary and indeed potentially risky. The lift chains worked noisily and brought them to a sudden halt before easing up through the next two feet or so to draw level with the exit door. Their companion waited for the door to lurch open before priming himself for the effort of pulling across the steel mesh of the outer door.

"Please, gentlemen…"

He beckoned them to leave the lift and performed the opposite manouevre to draw the lift gate closed again.

"Please. With me."

He set off down another dimly lit corridor. Fin counted four doors on either side before their guide stopped at the fifth. Without knocking, he swept the door open and ushered Fin and Michael inside.

"Please…"

He backed out of the door and closed it, his role, for now, accomplished. Fin and Michael found themselves alone in a room of the type that can be found in any one of the many gentlemen's clubs that hide themselves away behind the unprepossessing doors of anonymous buildings from Berkeley Square to St James'. The chairs were furnished in polished, gleaming, red leather and the walls were expensively papered in matching burgundy. The candle shaped bulbs of the dependent lights glowed and in the soft gloom the dark mahogany desk shimmered like the surface of a lake under moonlight. The lush carpet accepted their advancing steps and returned no sound. On the desk there were several bottles of water with writing in Cyrillic script, and half a dozen glass tumblers. Fin and Michael saw no other option but to sit down at the desk and pour a glass a water.

"A little bit of the hard stuff wouldn't go amiss eh Fin?" Michael's low words filled the otherwise silent room and relieved the tension. No sooner had the two settled into their chairs than a door in the wall to their left opened. Two men and a woman came in and wordlessly joined them on the other side of the table. The woman sat in the middle and looked long and hard at both Fin and Michael. The two men sat with their hands clasped on the desk in front of them. Fin felt that they were about to be fiercely cross examined, but the woman broke into a smile.

Evgeny please, offer our friends our warmest welcome.

With that the man to her left pushed back his chair, reached into the cabinet behind and brought out a bottle of "Wodka" and five shot glasses. He placed them on the table, twisted the top of the bottle and brimmed each glass in turn.

"Za Vstrechu! To our meeting."

The woman in the middle spoke next. She was wearing a white chemise and her black hair was scraped back and held in place by two slides each at an exact forty-five-degree angle above and behind her ears. From there her hair fell in generous swirls to her shoulders. She was lean, handsome. She had the dark complexion of many Eurasians and wore strikingly crimson lipstick.

"My name is Elmira and I am your contact. I am cultural attaché here at the Embassy."

Fin knew enough about the work that went on in embassies to know that "cultural attaché" was a euphemism and nodded to indicate that he understood.

"Let me tell you a little of our country. There have been many changes of regime since Independence; civil unrest is the curse of every day. We remain one of the poorest nations in the region and necessity drives us to find friends where we can. Economic crises have been relieved by generous financial assistance from our Russian neighbours. But that aid comes with certain obligations. It is only right that we offer them something in return."

Evgeny smiled. The man on the right introduced himself as Ruslan.

"Gentlemen we understand the nature of your struggle and have a very great respect for it."

"You are very generous" replied Fin. "Those of us who fight for justice, and freedom from repression, are united by a common bond."

Fin was well versed in the language of International Socialism.

"Indeed. We must do all that we can for one another" Elmira continued.

"For these reasons Evgeny and Ruslan will accompany you to a meeting with our friends who can help you. Gentlemen I bid you good day."

Instinctively all four men stood as Elmira left the room leaving only the sweet smell of her perfume. The atmosphere changed as soon as the room was left to the men. Evgeny reached for the vodka and replenished their glasses.

"Gentlemen we have ten minutes or so before we must leave for our meeting. So let us understand something of each other. As Elmira explained to you, we have certain obligations to Russia, notwithstanding our independence. This means that we are called upon to help them achieve their objectives. And they are very interested in your organization. And so it happens that we are to act as the Greek Pandarus once did, bringing the lovers together." He laughed heartily at his erudite literary allusion.

"But what is in it for them?" asked Michael when Evgeny had stopped chuckling. It was an obvious question, and Fin would have asked it himself had he had another vodka.

"The Russians like to disrupt. Interfere. Change the course of events. Influence affairs. This is their main strategy. They are propagandists and combatants in informal war."

"And occasionally they poison the enemies of the state" added Ruslan menacingly.

"They are capable of direct actions" agreed Evgeny.

"Your organization is similarly capable of direct action is it not gentlemen? "

Fin knew that Ruslan was asking for confirmation of this morning's blast in Lincoln's Inn Field. He wasn't going to give him the satisfaction and so said nothing. Ruslan laughed. Silence was confirmation enough for him. After a meaningful pause in which they all internalized the significance of Fin's tacit acknowledgement, Evgeny continued.

"The Russians are impressed with your disruption, both political and now it seems also physical. That is what is in it for them. It serves their purpose: the weakening of their perceived enemies, especially the allies of the United States. It is the covert war they have been fighting for twenty years. Ever since Lieutenant Colonel Putin became President."

Evgeny stood up and indicated that it was time for them to leave for their appointment. Ruslan led Fin and Michael back the way they had come. Evgeny took the stairs and was waiting for them when they exited the crowded lift in the vestibule. A black Prius met them outside the door; Evgeny sat alongside the driver for the short journey into Bayswater. Fin and Michael were escorted through the lobby of a hotel to a small meeting room at the rear. Evgeny and Ruslan took their leave and were replaced by two men who followed them into the room and addressed them in perfect English.

"There is coffee and tea. Help yourselves. My name is Pavel. This is my colleague Dmitri."

The four men settled around the table, each having shaken hands with is opposite number. As he stirred an implausible amount of sugar into his thick, black coffee, Pavel looked up at Fin and Michael.

"Gentlemen, that was a bold move this morning. You have our admiration and respect. There are not many organizations who could have done that. Not in London anyway."

"No-one has claimed responsibility" observed Fin casually, raising a smile from Pavel.

"Very good. Please be assured that we will not betray you: you are safe with us."

"Thank you" replied a slightly hoarse, discomfited Michael.

"We understand that we may be able to help you?"
This was Dmitri.

"With some information?" The rising cadence of Dmitri's sentence indicated that it was a question.

"Yes" replied Fin. "Which is why we are here this morning, at this unusually early hour."

"Of course. So, tell us, how exactly can we help?" Dmitri sat back in his chair as if awaiting a long and detailed story to unfold. Michael exchanged a glance with Fin which was to say "you are the wordsmith"

Fin leaned forward conspiratorially and began to rehearse the story of the nurse who had appeared in the pub which served as the informal headquarters for those dedicated to their cause. Fin explained that she had left with a pamphlet outlining the argument for the reintroduction of the Gaelic language in County Clare.

"It is an important subject" remarked Pavel. "The people of Ireland should be allowed to speak their native tongue and not the language of a foreign power. We understand the importance of ethnicity. It is why we had to liberate the Russian speaking people of Crimea."

"Well, yes" said Fin, who was not convinced that the Russian annexation of Crimea and the restoration of Gaelic in the west of Ireland were comparable. But he demurred.

"But you are not asking us to recover the pamphlet?" asked Dmitri playfully.

"No, no the pamphlet does not matter. What does matter is that two days later, the nurse disappeared."

"We think she was abducted" added Michael, for the sake of clarity.

"In our country" continued Fin, people are abducted for a reason and not at random. So we think that there may be more to her than meets the eye. We need to establish if she was sent to spy on us."

"In case your organization has been compromised?" Pavel leaned forward. Michael's raised eyebrow confirmed that that was indeed their concern.

"But if she has disappeared, does that not suggest to you that she was not working for the British?"

"Unless they thought she was in danger, her cover blown, and pulled her out and made it look like a kidnapping."

"They might have staged her kidnapping in order to convince you that she was not working for them?" asked Pavel. "Yes, it is not unknown for security services to do this."

"Well, that's what we were hoping you could help us find out."

Dmitri and Pavel exchanged glances.

"I am sure that we could have information you need in less than twenty-four hours" said Pavel. Dmitri nodded his agreement.

"But if it is the work of Mi5, as you imply, then there is not much more we can do to help you. We have to be mindful of our hosts."

"All we need to know is if it is in fact the work of British intelligence. If it is, we will take it from there."

"I am sure that you will."

"Gentlemen it has been a pleasure meeting with you." Pavel rose, offering his hand.

"We will be in touch. The driver will take you back to Marylebone."

Dmitri stood up, almost to attention, to indicate that the meeting was over.

Fin and Michael waited on the corner of Crawford Street. Fin's cheeks were suffused with the warmth of his early morning vodkas but he had to stamp his feet on the pavement to keep the chill at bay.

"Do you think Pavel and Dmitri were their real names?"

"Does it matter?"

"Probably not. Do you think they were FSB?"

"For sure."

"What about Evgeny and Ruslan? The only other Ruslan I ever met was a Ukrainian gun-runner."

"I think they are common enough names. Who knows?"

"Here you go."

Fin looked up to see the Peugeot slinking along.

"Turn the heater up will you Thomas?" said Fin, a little tetchily, as he climbed in. He felt the cold.

"How did it go in there?"

"I think that they will help us, Thomas. They are well resourced."

"They have certainly got plenty of feet on the ground here" confirmed Michael. "Big feet too, judging from the size of Ruslan."

"I hope they didn't offer you any polonium flavoured tea."

"That's not so funny Thomas." Fin was still cold and still tetchy. Fin was used to being in control and he felt both vulnerable and subservient this morning. And he didn't trust any of them. Thomas faithfully retraced their journey back to Kilburn.

Chapter 25

Sergeant Tindall arrived not long after Rob left for his meeting at the Home Office. Nick Booth arrived a few minutes later. Paul was impressed, knowing that Nick had not left until gone eleven the night before.

"Well, here we all are then."

"I should have the footage from Stevenage sir" offered Nick, pointing at his desktop, as if to explain his early arrival.

"You do indeed have it Nick. I am afraid I took the liberty of opening the file."

Louise smiled as she hung up her jacket and took her seat at her desk on the other side of the shared space. Nick will learn, she thought.

"Come and look at this." Paul corralled them together around Nick's screen. A passing colleague put three coffees down on the side of Nick's desk.

"There you go sir."

"Oh thanks Dom."

"What do you see?"

"I see the face of Lorraine Watson, obviously."

"But do you?"

"What do you mean sir?"

"Well look again."

"Ok. Two Lorraine Watsons. Two identical Lorraine Watsons." Nick was struggling to see where Paul was leading him.

"One image is from Lorraine Watson's Nightingale Hospital security pass: the other is taken from CCTV at Stevenage Railway station at four fifty-seven yesterday afternoon. Well done by the way Nick."

"Thank you, sir."

"So, we know that it is her, and that she might be somewhere near Stevenage" summarized Louise.

"All of which we knew yesterday. Today we also know that she looks well: there is no sign of any distress on her face in this image is there? But that is not really my point. What else do we know about Lorraine?"

"She came to London to study as a nurse" began Louise before Paul cut her off.

"But people's lives don't begin at twenty."

"What do you mean sir?"

"I mean where was she before 1989? You began the story of her life in 1989. But she is fifty-one. Why do we know nothing about her before 1989?"

"I see" said Nick. "I mean we should at least have a date and place of birth. Parents' address. A school record, GCSEs, A levels, that sort of thing."

"Exactly Nick. What does the fact that we don't have any of that information say to you?"

"Well, it could mean that she used another name" said Louise with disarming clarity.

"Which would mean that there are two Lorraines. Or rather, one Lorraine but two different people, one who existed before 1989 and one after. Start with the registers of deaths in 1989. See if there was a Lorraine Watson whose identity she could have assumed."

"On it right away sir" said an excited Nick.

"You start in January, Nick, and I will start in June" said Louise as they settled into the task at their respective screens. Louise knew that this would be a lengthy, painstaking assignment but she would do it thoroughly not least because she appreciated the way that Paul had attributed his own deductions about Lorraine firstly to Nick and then to her. Brilliant leadership she thought. She vowed to learn from it. They worked busily, silently, the only noise being the light tapping of the keys on their keyboards and the occasional slurp of cooling coffee.

After giving Louise and Nick their instructions, Paul made his way back to the bustle of the lobby. The media management team had released a series of wordy announcements that were designed to provide no real information beyond the fact that officers were responding to "an incident" in Lincoln's Inn Fields shortly before five am. Paul found the deliberate obfuscations of these press releases irritating and wondered why the general public did not rebel against them. He glanced over to the reception desk where Rob was talking to a receptionist. Paul pulled up alongside.

"This just arrived for you."

The receptionist pushed a white envelope across the desk. Paul and Rob knew exactly what it was. Against the backdrop of the glossy topped desk sat a familiar rectangle; the blue-black italic script seemed to stand proud of the envelope under the bright lights. "For the attention of Dr. Robert Martin. Metropolitan Police. Unsolved Historic Crimes Division." Rob picked up the envelope.

"Another letter from the Prince of Denmark?"

"It would seem so. By the way, which of us is Rozencrantz and which Guildenstern?"

"That's the joke, isn't it? No-one knows, least of all themselves."

"Better open the envelope then."

"Groundhog Day."

"But the event in Lincoln's Inn Fields is the adjustment, the flap of the butterfly's wing."

Paul was out of his depth so changed the subject.

"What did the Home Secretary have to say for himself this morning?"

"You know how these meetings go. The civil servants run them. Many words are exchanged but nothing is said. But the long and the short of it is that the location of the blast and the timing of the attack suggest a direct pre-emptive warning to the Inquiry. The retired judge who is chairing it has been given round the clock protection."

"Poor bloke."

"Quite." Rob pressed the button for their floor and continued,

"I am not convinced it is necessary. I mean while it is the obviously the case that in the 1970s and 1980s the presiding judge in such a court would have been seen as a legitimate target, the IRA has not assassinated a member of the British establishment for decades. It is not accidental that there were no casualties this morning."

"Perhaps they were merely lucky?"

"Perhaps; or looked at another way, that is if we assume that it was not a coincidence..."

"Because there is no such thing as coincidence..."

"Exactly. Then the conclusion has to be that the bombers were trying to avoid casualties. The attack was political, an attack on the legal establishment, not on individuals. I doubt that the judge needs be too frightened."

"Were there any other outcomes from the meeting? I mean is that all they decided?"

"The best guess of Joint Intelligence is that there could be further attempts aimed at disrupting the judicial system. The Home Secretary listened carefully and thoughtfully. He didn't seem in the least surprised."

"And what about your investigation?"

"After Guildford and Birmingham, the British government knew they had to stop the atrocities on the mainland, somehow. A ceasefire would at least buy time; the government responded quickly and a truce was in place as soon as February 1975. In effect the IRA had bombed their way to the negotiating table."

"Lightning strikes twice, then."

"Yes, although I don't think there is anything to negotiate this time. But this morning's bomb gives the investigation a new urgency: the cold case has suddenly heated up, the past has invaded the present, as it always will."

Rob sat at his desk, deposited his papers and reached for the white envelope.

"Now that is a Groundhog Day moment."

Rob gestured for Paul to open the envelope. It was exactly as before. In the centre of the otherwise pristine page was another seven-digit code: B847228. Paul stood up and made his way around to use Rob's computer to enter the grid reference, but Rob remained seated.

"I know where it is."

Paul returned to his seat smiling. He was not surprised at all.

"How did you work it out?"

"It was exactly as you said it would be. Our correspondent was indeed playing a game of Only Connect with us. I watched some episodes on the train home yesterday. I did not think earth had anything to show more fair."

"Victoria Coren-Mitchell?"

"Dull would he be of soul who could pass her by, but that is not what I meant. No, I meant the quiz itself. Pure Edward de Bono. And you were absolutely right. We had been set a Round Two question: you know, what would you expect to see fourth in this sequence?"

Paul had made the same deduction but unlike Rob, he could not find the connection.

"How did you work it out from the two grid references we had?"

"If our correspondent was playing the game in good faith then there would be a third envelope with a third clue. But then I remembered Pam Landy."

"What?"

"Pam Landy. You know you are much cleverer than you realize. You said we were being watched, like Pam Landy."

"In 'The Bourne Identity', yes. Great film by the way."

"I know. Better than the book."

"Psychogenic amnesia. An interesting phenomenon."

"Great chase scenes too" replied Paul.

"You fear we are being watched. In the film Pam Landy is being watched by Jason Bourne. The comparison is perfect."

"Is it?"

"Because we know that whoever is playing us somehow knows exactly what papers and files lie on my desk. And that was when I realized."

"Realized what?"

"We already had the first clue. In the files on my desk. In Oatley's official Mi6 note he describes how he brokered the meeting in Feakle for which he gives the Irish Grid reference, R585811. That was how I knew that the two codes I received were Irish grid references. Remember? But we had, in fact, the first three clues. Feakle, Kilkee and Limerick."

"From that you worked out what would come fourth in the sequence?"

"Carraig Airt, a small village in the Donegal Gaeltacht, where Irish is the vernacular. Or Carrigart in English."

Rob stood up from his desk and invited Paul to the computer to confirm it. Paul did not doubt Rob for a moment but nonetheless he, like doubting Thomas, put his hand out to prove it for himself. He typed in the code B847228. A map of County Donegal appeared and the location of the red dot marking the reference marked out Carraig Airt. Paul drew himself up to his full height. Feakle, Kilkee, Limerick, Carrigart.

"But I still don't know the connection."

"I can't not know the connection. For each of the locations you could substitute four surnames, those of Duggan, O'Connell, Butler and Doherty."

"On what grounds?"

"That those four locations are their home towns or villages."

"Should I know who they are?"

"Not necessarily, but there is no excuse for me. They were members of the Balcombe Street Gang, part of an IRA Unit operational on the mainland between October 1974 and December 1975. Someone is trying to tell me something. Ever been to Ireland Paul?"

"I went to Cork once, on the ferry from Swansea."

"Well, we are going right now, this minute."

"What?"

"Ten o'clock flight. Aer Lingus. Heathrow to Shannon. All booked. Come on."

Chapter 26

Tom and Lorraine made their way through the squared arch of St. Mary's and crossed over the river Cam to the waiting taxi. Lorraine had never been to Grantchester and her knowledge of it was drawn entirely from the television series that bears its name. She wondered if Professor Needham's house had appeared in the background and whether she might recognize it.

"The best way to arrive in Grantchester is by punt" explained Tom, "but probably not in November." Tom had punted to Grantchester on several occasions in his undergraduate days. Professor Needham used to host drinks parties for his undergraduates at the end of May and it had become a tradition that everyone arrived by punt. Drifting along through the overhanging branches of weeping willows, the banks enameled with fallen blossom, was a pastoral idyll, a hint of the eighteenth-century sublime. The return journey was a Rabelaisian picaresque, as Professor Needham was a generous host.

Lorraine could feel the chill in the air; the punts were becalmed for the winter, chained together in idleness bumping gently against one another at the foot of the steps. The Cam looked black and uninviting. As they walked the sun's rays escaped from the shadow of the colleges' buildings as if a stagehand had thrown a switch to flood the dark stage with light.

Lorraine remembered the keen easterly wind that used to follow her as she cycled to the site of Old Addenbrooke's Hospital, with the Fitzwilliam Museum silhouetted by the rising sun. London, she concluded, must be several degrees warmer. And for the first time she felt a tinge of homesickness. It had only been three days and three nights but she missed the domesticity of home. She wondered if this was another symptom of her recent sense of unease, a sense of the need to belong somewhere.

By now they were in the back of the taxi. The driver had the heating turned up far too high: the contrast between the crisp air outside and the perfumed yet unpleasant air inside made her feel faintly sick for a moment. She wound down the window a few inches to equalize the air temperature. Although there was space enough for three, Tom sat up against her, his physical proximity a reminder of her captive status but no less than welcome for all that. He sat so close she could almost taste the soap with which he had washed this morning. She wondered what it must have looked like in the taxi driver's rearview mirror but suspected that a taxi driver in a university town must have seen all manner of human couplings, many far more eyebrow-raising than this.

"Excuse me Lorraine."

Tom lifted his left leg slightly, tilting onto his right buttock, to reach deep into his coat pocket to retrieve his phone, whose screen was flashing with incoming messages. Lorraine did not mind: in fact, the sensation of his hand indirectly pressing against her thigh through both of their coats, was wholly pleasurable. She could feel a faint flush along her cheek and stared out of the window in case Tom saw her colour. But Tom was too busy to notice and Lorraine could enjoy her reverie.

Tom scrolled through his messages. One from Anthony confirmed that he had been watching Hermit Place and early this morning had followed the Peugeot to the Euro Car Park in Balcombe Street. Tom pressed the dial button.

"Where are you now?"

"Outside the 'Hart and Love' bakery on Kilburn Vale."

"Do they serve a mighty fine coffee?"

"They surely do. And right now, they are serving it to the guy from Hermit Place."

Tom smiled to himself.

"Ok. Speak soon."

Lorraine pretended not to notice, but she was sure that she could make what sounded like a familiar voice on the other end of Tom's call. If it wasn't such an absurd notion, she would have sworn it was Anthony. As the lanes of Grantchester were coming into view, she transferred her attention to the houses to see which, if any, she recognized as the home of the Reverend Sidney Chambers. She glanced across at Tom and imagined him in the role instead of James Norton.

"Most of the land here is owned by King's College," said Tom as the taxi came to halt at the top of Vicarage Drive. "Hence the Rupert Brooke poem: he was at King's. And lived in the Old Vicarage."

Tom paid the driver and led Lorraine to a cottage with white stone walls and a thatched roof. Tom unlocked the front door and invited Lorraine in. There were other houses nearby and it was only a couple of hundred yards from 'The Green Man'. It struck Lorraine as far less safe than the locked box they left behind in Stevenage.

"How do you know that I am not going to make a scene and start screaming?"

"I don't know; at least not for sure. But I strongly suspect that you won't."

"Why?"

"I think that we both know why, Mary."

Tom spoke the name slowly and carefully, his eyes fixed on Lorraine's. Lorraine once had a patient who had stabbed her with several syringes; she had been slashed across the arm by a drunk man wielding a broken bottle, but never had the blood drained from her as rapidly as in that moment. She felt as if her feet had been glued to the floor; she had lost the ability to move her legs. Her stomach flipped over and she felt her heart knock against her ribs. She tried to calm herself by breathing in deeply and out slowly. Gradually she regained her composure.

"So, you know?" she asked simply.

It was a rhetorical question.

Chapter 27

Just an hour or so later, Rob Martin and Paul Wilson were at the Europcar desk in the Arrivals Hall of Shannon airport.

"The car is booked in your name" said Rob.

"Would that be Mr. Rosencrantz or Mr. Guildenstern?"

"Which of you is Mr. Wilson?" asked the girl behind the desk.

"That's me."

"Welcome to Ireland. I need your driver's license and a credit card please sir."

Paul slid the license from its pouch in his wallet, together with his credit card. After receiving multiple copies of poorly printed yellow paper which he had been asked to sign in numerous places, Paul received the keys to the hire car.

"Have a lovely stay in Ireland."

Paul and Rob made their way out into the crisply welcoming air of the cold, clear morning. A few dark clouds loured above, patchily bruising the sky.

"We will be in Feakle in less than forty-five minutes, according to the guide" announced Rob.

"The Trip to Feakle" announced Paul as they turned out of Shannon airport. "Starring Steve Coogan and Rob Brydon."

He didn't expect Rob to be listening and even if he were he was sure he would not recognize the names of the two protagonists.

"They didn't do Ireland, did they?" asked Rob.

"You mean you have heard of the programme?"

"I watched "The Trip to Italy." On the iplayer thingy. On the train. You know you have influenced me much more than you might realize Paul."

Paul could feel that they were edging towards friendship.

"Shall we do the trip for them?"

"What?"

"The Trip to Ireland."

"I will read, like Brydon, while you drive along."

"Excellent."

Rob began reading. "Feakle rejoices in being the cultural centre of East Clare."

"Quite specific. Quite niche."

"You don't have to pretend to be Coogan you know Paul."

"Sorry. Go on."

"Feakle means the parish of the tooth. Today it is popular with anglers and artists, situated as it is in a region of lakes, rivers, mountains and deeply sheltered valleys. It is steeped in Irish music with the Feakle International Traditional Music Festival now in its second decade."

"Sounds idyllic."

"What the tourist guidebooks don't tell you is that this part of Ireland has a dark history. Did you know that Cromwell's troops were ambushed here on the way from Shannon to Galway and had to divert away? In 1920 the Sixth Battalion of the East Clare Brigade of the IRA ambushed the RUC. Houses were burnt in retaliation. Then there was that night in December 1974. And it is the birthplace of Harry Duggan."

"I recognize the name."

"Balcombe Street."

"Oh yes."

"It seems incongruous, doesn't it?"

Paul gestured at the long thin lane that stretched out before them, through low, green hills and valleys. There were no visible scars on the landscape, no signs of battle or struggle, just lush grass, gentle inclines and the occasional farm dwelling hugging the land.

"Oh, but your land is beautiful yet" said Rob, looking up from the guidebook and scanning the horizon.

After forty minutes or so they passed an arched stone set at a jaunty angle in the grass verge. It was the size and shape of a gravestone and it announced their arrival into Feakle.

"There are only eight hundred people" Rob explained as they drove along the empty road. Rob was imagining the Gardai heading for Smyth's hotel on a different winter night some forty-six years ago. His daydreaming became articulate.

"Smyth's Hotel closed and fell into disrepair but has been reinvented as an ecohotel to cash in on the International Music Festival. I doubt that we will learn much from visiting it. But there will be people who remember the way it was and remember the events of that night."

"How do you propose finding them?"

"I doubt that it will be hard. Pull over here."

Paul brought them to a halt opposite the church.

"Here's a good place to begin. Come on."

They made their way through the decorated, waist high cast iron gates up the gentle incline of the path to the gabled projecting porch. The walls were rendered and glowed in the late morning light.

"Looks quite modern" observed Paul

"1826. Is that modern?"

"I doubt that these are the original doors, said Paul lifting the latch."

Once inside and with the door clicked shut behind them Rob recalled the line in Larkin's poem "Church

Going" for a "tense, musty unignorable silence" filled this church too. The silence was fraught with the weighty cargo of its history, a silence heavying the dark air beneath the double height cruciform. Its air contained the voices of generations of County Clare men and women whose compulsion was to resist. In here they said mass; outside they talked the language of the tribe, firstly with Fenians and then with men who prophesied war and whose weapons of choice were the ballot box and the Armalite.

Paul's mind had taken an entirely different direction. He had been transported back to the wry and sometimes acerbic world of sit-down comedian Dave Allen whose litany was the ridicule of pompous catholic priests. Lost as they were in their own respective thoughts, neither Rob nor Paul had noticed that they were not alone. In one of the side chapels a small elderly man knelt in prayer. Two recently lit candles struggled to stay aflame, their glimmering light barely visible. It was Paul, who moved through the church more irreverently than Rob, who first registered his presence. He soft shoed his way back to Rob and nodded in the direction of the side chapel. Rob took the hint. The scene before him, he thought, could have played out on any day from 1826 until today and it would have been the same. Time stood still, as it often did in moments such as these.

"Wait" whispered Rob. "Let him finish his devotions. He is almost certainly offering up prayers for a departed relative."

Sure enough, the gentle click of clumsily fingered rosary beads echoed lightly in the roomy expanse of the church. A dependent Christ crucified, limp and forlorn, looked on from high above the altar. Shortly the elderly man smuggled his rosary back into his coat pocket and carefully drew himself up from his suppliant knees. He was no more than five feet and two inches; his face bore the lines of a lifetime of toil and cigarette smoke. He looked at the two strangers without interest.

"I am sorry for your loss. May the Lord grant her eternal rest."
It was Rob who had broken the silence. Paul was nonplussed. In the last three days he had discovered more about his colleague than in all the years that they had worked together. The old man stopped and looked at Rob.

"She is freed from the perils of this mortal life" he replied.

"Your wife?"

"That she was."

"Was she a Clare girl?"

"All her life."

"And you?"

"Ennis. But I moved here when we married, sixty years ago now." He waved his hand at the air and resumed his slow walk back to the entrance of the church. As he neared the main door he turned back.

"What are you two gentlemen doing in here?"
Experienced as they were, both Rob and Paul recognized this possible entrée. This could be the man they came to find; a man who had lived in Feakle for sixty years must have many stories to tell.

"Can we put you in the way of a drop of comfort sir?"
It was a longshot, but it found its target.

"Well, I was heading that way anyways. I don't mind if you do."

Rob had guessed as much. Paul was lost for words. Rob was disinterested in small talk, but here he was sweet talking a grieving widower in a small church in County Clare. But, of course, Holmes could be charming. Despite the relatively early hour the bar was open for business. By lifting his eyes and raising his weathered thumb the old man signalled his request to the barman who duly furnished him with a substantial measure of Jameson's.

"Two of the same please."

The old man shuffled over to the table in the corner and assumed what was clearly his usual seat. Paul and Rob hesitantly joined him; silence confirmed his consent.

"It's the wrong time of year for the festival so you must be here some other reason." The old man was direct and there was little point in being evasive.

"My name is Rob and this is Paul."

"English, eh?"

"Yes."

Paul was worried that this would bring down the shutters and that they would be shown the door but since the International Music Festival had brought tourists and more importantly, wealth, to Feakle, there was no lingering animosity towards strangers, not even English ones.

"Times have changed" said the old man as if to reassure them.

"You must have some vivid memories?"

"That I do."

The old man adjusted himself in his seat as if he were about to hold forth about the old days.

"I noticed that Smyth's hotel has been reinvented as an ecolodge" said Rob.

"That it has. That it has."

"Do you remember it well?"

"Served a fine stout in the old days. But when the landlord left it was never the same."

"So often the way."

It was Paul's first contribution to the conversation. He felt emboldened by the subject: a number of his favourite pubs in and around Westminster could no longer be relied upon to keep their beer properly.

"It was never the same after the Garda Siochana raided."

This was the grape dangling above their heads.

"The landlord never recovered. People distrusted the place. The business failed."

"What became of him, do you know?"

"Long since dead. And his wife."

That was a bitter blow. Rob was hoping that one or other of them might still be living locally. The old man paused to take a respectful drink in their memory. He lowered his glass to the Formica topped table.

"There was a daughter."

"What happened to her?"

"Went away to school in Dublin."

"Did you know her?"

"Not really."

Paul could see that the old man's glass was running low and went to the bar to ask for another. The old man nodded his thanks to Paul as he placed the glass on the table.

"Nothing for the young here. No jobs. No prospects. Farming is hard work. Young people wanted more. They went away to America. They say that there's more County Clare folk living in New York than live here." With that, the old man knocked back his Jamesons and made to leave.

"Thanks for the drink."

"I am sorry for your loss."

The old man nodded and made his way out of the door. Just as he did so he turned back to them.

"May your God go with you."

Paul and Rob watched as the old man made his way out and turned to make sure the door was firmly latched behind him. Satisfied, he shuffled on his way.

"Dave Allen" said Paul after the door closed. "That's how he signed off every show. May your God go with you." Rob wasn't really listening.

"There was a daughter."

"Yes. She will have gone to America with all the others."

"You are probably right."
They dutifully placed their empty glasses on the counter. The barman soundlessly thanked them with a brief nod and they made their way out into shafts of bright sunshine and soberingly cool air.

"Where now?"

"Let's walk and see what we can find."

"Dave Allen was born David O'Mahony."

"He would have understood all this" Rob affirmed as if to prevent Paul babbling on.

"All what?"

"All this. The landscape. The religion. The people. The past. The silence. The reverberation. The burden of history."

Chapter 28

The wall mounted television in Hermit Place filled the room with its gaudy colours. Conor, prone on the sofa, was watching with the sound turned down. It was less invasive that way. Uninterrupted coverage from Lincoln's Inn Fields swamped the airwaves. Conor had been watching from first thing and in that time all of the channels put out the same material and repeated it every fifteen minutes or so. It was formulaic. Each channel had an attractive female news presenter, each of whom was doing her level best to be earnestly concerned and at the same time alert for any new development. Conor found it much less enervating with the sound off. There were camera crews reporting live from the scene; there were camera crews outside Scotland Yard and in Downing Street. A succession of reporters was on hand for regular updates; each one was meticulously thanked by the anchor for their contribution. Live coverage from the scene consisted of interviews with passers-by, with coffee shop owners, with cleaners and refuse collectors, fireman, policeman and politicians. Opinions were sought and delivered sincerely. Presenters were grateful for them. "Thank you, James; James Johnson there reporting for us." In the studio the presenters, in their striking red or blue dresses, interviewed a succession of besuited so-called experts on all manner of issues; the BBC had an expert on counter-terrorism, an expert on middle eastern politics, and a transport expert outlining the disruption to road and rail links across London. Sky meanwhile had an expert on police procedure. Conor concluded that the television channels were more interested in how they were seen to be covering the story than the story itself.

"Will you look at all this? Conor complained as Fin and Thomas came in. It's been on for three hours non-stop and there are only three things to know. One: there was a big bang. Two: there was lots of damage but nobody got hurt. Three: they have no idea what caused it. I mean what a lot of nonsense."

"That's television news for you. All very self-important but nothing but piss and wind" agreed Thomas.

"Well, I am glad you have had a profitable morning Conor" said Fin playfully pulling Conor's legs off the sofa so that he had room to sit down next to him.

"Thomas. Will you put the kettle on."

"Already on, Fin."

As Thomas clinked and chinked away with teaspoons and mugs, the others settled into the sofa.

"You know as well as I do, that they can't broadcast the truth. This whole blanket coverage thing is a charade. They might as well broadcast the testcard and some soothing music."

Thomas brought over the coffees and a pack of Rich Tea biscuits and sat in the chair next to the sofa. He dunked his biscuit in his coffee so that half of it was the consistency of wet papier mâché.

"I need this" said Fin taking two or three noisy gulps.

"You know those fellas in the embassy drink Vodka for breakfast."

"Do they now?"

"They certainly did this morning" confirmed Fin.

"What were they like?"

Conor was keen to know.

"Friendly. They took us to meet two Russians."

"Thugs?"

"No. No. Far too smooth for that. They were well educated and smiled pleasantly."

"Spooks?"

"Almost certainly. They told us they liked us. They even wanted to congratulate us."

"They knew the bomb was us?"

"I don't think they were certain; they were fishing for confirmation. But they looked knowing when we didn't confirm or deny."

"But, Fin, can they find the missing woman for us?"

"They seemed to think so. Or at least they can find out if she was working for the security forces and whether her disappearance is suspicious."

"How can they do that?"

"Who knows how information is traded and exchanged. But exchanged it is. If you know who to ask."

Thomas had by now slopped his messy way through three biscuits; when his mouth was clear he decided to speak.

"I think we were followed all the way back from the car park."

"What? Are you sure?"

"Yep. A blue Honda. It stayed about six or seven cars behind us all the way."

"Do you think it was the Russians?"

"Can't have been. They didn't follow you back to Marylebone, did they? And they could not have known where I parked."

Thomas reached for another biscuit.

"Maybe the Kyrygs then?"

"Maybe. Doubt it though."

"But if it wasn't either of them……" Thomas took a bite from his biscuit and nodded; he had already reached his conclusion.

"Who else would follow you?" asked Conor

"And in a blue Honda? I think…."

"Here's what we do. Thomas, take some money from the fridge. Five thousand. Go to the usual garage and get another car. Park the Peugeot in the multistorey just down the road. Clean it and take the plates off. Disconnect the battery. Take everything out of it. Don't torch it: that will attract attention. Take Conor with you. Oh, and make sure you aren't followed. Especially by a blue Honda."

Thomas languidly reached for another Rich Tea.

"Well off you go then."

"When I have finished my biscuits."

Fin reached for the remote control and brought the sound up. There was nothing else for him to do but sleep off the effects of those early vodkas.

"I have made you a coffee Lorraine."

"Oh. Thank you."

She reached up and took the mug. Lorraine was sitting in Professor Needham's armchair looking out into the hedged, walled garden. It was private and comforting. The drawing room was elegantly proportioned and comfortably furnished; there were piles of books and postcards everywhere. Wherever she might sit down, on each side of the chairs and the sofa, there was a pile of books about two feet high. The bookshelves which lined the walls were crammed; the mahogany circular table was littered with papers that seemed to be growing up the stem of the handsome lamp, curling upwards where they rested against its ribbed surface. An antique clock ticked loudly. It was the only noise in the room. Lorraine's mind was in a state of considerable activity. She barely heard Tom say quietly,

"I have a few things I need to do."

He left the room and closed the door firmly. Lorraine was more than happy to be left alone with her thoughts. Life had been, until three days ago, a gentle stroll through a wooded glade on a warm, spring day. She had a secure job, no debts, no dependents, and time to herself. But now she had entered a different landscape, one littered with boulders, shrubs, stones and shriveled trees. How was she to make sense of what had happened to her? She was still reeling from the soft familiarity with which Tom had addressed her as "Mary." How did he know? She sipped her coffee. It was as fine a cup of coffee as she had ever had. If her relationship with Tom were coming to some sort of crisis, she would miss his coffee. Instinctively, she ran her hand along her thigh where Tom's leg had pressed against hers in the taxi. Far from intending her harm, Tom wished her to be comfortable and told her that he had arranged all of this for her benefit. Or had she made that up? Had she imagined that? Perhaps it was a symptom of Stockholm syndrome. She could not keep from herself the knowledge that she found him physically attractive. That complicated matters and seemed to go beyond anything she could remember about it; she had no recollection of a sexual element in the accounts she had read. She stopped herself from thinking any more deeply about it. In any case many psychologists and psychoanalysts refuse to acknowledge that Stockholm Syndrome exists. She told herself to shape up, to be more logical. The facts of the matter were stark. She had been kidnapped, efficiently and ruthlessly, in emerging daylight by a man who had administered a powerful sedative and then imprisoned her in a dingy flat above a Turkish run laundry somewhere off the Finchley Road. On the face of it that was hardly the behaviour of a benefactor. But then their day in Stevenage had been less intimidating and now, here in Grantchester, they were living in a way that resembled ordinary life. She could imagine living here; more to the point, she could imagine living here with Tom. But he was ten years younger than her. She did not really know him. And Tom wasn't even his real name, or so he said. She wondered what his real name might be. In the adjacent room, a large airy farmhouse kitchen that she had glimpsed briefly as Tom ushered her in to the house, she could hear the muffled sound of his voice, a siren's song. She sat back in the winged armchair and indulged a momentary flight of fancy. She had never felt such longing. Neither of her longer-term relationships had had this depth, this intensity. She wanted her ordeal to end here, here in Professor Needham's drawing room. To live happily ever after. She could play Barbara to Tom and they could live a good life. Grow vegetables. Tend goats. Walk on Grantchester meadow. She drew her coffee cup dreamily towards her lips; the aroma brought her sharply back to her senses. Of course, there would be no fairytale ending she told herself, but she couldn't bring herself to think of an alternative.

Chapter 29

At the same time as Thomas gingerly reversed the Peugeot out of Hermit Place for the last time, Rob and Paul were driving their anodyne hire car slowly through the centre of Feakle. There was little to see. The only striking building was a bar, boldly and childishly painted in red and yellow, like Noddy's car. There were a few low houses; behind them fields stretched into the middle distance. Rounding a bend, they saw a sign for the Clare Ecolodge, built on the site of what used to be Smyth's hotel.

"Paul, stop here."

Paul brought the car to a gentle halt.

Rob wanted to look around. He had read so much about this place it was as if he had been here before. But what he knew of Feakle was in the past. He was finding it hard to reconcile what he knew with the scene that lay before him now. As he looked at the buildings that now formed the Ecolodge he imagined the events of that furtive night in December 1974. He imagined the hurried hush, the whispers in the dark, the stealthy arrivals and sudden scrambled exit. He imagined the gardai bursting into the hotel, finding their quarry gone, if the IRA were their quarry that is. Rob had come to the view that as unlikely. He preferred to take the view that the Gardai had timed their interruption perfectly, allowing the IRA to make good their escape. After all this was Eamon de Valera country, the cradle and nursery of Republicanism. It seemed likely to Rob that the local gardai would have had Republican sympathies, drawn as they were from local families. The TD, Liam Cosgrave, was unpopular in Clare. Perhaps the Gardai were deliberately dilatory in acting on his orders. Perhaps the raid was all for show, to convince the British that the Irish were doing their bit. Or perhaps the raid was an attempt to sabotage the talks. Rob imagined the IRA men and women disappearing into numerous safe houses across the County, then vanishing, to make their way to Belfast, to London and to New York. The government papers he had read identified some of the IRA men thought to be there that night, but their identities had never been confirmed. Some of those named were long since dead and their secrets died with them. But he was sure that there were those who were still alive, perhaps only one or two, who knew long concealed truths, and who acted as guardians of the collective memory. This morning's blast in Lincoln's Inn Fields was proof that those memories would remain buried. They were not allowed into the light, and certainly not to be subject to the scrutiny of the British judicial system that had so egregiously failed to be just. Derry, Ballymurphy, Guildford, Birmingham: all travesties of British justice. Rob did not need to be a Republican sympathizer to acknowledge the truth of that. Perhaps he had been sent on a fool's errand. Perhaps the evidence, such as it was, that lay on his desk, was all that there was and all that there would ever be; the fading, tatty papers told a story without a sequel, a mystery that must remain so. He had hoped that the landlord of the hotel was still alive but the old man in the bar had gently extinguished that last hope. The only glimmer of hope he had was that there was a daughter. She would have been a little girl, but children remember. But what were the chances of finding her? A proverbial needle in a haystack. And Paul was almost certainly right: she is probably in America. He looked back at Paul waiting patiently in the car and decided that there was nothing further to be gained from their trip to Feakle. He walked disconsolately back to the car.

"Let's go."

"Where?"

"Something to eat and the afternoon flight back to London."

"Are we all done here?"

"We are."

Tom was preparing lunch in Professor Needham's well stocked kitchen. It was fastidiously neat and orderly. Racks of spices, in alphabetical order, stood above racks of herbs, also arranged alphabetically. The cupboards contained elaborately designed bottles of Extra Virgin Olive Oil, cider vinegars, and a box of Himalayan sea-salt. The granite work surfaces bristled with a standing army of culinary weapons: a juicer, Magimix, Nutribullet, coffee grinder and coffee machine, as well as a rack of the handsomest Japanese knives, glintingly sharp and menacing. Tom scanned the cookbooks: Tom was familiar with them all and pleased to notice that Delia Smith's 'Complete Cookery Course' was as battered and broken-spined as his own copy. Professor Needham had insisted that Tom use whatever he needed from the fridges (of course there were two), from the larder and from the wine cellar. Tom knew his way round the cellar; he had run many an errand there on those heady summer nights. Spoilt for choice, Tom had decided upon a mackerel and smoked trout salad, with apple cider vinegar. He chose a chilled Chablis to accompany it. He knew that it was not one of Lorraine's preferred wines but it was the best way to complement the fish. Lorraine must have fallen asleep. Tom was standing next to her inviting her to lunch.

"Is it that time already?"

"It is. Come on."

Lorraine had fallen asleep with her legs crossed and her arms folded. She carefully unfolded her limbs, arms

then legs, so that she could stand and then dutifully
followed Tom.

"Perfect."

Lorraine was disappointed that she had fallen asleep:
she would have loved to have watched Tom prepare this
meal. The anticipation was as delicious as the food itself
and she had missed out on it. Lorraine instinctively
reached for the wine.

"I am not sure if you will like it."

"Why, what is it?"

"A light Chablis. Evelyn Waugh claimed that he used
to clean his teeth with it. But Waugh wouldn't clean his
teeth with this one: it's too good for that. Doc Needham
is only interested in the best." Tom had reverted to the
familiar "Doc Needham."

"I thought he was a Professor?"

"He was Doc Needham in our day."

"I like this" said Lorraine after taking a tentative sip.
"Tastes of summer."

"The slopes of Fourchaume, where this wine is from,
face southwest, guaranteeing the most sunshine"
explained Tom.

Reassured that she had not said something asinine,
Lorraine drank some more. They sat opposite one
another at the long table which Professor Needham had
rescued from an old mill.

"Tom, how long will we be here for?"

"That all depends."

"On what?"

"How long it takes."

"How long what takes?"

Tom ignored the question.

"How's the salad?"

"Very good. Thank you."

"Lorraine, why did you go into Kilburn last week?
You know, to the Campbell."

"Why?"

"It matters."

"How could it? It's just a pub."

"Kilburn is in the opposite direction to Southwark from Marylebone. It is not on your route home."

Lorraine sensed that Tom was putting her on the spot.

"No, it's not directly on my way home, but it's only a short walk from the Nightingale. I had heard some of the other nurses talking about it. It sounded fun; a place with live music and a great atmosphere. Thought I would go and see for myself. I fancied a change of scene, something different from the super-smart wine bars of Marylebone High Street."

"It is an Irish pub."

"There are loads of Irish pubs in London."

"Not like the Campbell."

"What do you mean?"

"Did you talk to anyone?"

"In the pub?"

"Yes, in the pub."

"Yes. Why does that matter?"

Tom paused to savour his Chablis.

"I spoke to a middle-aged woman."

"Did she tell you her name?"

"I can't remember."

"Was she Irish?"

"Well, that's as daft a question as I have heard Tom. As you just said, it's an Irish pub."

"Yes. But can you remember?"

"I think she said her name was Maud."

"Maud Byrne?"

"She didn't tell me her last name. Why, do you know her?"

"No, not really."

"Meaning?"

Tom demurred. "How did your conversation go?"

If Tom hadn't been so good looking (really so good looking) she would have resented this cross examination.

"I don't remember all that much. We exchanged pleasantries about Ireland, I think. There's quite a little library of books and articles on the shelves and tables in the pub."

"And copies of 'An Phoblacht'. Maudy Byrne is the leader of the London branch of Sinn Fein. The Campbell is the preferred meeting place of Sinn Fein members, their political friends and allies."

There was a pause as they both enjoyed generous mouthfuls of Chablis.

"Did you see the news this morning Lorraine?"

"Yes. Why?"

"There was a bomb in Lincoln's Inn Fields."

"I know: it was pretty much the only story on the BBC and Sky."

"Who do you think might have been responsible?"

"I don't know" she said disingenuously. "Al Qaeda?"

Tom smiled.

"No. Not them, as you well know. It had all the hallmarks of the IRA. It was a specifically targeted and designed to convey a political message rather than maximise casualties."

"Oh." Lorraine put down her glass and sat back in her chair.

"And there is every chance that Maud, and those of her circle, know exactly how it was planned and executed."

"She might know nothing about it. You said she is Sinn Fein, not IRA."

"You mean in the way that Gerry Adams is? And how many people believe that, other than as a convenience?" Tom gave her a look which told her that he knew she, of all people, must be one of those who knew the porous nature of the boundary between those two organisations.

"More than that, it may well be that one or more members of an Active Unit was there, right there, next to you, in the pub. Which means that you might be able to identify them."

Lorraine looked into the contents of her glass as if silently acknowledging the truth.

"Did you speak to anyone else?"

"Only Maud. She called herself Maudy."

"Are you sure she was the only one you spoke to?"

"Yes. Completely sure. I was looking at some of the books and papers and she came over to me and asked me if I was Irish."

"Which means that she was suspicious of you. You were new, a stranger. Did anything else happen?"

"No. Only…"

"Yes?"

"I took one of the pamphlets home with me. It was in Gaelic. I didn't really understand that much but I recognized the word Chlair."

Tom gave her a meaningful look. Lorraine could not hold out any longer against such beauty.

"What do you want from me Tom?"

"The truth."

"I suspect you know most of it already."

"Maybe. Try me. We have all day."

They drank more wine.

"So, tell me, what did you do with the pamphlet?" This was an easy question to answer. Lorraine was grateful to Tom for that.

"I left it on top of the bookshelf by the front door. It will still be there."

"Lorraine, do you mind clearing the table?" She reached across to take Tom's plate, put it on top of hers and took the pile through to the kitchen.

"Shall I make some coffee?"

"Yes please."

Tom could hear Lorraine busy with the coffee machine. He made a call.

"Anthony. Where are you now?"

"On my way home."

"Good. I need you to do something. When you have a moment, can you let yourself into Lorraine's flat and look on the top shelf the bookshelf just inside the front door."

"What am I looking for?"

"A small pamphlet with a Gaelic title."

"Any more detail?"

"It has the word 'Chlair' in the title. As in the Gaelic for County Clare."

"Will do."

"Any news from Hermit Place?"

"Two of them left the flat talking about ditching the Peugeot; they must have known they had been followed. There was another car tailing them too. I followed safely behind both."

"Ok. Let me know as soon as you are back in Wooler Street."

Tom rang off. Lorraine carried the coffee through into Professor Needham's drawing room.

"Black?"

"Yes please."

Tom settled himself into his chair like a priest, ready to hear Lorraine's confession. She was nervous, but she was convinced that Tom was on her side. She thought that even if her feeling of security was some kind of psychological aberration, she had few other choices, indeed no other choice, other than to rely on Tom. Being alone with Tom in Professor Needham's gracious home was balm to her anxious mind.

Chapter 30

As Paul parked the hire car at Shannon airport, Sergeant Tindall called to say that she had good news. This development, combined with the news that their flight into London would arrive ahead of schedule, inclined Paul to think that the stars were beginning to align, and he said as much.

"They don't align. That is mere superstition," corrected Rob.

"It's just a figure of speech" replied Paul defensively. "Like the sun going down. I mean nobody says "the earth is coming up" because to us it appears as if the sun is sinking below the horizon."

"Perhaps, then, you should have said it appears as if the stars are aligning in our favour."

Paul shook his head wearily. He forgave Rob his pedantry because he knew that he had hoped to find that crucial something in Feakle and his disappointment was palpable. As they made their way from the gate into the terminal, a customs official unclipped an orange elasticated band and waved them through the newly opened fast track channel.

"Thank you" said Paul rushing past.

"What do you think Sergeant Tindall might have found?"

Paul's explanation was as hurried as their bustling walk.

"The image of Lorraine Watson from the CCTV at Stevenage station and the one from her hospital security pass are a one hundred per cent match. But we still do not know who she really is. How do you explain the fact that we can find no trace of her before she was about nineteen? She could not have come into existence as an adult female?"

"Like the Birth of Venus?"

"Hmm?"

"The Botticelli painting. Venus springs from the scallop shell as a fully formed and beautiful young woman."

"Yes, yes. But Lorraine is not a mythological woman. She is real. I have been thinking about this all day. I have tried a number of explanations and there is only one that I cannot rule out."

"Which is?"

"Lorraine Watson is in fact two different people; one who lived before 1989 and a different one who lived after 1989."

"It has a certain arithmetic appeal."

"I left Tindall and Booth with the task of trying to find the second Lorraine Watson, the one who existed before 1989."

"And it sounds as if they may have found something?"

"I hope so because we desperately need a lead."

The Aer Lingus flight, which had been helped over the Irish sea by a strong south westerly, arrived into London twenty minutes early. PC Nixon was waiting for them in the Volvo.

"Are we in a hurry sir?"

"Yes, we are Nixon."

PC Nixon smiled into the rear-view mirror and launched the willing Volvo onto the Heathrow perimeter road. The M4 was running well enough but Nixon wasn't going to miss this opportunity. He pulsed the blue lights briefly to make sure they had a clear run in the outside lane, accelerated firmly, and settled the red tip of the speedometer's needle at ninety-five. Paul developed his argument.

"Think about what we cannot rule out. We know that "Tom Eliot," the owner of the now burnt-out Honda, must be your correspondent because he left two envelopes, one at the recorded keeper's address and one in the car itself. The third envelope was delivered directly to reception so we don't know where it came from. But it had the same handwriting, so we can assume it is also from Tom Eliot. He must have known about the highly classified documents on your desk."

"How?"

"It could be that Tom Eliot, like Jason Bourne, is someone who was, or still is, on the inside and he knows something that he wants you to know, and like Pam Landy, expose it. Think about it. Didn't you tell me that the four men arrested in Balcombe Street claimed, at their trial, to have been responsible for the Guildford pub bombings? But that no-one took the claim seriously? Right?"

"Right."

"Because two of the four were still in Ireland at the time."

"Yes. It could not have been them. We are sure of that Paul."

"Let us suppose that your correspondent knows that you know that."

"How does that help?"

"Rob you are supposed to be the genius here, not me."

"I am following Paul, but I want you to spell it out. Make it obvious. Like you usually do."

"Ok. So, your correspondent knows that you know that the Balcombe Street gang did not carry out the pub bombings in Guildford or in Birmingham. But he might be trying to lead you to those who might know."

"You mean people on the inside?"

"Yes. Former government ministers, former Prime Ministers, security service chiefs. Civil servants. Who knows how many might be implicated in a cover-up."

"I see."

"If that were the case, and you had compelling evidence from your correspondent, then you would be obliged to tell the Home Secretary. The Home Secretary would then have to take the matter of the Inquiry offline as a matter of national security. He would have to delay it at least."

"In those circumstances he would have no choice, yes."

"The identities of those involved in the bombings, and those who knew who was involved, would have to be protected, that is to say kept secret. And because of that, the identities of those IRA members at the meeting in Feakle would also have to be kept secret in case they were among those responsible, or knew those responsible."

"That part may be easy. As you heard the old man say this morning, the landlord and landlady are both long dead and no-one else is talking."

"But it is reasonable to believe that there may be somebody, somewhere who can shed light on it. And perhaps that person is your correspondent. Does that make sense?"

"It does. And I am still with you. Go on."

"Let us look at the problem another way. Why has Lorraine Watson, a person with no apparent connection to any of these events, been taken?"

"Because she is, in fact, connected in some way? But how?"

"That I don't know. But if we could find out the former identity of Lorraine Watson, I mean who Lorraine Watson was before 1989, then we may be closer to an answer."

"If your doppelganger theory has any merit."

"Rule everything out until only the truth remains. Isn't that what Sherlock Holmes said?"

"And Euclid before him."

"Well then."

"Paul, I think that you might well be on to something."

"So much depends on what Sergeant Tindall has found."

"It does."

Nixon swept the Volvo into the underground carpark.

"Twenty-two minutes Nixon. Impressive."

"Thank you, sir."

"Remind me to approve your next pay rise."

"Yes sir."

Chapter 31

Fin was watching the dying embers of the BBC's ashen-faced coverage of the bomb blast. There was no new information and the looks on their faces betrayed the fact that the desperate presenters knew that they were filling time and space. Fin must have dozed off, as a couple of hours had drifted past. He was awakened by the noisy footfall of Thomas and Conor. Fin roused himself.

"Are we all good?"

"We are all good. We are the new owners of a fifteen-year-old Vauxhall Vectra B. No careful owners and several very clumsy ones from the look of the bodywork. Knackered, but not dead yet."

"I know how it feels. Does it run properly?"

"That it does. And in Kilburn a clapped-out Vectra blends in just perfectly."

"I didn't hear the garage door open."

"You were asleep by the looks of it, Fin. But I left it around the corner. Just in case."

"Good. Will you look at this though?"
Fin gestured towards the television. The screen was filled with the image of a shopkeeper sweeping up shards of broken glass and debris.

"I mean in what way is that news?"

"What did you expect?"

Why do they bother? I mean there's bombs going off all over the world, from Azerbaijan to Yemen, bombs that kill thousands every year and you are lucky to get two minutes on Channel Four. But because this explosion happened in London, we have to watch footage of people being interviewed because they know how to use a brush."

Fin switched the TV off and threw the remote control onto the table in disgust.

"It makes the Brits nervous though, doesn't it?" said Conor.

"Because it is too close to home. Bombs claim the lives of thousands in Iraq but one stabbing in London and the papers are full of stories of Jihadi barbarians storming the gates."

"Do you think the Brits really think this was the work of the mad mullahs?"

"Not for one second. But they aren't letting on yet." As Fin warmed to his theme his phone danced to life on the low coffee table. Fin picked it up and pressed it secretively to his ear. It was Michael.

"Fin, meet me at the usual place with the car. Bring Thomas."

"Why?"

"We have been called to a meeting. By Elmira."

"No shit."

"No shit, Fin."

"That was quick work. It's only been a few hours."

"She didn't say what the meeting was about."

"I'm on my way. Oh, Michael, we have a different car. Look out for a Vectra. We ditched the Peugeot."

"Why?"

"Thomas thought we were followed back from Marylebone."

"Ok."

He rang off and put the phone in his jacket pocket.

"Thomas, that Vectra better work. We are on the move. Just you and me."

Thomas' quick feet skimmed the surface of the steps as he raced down the stairs and out into Hermit Place. He had parked in Priory Road.

"How much did you part with for that heap of shit?"

"Eight hundred and ninety."

"I gave you five grand. Where's the rest?"

"Don't worry. I have it here in my pocket. When we were done cleaning the Peugeot your man at the garage said he knew a man who could put it in a crusher for a monkey."

"A monkey?"

"Five hundred. Money well spent. So, I have about three and a half left."

They had reached the moodily dark blue not quite black Vectra.

"Perfect" said Fin pulling the reluctant safety belt across his torso and into the waiting clip. It pinged straight out again. Fin gave Thomas a look.

"Don't worry Fin. She won't go fast enough for you to need it" replied Thomas as he turned the key. The banshee of a fan belt screamed briefly before giving way to a steady engine note. Fin burst out laughing. Michael was waiting at the usual place and had the rear door open before Thomas had come to a halt.

"Is it that urgent Michael?"

"It might be. Come on. Let's go. Same place as before."

"Michael, have you seen what they are putting out on the BBC?"

"That's their job Fin. It is a distraction; it allows the security services to get on with their work while the BBC fuss and cluck at nothing."

"How long do you think we have got?"

"Couple of days."

They arrived in Crawford Street without incident. Thomas had been vigilant: they had not been followed. Michael and Fin were admitted through the black front door and were accompanied into the lift by a burly man whom they had not seen on their previous visit. He performed the function of lift operator in the same wordless manner as their first acquaintance and led them along the same dark, barely lit corridor. They were shown into the same paneled room as before but this time it was not empty. Elmira sat alone, looking over her papers, the scent of her perfume drawing the two men in.

"Come. Sit down."

Elmira nodded redundantly at the chairs opposite her, there being no other choice of seating.

Lorraine was ready for confession; her conscience was serene. She had known that this moment might come, that disclosure would be necessary. She remembered the words from her childhood and spoke them softy.

'Confiteor Deo omnipotente, beatae Mariae semper Virgine………'

"I was enjoying life in London" she began. "I was enjoying the freedom London offers a single midlife female. I could come and go pretty much as I pleased. Every evening and every weekend were a blank canvas. My work was rewarding. People think that nurses find what they do rewarding because they are kindly, compassionate souls who have abundant good will to share with their patients. But for me it wasn't only that: it was also rewarding intellectually. It was exciting to see how trials turned out. Many of the patients were as intelligent and articulate as the consultants: the only difference between them was that they suffered from a confounding mental illness. It was so rewarding when successful trials of new treatments, drugs and therapies alleviated people's pain or took them a step closer to functioning normally. Everything about my life was hunky-dory. Even my commute to work, until a couple of mornings ago, was painless."

"I am sorry about that Lorraine. Think of it as a necessary evil." Lorraine was about to continue when Tom's phone rang sharply. Tom went to silence it.

"No please take it. I need to refill my cup anyway."
Tom went through to the kitchen to take the call.

"Anthony. What news?"

"No sign of the pamphlet anywhere in the flat."

"Are you sure?"

"Certain. I looked everywhere. I found a large format English book with the title "The Castles of County Clare" but nothing written in Gaelic."

"They must have taken it, which means that they were looking for Lorraine."

"Want me to track them?"

"Too risky. Let's stick with the original plan. Work with Paul Wilson and Rob Martin."

"Will do."

In the time it took Tom to end the call and to walk back from the kitchen to the drawing room he had decided that he would not tell Lorraine that the pamphlet was missing. Not yet anyway. Lorraine was standing at the window looking out across the wall-bordered lawn which was yellowing in the ochre light of the late afternoon. Though she couldn't see the church clock, she guessed it wasn't far off ten to three; the light was already fading. She heard Tom come in from the kitchen.

"We should have honey for tea" she said without turning around.

"You know that Brooke died from an infected mosquito bite?"

"Sepsis is the cause of one in five deaths."

"Maybe. But you might argue that it is evidence that the good die unluckily."

"Was Rupert Brooke one of the good? I mean was he a good man?"

"In the world's terms yes, I think so. And he wrote some easily memorable lines about honey, tea and church clocks."

Lorraine resumed her chair and made ready to continue her confession.

"It has been ten minutes since my last confession" she said ruefully.

"More people would call it therapy these days."

Lorraine laughed.

"Where were we?"

"You were describing your hunky-dory life, a comfortable life rudely interrupted, by me."

"I had everything that I wanted. And before you ask, I didn't feel that I had missed out by not having children. I do not have any regrets about any of my relationships. But I was beginning to feel lonely. It is hard to explain really. I had friends, but one can be lonely in a crowd. I felt disconnected. I was not connected to anything or anyone. At night I would dream of being a little girl running through lush grassy fields, across farmland and in and out of other children's houses. It is all I remember of being a little girl. My parents died when I was seven and I do not really remember much before that. I was sent away to school in Dublin and the days and years before that exist only in glimpses. But those images kept popping up in my dreams. Not in any sequence or order but more and more frequently. It was like watching an old reel to reel tape, every colour faded and the images jittery. But I wanted to reconnect with my past, to reconnect with the carefree little girl who made herself known to me in my dreams. She wanted my attention. Then at work one day I overheard the cleaners at the hospital talking about a pub in Kilburn. I asked them about it. They said that many of the people who drink there regularly are originally from the west and south of Ireland and that it was a great place to meet. And I knew that I had to go there. I wanted to hear the lost sounds, the accents, the rhythms of my childhood. I wanted to be that little girl again."

Lorraine paused, as if to listen to those voices.

"Did you not realise that you were putting yourself in harm's way?"

"Not really. I had no idea that it was a Sinn Fein meeting place until you told me earlier. It seemed like a regular north London Irish pub to me, you know, like the ones in Crouch End and Highbury."

"The woman you spoke to, Maudy?"

"Yes."

"She noticed you were a stranger. That's why she came up to you. "

"Yes. But we only talked superficially."

"But she asked you directly if you were Irish?"

"Yes."

"And you took a pamphlet which was written in Gaelic, which she would have noticed. She would have had her suspicions and almost certainly talked to the others about you."

"So?"

"What if they find out who you really are, Mary?" Like a skier suddenly and unexpectedly catching an edge on an icy slope, Lorraine lost her balance for just one fraction of a second; she was metaphorically thrown sideways, skidding and banging across the compacted ice. Everything hurt. Tom could see her pain.

"That's why we had to intervene."

"We?"

"Well, specifically, me."

There was a momentary silence. Tom broke it.

"You took the pamphlet because you thought it would connect you to Clare?"

"Yes. I was trying to reach out to the little girl in my dreams. To bring her something that she would recognize."

"Was Mary a Gaelic speaker?"

"We spoke Gaelic in games and between ourselves. English was the official language. In the sixties few people spoke Irish in public because it was seen as the language of the rural poor. But it lived in our childish play, in our nicknames and in vulgar terms. I thought Mary would recognize the words."

"Did she?"

"Yes, she did. The more that I read, the more words and phrases came back to me. And its cadencies brought back memories, as if each word conjured a scene; the low bellow of cattle across the misty morning on the strand, the crackling cackle of geese in the yard. Reading the pamphlet made me homesick. And that made me realize what was missing from my life: a sense of place, of belonging, of my past."

"Maud would have been suspicious. People have a reason to be at those bookshelves. Not many people are invited into the inner sanctum: fewer still wander into it out of curiosity. Maud acts as gatekeeper. That is why she asked you if you were Irish."

"Well, it is hardly unusual to be Irish in north London."

"But it is unusual to take a pamphlet on such a specific subject as the restoration of the Gaelic language in County Clare. The title is so precise in terms of geography and politics that it could have put you at great risk. It could place you exactly. And it might still. It offers the acute observer interpretive possibilities."

Lorraine felt the force of the priestly rebuke.

"Mea culpa" she whispered to herself.

Chapter 32

Elmira pushed a file across the desk with the tips of her fingers. Her nails were varnished Persian red. The looped, gold circles of her bracelets jingled as she withdrew her hand. In another time and another place Fin could have been looking at the bewitching hands of a clairvoyant in a caravan at a fair. Michael looked down at the manilla folder. Elmira rested her elbows on the desk, her fingertips touching as if in prayer. Her sharp features and languidly black eyes were framed by dark borders of eyeliner which flicked upwards at the outer edge of each eye. In amongst the swirls of her black hair were silver earrings which descended from the fixings in her lobes in three watery streams; the streams gave into a triangular lake. The ends of each dependent brushed against her shoulders. Fin was uncomfortably aware that his eye had followed the watery silver downwards to her shoulders and there he could make out the straps of her bra, visible through her white blouse. Bind me to the mast, stop my ears with wax, thought Fin. Fin had been schooled in a world of craggy faced men who spoke sparingly: men who were brought up to hard labour, cutting peat and harvesting potatoes, men who knew how to handle both spade and gun. But here he found himself in a room of alluring fragrance and beguiling jewellery.

"Please, take some time to read through the file."
Elmira stood and moved away from the desk. Fin expected her to leave the room, but she simply turned her back to them, like a schoolmistress who has assigned the class some quiet reading. Michael opened the file. On the inside cover was the same image that DCI Wilson had so carefully pasted together on his computer screen,

the image he had christened "the two Lorraines". Fin nodded his recognition to Michael, as if to say, "that's her." The only sound in the room was the quiet swish of Elmira's skirt brushing against her legs as she slowly paced the room. The file's loose bundle of pages set out the timeline of Lorraine's life from enrolling at University College, London in 1989 to her disappearance just a few days ago. There were pictures of the flat in Wooler Street and stock photographs of the Nightingale Hospital. There were also copies of bank statements, credit card bills, and a print-out of the dates and times of Lorraine's most recent mobile phone calls. The documents were an exact facsimile of the file which had been compiled by DCI Paul Wilson, PC Nick Booth and Sgt. Louise Tindall. Michael and Fin were familiar enough with this kind of documentary evidence to know that what they had been given was a police file. Fin wanted to ask the obvious question but thought better of it. Michael, who was less subtle, could not help himself.

"Where did you get this?"

Elmira had anticipated the first question.

"There are leaky people in every organization, people who accidentally grant access to their computer systems."

Or deliberately thought Fin. Elmira continued.

"Hackers have no scruples; they work for whoever pays them."

"Your people work very quickly" said Michael.

"It is a routine case; not difficult" explained Elmira.

"What does this information mean to you?"

"This is definitely the woman we are looking for. But I am not so sure that it tells us anything about her that we did not already know."

"That may be true" replied Elmira, returning to her seat, "but what the file does not contain is perhaps more important than what it does."

Fin could feel himself being lured dangerously close to the rocks.

"If this lady" continued Elmira gesturing at the image of Lorraine, "had been connected to the security forces, then there would be evidence: it might be a phone call, or a text, an email. There is always something."

"A smoking gun?"

"If you like. And if she had been taken by the security forces then once again there would be evidence of that."

"So, you are confident that her disappearance is not the work of Mi5?" Michael asked the direct question.

"As confident as I can be, yes."

"But she disappeared immediately after she had been seen acting suspiciously in Kilburn. Are you telling us that it is just a coincidence?"

"I am not telling you anything. I am showing you the evidence."

Michael was heading for the rocks. Fin grabbed the tiller.

"I think what Michael means is that there is no evidence linking her with the security forces in any way?"

"No. But look at the last page in the file."

Fin turned to the last page, a page he had not really taken any notice of when first glancing through the papers. It was a list of internet searches made by PC Nick Booth. Fin's quick eye ran down the list.

"These are all searches for the record of the death of Lorraine Watson in 1989."

"There is no trace of the woman that you know as Lorraine Watson before 1989. It seems that the police were working on a theory that she had assumed, or stolen, that identity from another Lorraine Watson who had recently died."

Fin closed the file and made ready to leave.

"You have been most helpful Elmira. Thank you. We can see ourselves out."

"Gentlemen."

Elmira gathered up the loose papers into the folder and watched the men go. Fin led Michael back down the gloomy corridor and wrestled the lift gate open.

"Why the sudden exit, Fin?"

"Not now. When we are out of the building."

Fin pressed the button to take them back to ground level. They emerged blinking into the oblique light of the fading afternoon. Fin, whose seatbelt would still not click into place, turned to face Michael. He knew he owed him an explanation.

"You heard what Elmira said?" he began.

As soon as Paul stepped out of the lift, he shook off his coat as if it were on fire. A combination of the short sprint from the car and the building's overzealous central heating system had raised his temperature to summer heights. He threw the coat towards the hook on the back of the door. It fell into a crumpled heap on the floor where it lay like one of London's rough sleepers huddled in a doorway. PC Nick Booth looked up to witness the debacle and had to look quickly down again for fear of catching someone's eye. Then wordlessly, the office, responding to Paul's somewhat comedic entry, came alive with movement.

"Over here sir."

Louise Tindall rose and positioned herself behind and to the left of her chair. Nick moved around from his desk and assumed a similar position on the right. Paul assumed the captain's position: his co-pilots leaned in and down so that their heads were all in the same horizontal plane.

"Nick found this" said Louise clicking on the mouse.

"Girl collapses and dies from asthma attack" read Paul.

"A nineteen-year-old girl, named by police as Lorraine Watson, suffered an asthma attack on the Fulham Palace Road. The tragic incident, which happened at about two pm yesterday afternoon was witnessed by passers-by. "It happened so suddenly, said one eye witness, "She fell to the floor and was obviously struggling to breathe. I ran over and tried CPR but I could not revive her. It was devastating." A spokesperson for the hospital said, "Lorraine had severe childhood asthma and attended regular clinics here. Our thoughts are with her family at this tragic time."

Paul sat back in his chair. He then leaned forward again to check the date of the article. August 1989.

"So sad" he said quietly to no one in particular.

"I checked the records at the hospital" said Nick. "And the death certificate."

"And?"

"Her date of birth is the same as Lorraine Watson's."

"You were right sir; there are two Lorraines, or rather two people sharing the one identity." Paul thought for a moment.

"Well done you two. Brilliant work." Nick and Louise exchanged satisfied glances.

"Thank you, sir."

"The thing is" continued Paul, "the thing is that it doesn't tell us who the second, later, Lorraine Watson is."

"But she must be somebody quite important" said Louise.

"Why do you say that?"

"Because she assumed, or was given, a whole new identity when she was nineteen or twenty. You would have to be somebody quite important for that to happen."

"Maybe." Paul pushed his chair back causing Nick and Louise to move swiftly aside. Paul looked across and saw his lifeless coat gathering dust on the floor.

"What do we do now?" asked Louise pragmatically.

"We go back to Wooler Street and examine every thread, every fibre, every nook, every cranny. There must be something we missed, a footprint in the hearth, a body in the attic, a reflection in the mirror…" He was running out of analogies, "…something that gives us a lead. There has to be a chance that she will have kept something that connects her with her former life. It might be an entry in a diary. It might be a postcard or a photograph. But whatever it is it will be well hidden, you know, like an Anglo-Saxon coin lying undiscovered for centuries in a Suffolk field."

Paul may have run out of analogies but he had not exhausted his cache of similes. Not yet anyway. Louise exchanged glances with Nick.

"I will assemble a team straight away sir. How many do you think we will need?"

"Five or six. At least two from forensics."

"I'm on it" confirmed Louise.

"I don't want them in those white body suits. The flat isn't a crime scene, so no yellow ticker tape or any of those small marquees that forensics love to erect. We absolutely must not draw attention to ourselves. We just need very good detectives. Have you still got Mrs. Nair's keys?"

Paul knew the answer because he had, only yesterday, put the keys back in Louise's drawer himself, but it was a necessary pretence. Louise hesitated. She should have returned them and did not want to admit she hadn't.

"It helps if you do."

"There are in my drawer sir."

Chapter 33

Evening fell quietly in Grantchester. Light retreated diagonally across the walls of its houses, its pubs and its church. Fronds of watery blackness elongated themselves across the meadows and reached into the village. Weeping willows hushed their swishing branches; the incoming tide of night crept secretly up the lanes and between the buildings. The darkness in Grantchester was as soft as the delicate limbs of Morpheus. Lorraine had fallen under his spell as daylight retreated from the garden doors. Tom was in the kitchen orchestrating the ingredients gathered from Professor Needham's ample stores. One of two phones to his left sounded the opening notes of the overture. Tom glanced at the screen's incoming message. He put down the knife on the chopping board, sluiced his hands under the hot tap and wiped them on the tea towel that he had tucked into his trousers like a professional chef. As soon as his hands were dry enough, he pressed the button to reveal the message.

"They took the bait. Elmira x"

Tom allowed himself a brief smile. He picked up the knife and with a swift, delicate, rolling motions, moved the blade rapidly from tip to base to fine chop the onions, then the garlic, then the peppers. He placed the fragments into a pan of olive oil which sizzled its pleasure. Tom seasoned the lightly bubbling mélange. I can leave it to simmer for ten minutes he thought; he had an important message to send and he needed to select a wine from Professor Needham's cellar. He picked up the second phone and pressed speed dial.

"Hey, Tom."

To those who did not know him, and even to those, like Lorraine, who did, Anthony gave the impression of meandering gently through life. He seemed to ask the world to look at him and see a stereotypical second generation, British born, Jamaican. And although it was true that Anthony was a second generation British born Jamaican (and proud of it) and although he had a huge collection of reggae music, Tom knew that Anthony's persona was a camouflage. It was not really who he was. Or rather it was only a part of who he was. But every time he rang him, Anthony would pronounce Tom's name the American way, as if the vowel in the middle was nearer an 'a' and an 'o'. It made Tom smile.

"Anthony. Elmira has been in touch. Wooler Street will be busy tonight. Visitors. Police and thieves."

"Fighting the nation?" added Anthony before swiping right to end the call. He knew what to do.

Night fell suddenly in London. Darkness dropped from above with the dramatic flourish of a theatre curtain. London responded by lighting itself from the footlights upwards: cars switched on their headlights, streetlamps flickered themselves on, district by district, and tall buildings began to glow. New Scotland Yard was particularly brightly lit by the floodlights of the TV stations whose crews were waiting patiently for news. The media briefing team had kept them interested with occasional titbits. The news was that, although the forensic teams had gathered enough evidence to identify the size and type of explosive device used, they had much work to do yet. The truth was that those with years of service knew the truth, but could not say so publicly. The Commissioner and her Assistant had briefed the Prime Minister that it was likely to be the work of the IRA and that it was deliberately timed to coincide with the latest inquiry. But they advised the government not to say so and the government agreed that it was in no position to start hares running. Instead, the Assistant Commissioner was tasked with releasing a limited amount of information in a news bulletin to be broadcast at six o'clock. He told the waiting world that the Counter Terrorism Division had called in all available personnel and that they were using every resource to find the perpetrators. There was no further threat to public safety but everyone should remain on high alert.

Paul let out a dismissive sigh as he watched the screen in Rob's office relaying the images from forty or so feet below him. The medium is the message; he agreed with McLuhan about that. For the Met. the way news is released is more important than the news itself. He had some real news, that Lorraine Watson was not the young woman baptized as such. Everything was somehow connected: the fire at Marylebone station, the disappearance of Lorraine Watson, the bomb blast in Lincoln's Inn, the files on Rob's desk, the events of 1974 and 1975; somehow, they existed simultaneously, time present and time past. But the kaleidoscope is still turning, the pattern changing.

Gregory Isaacs' "Babylon too Rough" eased its lilting way through Anthony's flat in Wooler Street. Anthony knew the song well; it did not disturb his concentration as he studied the pages of the file that Tom had entrusted to him four days ago. Anthony's memory was near enough photographic; he had committed its contents to memory. The file was a little dog-eared and tatty. Every page bore the familiar crimson double underlining which underscored "Top Secret" at the top of each page. Like the similarly aged files on Rob's desk, the edges of each sheet had yellowed, the paper clips bled rust where their edges scored and etched the paper, and the typescript had worn away in places. Tom and

Anthony had been through the file together. Anthony knew exactly which document to select and precisely what to do with it. He turned the pages until he came to a sheaf of photographs. There were four or five. They were all pictures of the same young girl, progressing through her young life. The last was a school photo in which she proudly wore the red and white uniform of Alexandra College, Dublin. But this was not the image Anthony needed. No, the one he selected was one which bore on the reverse the legend "My First Communion,1976". It depicted a girl in a white dress standing before a low brick wall. A short distance behind her stood the double-height Roman Catholic church with its gabled projecting porch and pitched slate roof. Anthony slid the picture carefully into a clear plastic sleeve and returned the folder to its document case. He was looking forward to his next task. He left his flat and made his swift way to the back door of Lorraine's. He carefully opened the window which Fin had prised open only the other night. Anthony reached through the window and pulled himself through. He landed in the kitchen with the lightest of taps of his feet as Anthony instinctively cushioned his landing. He made his way through the darkness towards the front door. His eyes had adjusted enough by now to be able to make out the shape of the bookcase to the side of the front door. He stood as close to the bookcase as possible and reached for the weighty volume which he knew would be on the top. It was too dark to read the text but he could make out the outline of the familiar tower house of Bunratty Castle, the image on the back cover of "The Castles of County Clare." He lifted the hard cover just a couple of inches and slid in the plastic sleeve containing the image of the girl. It had to relatively easily discoverable, so there was no need to try that hard to conceal it. He patted the cover down softly and let himself out through the front door. Back in his flat, Anthony lightly clicked the switch on the front of his turntable and Gregory Isaacs began to sing "Rumours dem spreadin'". It was no more than seven minutes since "Babylon too rough" swung the air.

Chapter 34

Maudy carried her drink to the rearmost table of the 'Campbell Arms' and took her seat between Gerry and Fin.

"The folder which we were given was almost certainly a copy of a police file" explained Michael.

"How do you think they accessed that?" asked Maudy.

"Someone was happy to leak it."

"You mean someone was keen that we should have the file?"

"Yes. A bit too keen for my liking." said Fin.

"What's in it?"

"Not much though it seems that our nurse was not all that she seemed."

"I could tell."

"It seems that the woman, who came to the Campbell and whom we tried to visit in Wooler Street, the woman we know as Lorraine Watson, assumed that identity as a student."

"There was a document in the file that showed that the police were looking for the death notice of Lorraine Watson. And they were searching, exclusively, in the year 1989."

"Do we know if they found anything?"

"No. That was all that they wanted us to know. Elmira told us that they could find no trace of our Lorraine before 1989 when she assumed that name."

"So, we have to conclude that this Lorraine is someone with a past to hide."

"Yes. But that was as far as they allowed us to go."

"But there was nothing to suggest she was an undercover agent?

"No. In fact Elmira was insistent that there was nothing to connect her with the security services in any way."

"Well, that's a relief."

"May be. But why had she assumed a false identity?"

"O come on now Fin. Loads of people change their names, or take other ones. And taking on the name of a dead person is on page one of the fraudster's handbook."

"I know. And it may come to nothing. But Elmira was giving us the brush off all right."

Michael had been living in London for nearly twenty years without attracting so much as a parking fine. He didn't want his anonymity to come to an end. Not now, not so close to the completion of their mission. He felt reassured that whoever this Lorraine was, she did not seem to represent an immediate threat to his discovery and exposure.

"And we still don't know what was she doing here. Nor why she took the pamphlet?

"Both good points Maudy" said Fin. "I have been thinking about them too. And I may have an answer." Maudy gave Fin one of her sceptical looks.

"Well, think about it" continued Fin. "She took away a pamphlet about the case for the reintroduction of Gaelic in County Clare. It is an odd choice from all the literature we have available or for sale."

"Maybe she had been to a music festival in Clare."

"Maybe. But maybe her connection is deeper than that. I mean the pamphlet is in Gaelic."

"Are you suggesting that she is actually one of us? I mean that she is from the west of Ireland?"

"I don't know. But if, when she came to London, she was given or assumed a new identity, as the police seem to think, then it follows that she was and is someone with a past identity to hide."

"What do you propose we do?" asked Maudy,

"We need to go back to her flat. Tonight. Find out for sure who she really is. Gerry, are you all set?"

"Sure."

"Good. We need to be extra vigilant."

"When we have finished our drinks, Gerry and I will leave. Michael you stay here with Maudy."

"Mine's a vodka then" said Maudy shaking her empty glass at Michael who smiled and made his way to the bar.

Visitors. Police and thieves. Anthony allowed Tom's words to echo around. He knew well enough who all of his visitors would be, but he did not know in what order they would arrive. Would the thieves arrive before the police or vice versa? His money was on the thieves.

Thomas made his way to Kilburn High Road as soon as he received Fin's call from the Campbell. Conor was in the back, lying awkwardly across the seats of the Vectra, partially hidden. Fin slid into the passenger seat and instinctively reached for the seat belt. Thomas gave him a look.

"You haven't fixed it then?"

"Like I have had a chance."

Fin let the belt slide back into its halter.

"Have you everything we need?"

"We don't need much if last time is anything to go by."

"True enough. But someone may have secured the window and we might need to force it."

"We don't want to disturb the fella next door" whispered Conor from his prone position in the back. "There's a good chance he will recognize us. He clocked me before."

"Different car this time" offered Thomas.

"Doesn't matter. He got a good look at me, didn't he? Why else would I be acting the fugitive in the back here? I can't afford to be seen."

"Conor's right Thomas. We can't be too careful. On the other hand, you could try and get us there before dawn." Thomas changed down a gear and sped alongside Regent's Park.

"You better cut down through King's Cross: the area around Holborn is bound to be cordoned off."

"And whose fault would that be now?" teased Thomas. The Vectra fell silent as each man reflected on the day's events. Fin typed Wooler Street into Waze.

"ETA twenty minutes" he announced, breaking the silence.

Anthony knew that his 'visitors various' as he categorized them would be on their way here by now. He slipped out into the darkness of Villa Street. To his experienced eyes, unmarked police cars were as obvious as marked ones and he would know them straight away, but he didn't know how the thieves would make their appearance; he was not expecting to see the brown Peugeot though. He knew they had dumped that.

In the underground car park of New Scotland Yard, Louise Tindall was addressing the forensics specialists that she had hastily assembled to help her and DCI Wilson carry out a more comprehensive search of Lorraine's flat. Wilson had proposed a team of five or six but she reasoned that the flat was not large enough for that number. Once briefed, the group divided into two unmarked cars with Paul in the lead car. A few minutes later, two plum coloured Ford Mondeos were heading across Westminster Bridge.

Anthony smiled when he saw a car whose right indicator was flashing too frequently, as if overwhelmed by electrical current. Here come the thieves, he thought.

Thomas came to a halt in the same place that he had previously berthed the brown Peugeot. Anthony typed the Vectra's registration number into his phone and repocketed it in his long coat. He would have remembered it in any case. Nothing but his left shoe was visible as he hid in the canopied doorway like Harry Lime in 'The Third Man.'

Fin and Conor left Thomas behind the wheel and scurried their familiar way to Lorraine's flat. Fin was relieved to find that his handiwork from the other evening had not been undone and made quick work of entering without breaking, in exactly the manner Anthony had done an hour or so earlier.

Once inside Fin made straight for the bookcase near the front door: he was convinced that the sloping ranks of books would hold clues about Lorraine's past life. Conor meanwhile searched the bedroom looking for anything of significance, perhaps a bundle of letters or a diary, a keepsake, a memento, or a piece of jewellery. He examined each object on Lorraine's dressing table then replaced it carefully in exactly the position he found it. Conor moved quickly through the room. He noticed that the drawer of the bedside table was ajar. He levered it fully open, saw little of interest inside, just a handful of hairgrips and an eye mask, and wiggled it back to its original position before dropping to a press up position to look under the bed. He saw boxes: Conor reached one out and opened it. Inside, cradled in tissue paper, were a pair of red shoes with long, angular, pointed heels. Conor briefly wondered if there were another side to Lorraine before putting the box back and selecting another one from the cache.

In Villa Street a cat blithely licked its left front paw a few inches from Anthony's feet, oblivious to his quiet presence. The stillness of the scene was broken by the approach of two Mondeos making their way past the parked Vectra. From their different positions Anthony and Thomas both understood what the arrival of these vehicles meant. Anthony had been expecting them but Thomas was not so prepared. He pulled his phone from the charging cable which was plugged into the cigarette lighter and messaged Fin.

"Incoming. Leave now."

He watched the green screen anxiously and was relieved to see the double tick that confirmed that the message had been received. The passengers from the two Mondeos were laboriously retrieving their baggage from the cars' boots and seemed in no hurry. Paul Wilson was on the move, keys in hand, anxious, excited. Thomas watched him in the rearview mirror; he calculated that if Fin had reacted immediately, then he and Conor would have time enough to get out through the back door and down the side of the building. Inside the flat Fin was leafing through the books in the bookcase, checking between each one for any hidden letters or notes, but his search was proving fruitless. He stood up and was about to give up when his eye was drawn to an image on the cover of a substantial volume, an image which he immediately recognized. He experienced a momentary quiver, like a sudden chill, of homesickness and turned the book around so that he could see it more clearly. He could not help himself but turn its beguiling pages: Bunratty, Knappogue, Carrigaholt, Newtown, Dromoland. For a moment he was transported back to a landscape of Celtic crosses, Franciscan Friaries and Gothic towers.

Now why would Lorraine have such a book? he thought to himself. And as if in answer to his question he turned the next page and discovered the photograph that Anthony had placed there twenty minutes earlier. Fin used the light from his phone to scrutinize it. He found himself looking at a young girl dressed for her first communion standing outside a church, a church that he knew that he had seen before, but which he did not have time to place before Thomas' urgent message shook the phone in his hand. Fin had the presence of mind to press the camera button and took a screenshot of the photograph before closing the book and running through to the bedroom.

"Conor. Out now!"

Conor pushed the box that he had been about to open back under the bed, sprang to his feet and soundlessly followed Fin out through the kitchen. From the dreary cover of the alley Fin watched until he was sure that the police team was safely inside the building then signaled to Conor to retreat. Thomas rode the clutch until they slithered away.

'Neat exit' thought Anthony, who looked on appreciatively. But did you get what you came for? He couldn't know for sure whether Fin and Conor had been disturbed too soon, but time would tell.

Inside the flat the forensic team began their tedious work, mapping and cataloguing the impedimenta of Lorraine's life. Paul did not like this part of the job and didn't really understand the caste of mind required to be in forensics, so he left them to it. Instead, he took a leisurely tour of the flat. He lingered over each item that his eyes fell upon and created a possible narrative of its history, how it might have come to be there, how it fitted into Lorraine's life. As the others set to work pinning and mounting Lorraine's life like a collection of butterflies and moths, each item labelled and given a number, he found himself drawn back towards the front door. He knelt down next to the bookcase. He knew the value of books: he knew how to construct a profile from someone's reading, the old-fashioned way of examining someone's interior life before google searches. Books were often far more intriguing and ultimately more revealing. The bottom shelf was home to familiar airport thrillers. All of the paperbacks showed signs of having been read on holiday, with yellowing pages and broken spines. He eyes moved up to the next shelf which housed medical textbooks and journals, the accumulated evidence of Lorraine's professional practice. 'The Divided Self' R.D Laing. Of course she would have read that, he thought. These books post-dated Lorraine's arrival in London and so he was sure that there were no clues about her past to be found within their pages. The top shelf was, as is so often the case, a much more eclectic mix. Here he found a couple of cookery books, some travel guides, a couple of biographies, and some novels. He read the titles on the spines: 'The Country Girls' by Edna O'Brien; 'The Old Jest' by Jennifer Johnston; 'Foster' by Claire Keegan. He knew the O'Brien, so he pulled out 'The Old Jest' which he didn't know, though he had heard of Jennifer Johnston, and read the description on the back cover. "The violent backdrop of the Irish rebellion threatens Nancy's innocence as a fugitive IRA rebel seeks shelter….." He pulled out the Foster. He did not know this novel and had not even heard of Claire Keegan. He turned the book over and read the blurb, "Set on a farm in County Wicklow, 'Foster' is a brilliantly rendered account of a young girl who is placed with her aunt and uncle….." He broke off reading as the truth dawned; these novels were all about young girls growing up in Ireland.

'Shit' he whispered. 'Shit'. The blood drained down to Paul's feet. He noticed the large volume that rested at an angle across the top of the other books, where Fin had left it. He picked it up rather too quickly and did not have a firm enough grasp. It fell to the floor splayed out spine upwards revealing to the right a glimpse of the image that Fin had captured on his phone about ten minutes ago. At first Paul was almost too stunned to move. He slid the photograph clear of the clumsy book and turned it over.

'Shit'. The word escaped from him involuntarily; he knew immediately what he was looking at. His eyes looked beyond and behind the girl at the picture of the rendered church of the grieving widower in Feakle.

"This is what we are looking for Louise" he called out. She was at his side in a moment

"Sir?"

"Look at this."

Louise stared at the photograph.

"It fell out of the pages of 'The Castles of County Clare'" he explained unnecessarily.

"Do you think it could be a picture of her?"

"Yes. And look at the titles of the novels. What do you see?"

"All by women?"

"All by Irish women novelists and all about growing up in Ireland." Louise diverted her attention and her gaze to Paul.

"This is her, isn't it?"

"Come on. Scramble the teams; let's get out of here." Paul put the photograph, still in its plastic sheath, into his jacket pocket. His trip to the west of Ireland had not been wasted time after all.

Anthony watched as the identical twin Mondeos were hurriedly, unceremoniously, repacked. Doors and boot lids were slammed in noisy percussion; engines were revved hard. As Anthony stepped from his hidden canopy, the soft streetlight washed across his feet, and a light came on in a window in the eaves of a house on the opposite side of Wooler Street. The casement opened; an elderly woman's face appeared. She glanced down the street at the rapidly retreating Mondeos, tutted to herself, withdrew and closed the window. Anthony thrust his hands deep into his coat pockets and made his quiet way back to his flat.

Chapter 35

As silence returned to Wooler Street, the cloak of night muffled Grantchester meadows. Lorraine finished the washing up: she insisted, it was the least she could do. Tom poured the last glass of Chateau D'Issan. Lorraine understood that they were drinking a fine wine but did not really understand what 'Third Growth' or 'Grand Cru' meant, despite Tom's comprehensive description of the undiscovered treasures of Professor Needham's cellar. Lorraine was still trying to understand what had happened to her in the last few days. She had made her confession, which is what Tom seemed to demand of her. Their conversation over dinner was convivial and harmless; Tom had not raised the subject of her past again. She was a little startled when Tom leaned forward in Professor Needham's armchair.

"Lorraine, do you mind if we talk further about Mary?"

Lorraine knew now for certain that it was on account of Mary that she had been taken. It was always a possibility. All those who live an assumed life or live in witness protection, must suffer a kind of imposter syndrome, she thought.

"What do you want to know?

"Everything. I want to know everything that you can remember about your childhood up until the time you went to school in Dublin."

"Well, it's much as I was explaining to you earlier. I can piece together certain elements; sights, sounds, voices, but not a continuous narrative. In the last couple of years, the memories have become more vivid and more compelling. Irish words float uninvited into my mind and I see Mary. I remember my first communion.

I remember the three of us: Maeve, Niamh and me all learning our catechism together. We rehearsed it for hours.”

“Who were Maeve and Niamh?”

“Girls from school. We did everything together. Until I was sent away.”

“Do you remember why you were sent away?”

“My mother died and my father thought it was for the best. He did not have the time for me, what with running the hotel and everything. And he was a man’s man: he did not do daughters.”

“Like King Lear?”

“The hotel bar was not a place for a young girl to be brought up in, he said. There were too many things that went on there, things a young girl should not see or hear. So even in the school holidays I was sent away to stay with my aunt and uncle in Tipperary. I kind of left Feakle at the age of seven.”

“What sort of things did he think that you should not see or hear?”

“Bad language. Ugly talk. That sort of thing I imagine. I don’t know. There were a group of men who drank there regularly, men my father seemed to be nervous of.”

“What sort of men?”

“Local men. Men from the village, from the parishes of Feakle. But sometimes men from further west, from Ennis and West Clare. My bedroom was above the main bar and I could hear the steady drone of their voices below. It was quite comforting in a way. There was always a huddle of men drinking late into the night, especially on Fridays and Saturdays.”

“Can you remember any nights in particular?”
Tom did not want to push too hard but so much depended upon Mary’s memory.

"I can't quite place it in context but I do have a vivid sense of one night."

"Can you remember when it was?"

"No but I think I would have been about five because it was before mum died. It exists in my memory only as a set of impressions, of colours, lights, sounds. I remember that it was a frosty, windless night, one of those still nights when sound travels effortlessly across the ground and up into the air: I could hear everything very clearly from my room. I heard several cars arrive together which was unusual. I remember looking out of my window and seeing several men all wearing black suits. They spoke in English, but in an accent I had not heard before, a harsh, almost rasping sound. I heard my father welcoming them politely and taking them through to the dining room. Then more cars and more men arrived. I could tell from the manner of their greeting that these men knew my father and I had seen one of them in the hotel bar many times. Their soft voices were familiar to me. I could hear my father settling them into the dining room. Then everything went quiet for an hour or so. The next thing I remember was the sudden scrunch of feet running across the courtyard and two or three of the cars leaving. Shortly after that several armed gardai came rushing into the hotel. There seemed to be no end of them. There was a lot of shouting at first but it quickly died down. Then the cars were driven away. That's all I remember except that the next day an English man came into the hotel asking to speak to my parents."

"Do you think you would recognize any of the men you saw that night, particularly the ones who arrived last and left first?"

"I would be more confident of recognizing their voices."

"That would do just as well."

"Why does any of this matter Tom?"

"It shouldn't matter really. It is a morsel cold upon dead Caesar's trencher."

"But it does matter?"

"If someone thought that you could identify the voices that you heard that night then it would matter very much."

"Why?"

"You could rewrite history."

"How could I do that?"

"If you identified the men whose voices you heard that night, it would change everything. There are many vested interests who will go to great lengths to prevent that happening."

"Lengths such as planting a bomb in Lincoln's Inn?" Mary was beginning to understand.

"It is a timely reminder."

"A reminder?"

"Yes, to let sleeping dogs lie. The Republicans will argue that they have kept their side of the bargain and the British must do the same."

Mary thought for a moment.

"People who imagine themselves to be oppressed will always claim the moral high ground."

"Without a doubt. And the British government knows it is skating on meltingly thin ice because of the wrongful imprisonment of the Guildford Four and the Maguire Seven. If the ice cracks beneath their feet they drown in freezing water. No minister can afford to take that risk. And they will be worried about what you remember."

"Neither side wants the sleeping dog to wake."

"That is the inconvenient truth, Mary."

"What do you mean?"

"Despite all that has passed over the last five hundred years their interests are mutual. They are effectively on the same side. Neither side wants any further revelation."

"But how does that affect me?" asked Lorraine

"You are the only surviving witness, the only one, who if prevailed upon, could lift the veil. But up until now, nobody knew what had become of Mary Maloney."

"What do you mean up until now?"

"Until you the moment that you walked into the Campbell."

Tom paused for Lorraine to digest the significance of his words.

"Could they find me?"

"Without a doubt. And there is a very strong probability that they would want to guarantee your silence."

"Which is why you plucked me from Baker Street?" Tom swirled the last mouthful of wine around the glass before lifting it to his lips. Mary's eyes followed the up and down movement of his glass as a devout communicant follows the raised and lowered chalice. This is my body. This is my blood.

Chapter 36

Fin wondered what to do with the image of the girl imprisoned inside his phone. He was sure that he recognized the church in the background: it looked so familiar. Perhaps he should recognize the girl? But he couldn't place her. How could he identify who she was? Maybe Elmira's contacts could find out for him. But he didn't trust her. Elmira moved in the shadowy world of former soviet republics. That made Fin nervous because he thought that you couldn't be sure whose side they were on. But he was also nervous of Elmira as a woman because she stirred something in him and that, more than a fondness for whiskey, was the ruin of many a good man. Parnell's affair with Kitty O'Shea marked the end of any chance of All Ireland Home Rule. Fin convinced himself that the slightest hint of sexual feeling was therefore a distraction and a weakness. No, he could not risk another meeting with Elmira. Fin decided that his only course of action would be to WhatsApp the image to Maudy. There was a good chance Maudy would recognize the church, if not the girl. Fin sent the image, pocketed his phone and waited patiently for Thomas to steer them safely home.

In Wooler Street, Anthony was also sending an encrypted message. Once he was sure that his visitors had vanished, as the cat that kept him the briefest company in the Villa Street doorway had vanished, Anthony let himself back into Lorraine's flat and made his way to the bookcase. 'The Castles of County Clare' lay there innocently enough, spreadeagled across the books on the top shelf. However, it was lying with its spine against the wall whereas Anthony had deliberately left it the other way around, spine outwards. He smiled. The fish had taken the bait. Just to make sure, he lifted the well-handled tome from its resting place and confirmed the disappearance of the photograph. Anthony reasoned that the image would now be safely in the hands of DCI Wilson. He came to this conclusion because he had seen the police move in with the deliberate air of those who were used to long hours poring over crime scenes. But they left in a disorderly hurry which must mean that they had made a discovery so important that they could bring the search to a premature end. Their hasty departure must mean that they had taken the photograph. It followed therefore that his other visitors, the thieves, did not have the photograph. But that did not mean that they had not seen it. He felt that he knew these men, knew how they worked. He had watched their stealthy comings and goings in Wooler Street. He had witnessed their sangfroid as they waited patiently for the opportune moment to exit the alley, and the driver's equally nonchalant departure from the scene. Further, they had not been back, which might suggest a mission accomplished. If it had been him, he would have taken a screenshot of the photograph and left it exactly where he had found it, to minimize any risk of discovery. He concluded that Fin had done the same.

Tom let the last drops of wine linger at the back of his mouth before reaching for his phone and reading Anthony's message:
"The visitors left with souvenirs of their visit."
He texted back just the one word.
"Endgame."
He scrolled quickly through the menu and sent the same single word message to Elmira. Lorraine saw Tom's features suddenly enlivened.

"What is it?"

"Tomorrow to fresh woods and pastures new."

"What?"

"The closing line of 'Lycidas'. Milton."

"Why do you always talk in riddles and quotations Tom?"

"It isn't a riddle. Tomorrow we must make our way to pastures new."

"I thought this was too good to last."

"Grantchester has its charm, but we can't stay here."

"Why what's happened?"

"Exactly what I had hoped would happen."

"Which is?"

"Remember I mentioned to you the two detectives at New Scotland Yard?"

"Yes, vaguely."

"Their names are Robert Martin and Paul Wilson."

"Unremarkable enough names."

"Remarkable enough detectives though."

"How do you know them?"

"Serendipity."

"What?"

"The result of beneficial chance. Robert Martin was at St Mary's."

"That's doesn't sound like chance. That sounds like the old boys' network."

"We didn't overlap: I mean we didn't know each other. The important thing is that within the next few hours he and Wilson will piece together the remaining pieces in the jigsaw and see the picture in full for the first time."

"What will they see?"

"They will see a portrait of you, Mary."

"Ah."

"Once they are sure that they have established beyond doubt that Lorraine Watson used to be Mary

Maloney, then it will become a matter of greatest urgency for them to find you.”

“Why?”

“Because they will know that they have to find you before others do.”

“Others?”

“Yes.”

“You mean Maudy’s people?”

“I knew you would understand.”

Lorraine did indeed understand and it occurred to her that she had, deep down, understood all along. It was the reason why she had been so composed since coming to her senses in that gloomy flat in Finchley; it was why she was neither panic stricken nor terrified. It was the reason why she had not been afraid of Tom. She knew that her life as Lorraine Watson was a fiction and that like all stories it had to have to have an ending. She had been feeling that sense of an ending for some time. There was a kind of ennui, an existential boredom, that had overcome her in recent months. The well of Lorraine had run dry. Mary had exhausted all that Lorraine could give her. It was why she had started dreaming of home, of the life she lived before she became Lorraine. She took the pamphlet from the pub because she hoped the unfamiliar words would seep into her subconscious mind and unlock buried dreams, the inaccessible memories of her life as Mary Maloney. She knew that they were in there somewhere. She just needed a catalyst to release them. The more she willed the recovery of Mary the more Lorraine receded. Now she was finished. As the truth settled upon her, she looked imploringly at Tom.

“I didn’t know, you know.”

“Didn’t know what?”

“I didn’t know about Maudy and the others. I mean I took the pamphlet because it was in Gaelic and it was about County Clare, but I didn’t know about them. Tom,

I need you to believe me. I went to that place to find myself, for that reason alone. I need to know that you don't blame me for doing that. For putting myself in danger."

Tom found himself moved by her appeal to his emotions. And he believed her. He went over to the window to recollect himself. Outside, the garden shimmered under the light of a waxing moon. After a few moments Tom recovered his dispassionate professionalism.

"Let us look at it as an example of Zemblanity."

"More riddles, Tom?"

"It's the opposite of serendipity. Coined by William Boyd."

"I read a book by him; 'Any Human Heart'"

"He also wrote a book called 'Armadillo.' The main character is an insomniac who spends many nights in the 'Institute for Lucid Dreaming.'"

He paused to allow Mary to reflect on the relevance of that to her own lucid dreams. The irony was not lost on her.

"But it is also the novel in which he coined the word 'zemblanity'. It is the opposite of serendipity. It means those things which turn out unhappily and unluckily, but by design. Boyd named it after Zemblan in the Russian arctic circle, because it is the opposite of Serendib, in terms of climate."

"Where on earth is Serendib?"

"It is the old name for the island of Sri Lanka."

"And my visit to the Campbell is an example of zemblanity?"

"It fits the definition. You went there by design but in doing so met with ill-luck; you were ill-met by moonlight."

"You don't blame me, then?"

"No, I don't."

"Thank you. That matters a great deal to me."

"Think of it another way. It was always likely that, one day, Mary would make her presence felt. Time past is inscribed in time present. Mary was bound to step out from the past. The timing of her appearance was unlucky but not unexpected."

"Yes; I didn't know, I mean, not in any conscious way."

"No, you didn't know."

Tom's smile reassured her that he was not judging her.

"I suppose I knew that one day Mary would resurface. After all she is me, much more so than Lorraine is. Give me the child until he is seven and I will show you the man. Or in my case woman: the Jesuits didn't do female. I was seven when the real Mary began to disappear. I mean I was still Mary Maloney, by name, at school in Dublin, but I was no longer the little girl from Feakle. That little girl was, at seven, the woman I am now. Not Lorraine Watson. She was an imposter. A part I had to play. But Mary had been fading away for some time. I was an orphan, living in a girls' boarding school in term time and at my uncle's house in the holidays. I had no identity. When I finished school, I explained to my uncle that I could not go back to Tipperary. There was nothing for me there. I thought I could go to America. On a green card. He said he could arrange for me to go to England, but not America. And on one condition. That I must change my name."

"How did your uncle persuade you?"

"He explained that there was so much prejudice against the Irish in London because of the political situation that I would have a much easier life if I had a name that did not sound remotely Irish. A Protestant sounding name. He said he knew how it could be done. A few weeks later we met an Englishman in Dublin who gave me a British passport and a ticket to Heathrow. Mary had become Lorraine."

"Did you ever wonder how and why your uncle had the means to do that?

"My uncle was not the sort of man you questioned."

"You know that you can never go back to Wooler Street don't you?"

"It doesn't matter. It was only a place to stay. It wasn't a home. The only thing I will miss about the place is Anthony."

"Who?" Tom dissembled, not for the first time.

"My next door neighbour."

"Oh. I see." More dissembling, which made Tom feel slightly ashamed.

"What will become of me, Tom?"

"Someone else will become of you Mary. Someone good, someone new."

"This is the end for Lorraine?"

"I am afraid it is, yes."

"She had it coming!" she exclaimed.

Lorraine laughed, easily, freely, as if laughter itself, like Mary, had been released from within her.

Chapter 37

On their return from Wooler Street, Paul Wilson and Louise Tindall waited impatiently for the lift to come down to the underground Car Park. Paul knew that Rob would still be in the building as he would be required to be on duty all night as the investigation into Lincoln's Inn gathered momentum. He knew the routine. Rob would be closeted in small meeting rooms whose rank air would smell of stale breath and sweat, its occupants fueled only by stewed, murky coffee. Paul imagined having to interrupt and drag Rob away. How would he explain? Despite this troubling distraction Paul was concentrating enough to be able to thank the team for their hard work, another managerial lightness of touch noted by the ambitious Louise. As they made their stately way up through the airy space of the building, Paul could see that the lobby of New Scotland Yard was, even at this late hour, brightly lit and busy. He recognized the BBC Politics editor, notepad in hand, biro poised, in a discreet huddle with both uniformed and plain clothes officers. As the lift rose further through the glazed void of the atrium, Paul thought that the oddly shadowless people below resembled Lowry figures. Paul had lingered, beguiled, in the Tate, in front of the apparently artless "Sunday" on any number of his lunch breaks. The lift slowed before drifting noiselessly to a halt. The doors seemed to Paul to take an age to register the fact that the lift had come to rest.

The swish of the stiff nylon fronds fringing the bottom of the lift door granted them their release and Paul made straight for Rob's office. There was a polystyrene cup of coffee lightly exhaling on the desk, a plume of warm air meandering upwards. Paul instinctively picked it up. It was warm. Louise was leaning against the door and in the mood for police business.

"Shall we make a start? Scan the photograph, check it against databases. That sort of thing?"

"No need. I know that the photograph was taken in County Clare."

"How on earth do you know that?"

"Rob and I were there less than twenty-four hours ago."

Louise had wondered where he had been and realized that there must be much more to this case than he had been able to say.

"In fact I stood on the exact spot where the photograph was taken, but that doesn't really help. We need to know who the girl is. Scan the image in and magnify it as much as you can. Then compare it with the image of Lorraine Watson."

"Do you think it is her?"

"It was in a book in her flat."

"Yes, but it could be a friend, a god daughter, a relation."

"It could. But equally it could be her. I know I am asking you to compare a photograph of a seven-year-old girl with one of a middle-aged woman, but if there is any resemblance in the features, chin, nose, shape of the jaw, eyes, anything, then let me know. Can I get you a tea or coffee?"

"Tea please. No sugar and just a little milk."

Paul went to make the drinks and Louise did exactly as Paul asked. She manipulated the two images until she had them scaled to the same size and resolution. She placed the image from Stevenage station and the scanned photo from Wooler Street side by side. The eyes were the same colour. The jawline was broadly the same. They could be mother and daughter. Louise had an idea.

She crabbed her way around the table and brought up the scanned image on Nick's computer. She opened the photo editing software and began to age the picture, year by year. Paul returned with the steaming cups and was looking at the screen over her shoulder. As the software aged the photograph by thirty years, there, unfolding before them, was the unmistakable likeness of the adult Lorraine Watson. Paul put the cups down carefully. Louise looked up at him.

"Are you thinking what I am thinking?"

"What else is there to think Louise? It is her. She is the girl in the photo." Paul ran from the room. Louise guessed where he was going.

"He is in with the Assistant Commission……"
Louise did not bother to finish her sentence because Paul was already out of earshot, making for the glassy cage of the lift.

Chapter 38

The shadeless, yellowing lightbulbs of Hermit Place cast a nicotine stained gloam vaguely through the flat. Beneath one of the dim lights Joe and Conor sat at the kitchen table playing cards. Thomas lay across one of the sofas: on the other, Fin was reading. He could not really concentrate and every few seconds he glanced down at his phone. It had been about an hour since he had sent the message to Maudy, but it seemed far longer. The only sound in the flat was the regular snap of plastic playing cards being placed firmly on the flimsy kitchen table. Fin surveyed the room. The set of a Pinter play, he thought. He had seen a production of 'No Man's Land' at the Gate Theatre in Dublin about fifteen years ago, with Michael Gambon. Four men in a room. That was pretty much all he could remember of it. Perhaps that was all there was to remember of it. Conor sat back in his chair, which creaked its displeasure at the disturbance. The sound was a welcome distraction. Joe started to laugh.

"I need a drink."

"Me too."

"Go easy: our day may not yet be done" warned Fin. Joe reached for the Jameson's and poured out two measures. He pointed the bottle's nose at Fin inquiringly.

"Go on then."

Joe poured a third and took it over to Fin on the sofa. They both looked across at Thomas who was oblivious to them, cut off from the world by noise cancelling headphones.

"Leave him. He might have to drive" cautioned Fin.

Joe returned the bottle to its place, sat down, and scooped up the cards.

"My deal?"

"Your deal."

Fin reached down to pick up the tumbler; the screen on his phone lit up. He grabbed it and put it to his ear as quickly as he could. It was Maudy.

"Hey. How are you? The picture was taken outside St Mary's, Feakle."

"I knew I recognized the church." Fin was angry with himself for not being able to place it.

"I must have driven past it hundreds of times."

"And I know who the girl is. It is Mary Maloney."

"Maloney?"

"Yes."

"Are you sure?"

"Yes. Niamh recognized the photograph. It was taken at their first communion."

"I thought Niamh was in New York."

"She is. And she was at work. I had to wait an hour for her to pick up the message. She replied as soon as she left the office."

"Has she stayed in touch with Mary? Does she know where she might be?"

"No. No-one has seen Mary since she left to go to school in Dublin."

"So, the missing nurse is the Maloney girl?"

"It would seem so. This may sound really funny Fin but I thought there was something familiar about her when she came into the pub. And she was looking at pictures of Clare. I should have realized."

"How could you have made the connection? As you say no-one has seen her since she was seven."

"But she was looking for something. She was looking for herself. I should have known."

"You know what this means though?"

229

"It means that somebody else knows who she is."

"Which means we have to find her."

"She was very young. Just five. She may remember nothing, Fin."

"We can't take that risk. Meet me at the all-night café in twenty minutes. Sooner if you can."

"Ok."

He dropped the phone onto the table and sunk back into the sofa. Bloody hell, he thought. The Maloney girl. As soon as they heard the name Maloney, Conor and Joe were stilled. Fin looked across at them.

"Did you hear that?"

"I did" said Conor.

"The Maloneys ran Smyth's hotel" Fin explained to Thomas, who had removed his headphones.

"Bloody hell." Thomas understood the significance.

"Somebody has taken her. They think that she might know something. Might name names."

"She might. But she was only a girl."

"Children remember."

"How are we going to find her?" asked Conor reasonably enough.

Fin's mind was running through the events of the last couple of days. He could not stop thinking about Elmira. She was so polished, so assured. Capable of manipulation. What if she was lying? What if she knew exactly who had taken Lorraine? What if the elaborate charade at the embassy was designed to mislead them? Put them off the scent. Did she know where Mary was? Why would she? She was under orders to send us away with nothing. He had felt instinctively at the time that she was playing them. He was sure now that she was. He felt stupid. Why did he not realize? He gathered himself and beckoned Thomas to follow him out of the flat.

In the café Maudy stirred her latte languidly, melding the foamy white milk and the dark brown coffee, the alternate stripes of caramel and cream gradually amalgamating into a light brown. Fin assumed the seat opposite.

"I heard that Gerry landed safely in Galway" said Maudy, absentmindedly stirring her latte. Fin nodded his approval.

"That's good."

"And Michael worked his last shift in the sorting office today."

Fin nodded again.

"He deserves the rest."

Maudy looked deep into Fin's eyes, as her namesake once looked deep into the eyes of Yeats.

"This is no country for old men" she whispered. Fin imagined the mackerel-crowded Irish sea. Michael would be standing on the deck of the night ferry to Cork under the starlit dome. Leaning forward across the table, Maudy gently brought Fin back from his reverie.

"We have to find Mary Maloney" she whispered.

"I know" replied Fin softly. "But how? What can we do?"

Maudy rounded on him.

"Resignation is the enemy of action" she snapped at him. Yeats, rebuked by his Maud, thought Fin. Fin repented.

"There may be something we can do."

"I am glad to hear it."

"It is risky."

Maudy looked at him with an expression of mock incredulity and her arms half outstretched. Fin was humbled.

"Yes, obviously, it would be risky."

"Well go on" insisted Fin's muse.

"We know that the police are looking for her. They came to her flat. Let them find her for us."

Maudy thought about it for a moment. Fin warmed to his theme.

"They must have found the same photograph as us."

"Can we be sure of that?"

"They arrived with a forensic team: they would have been blind and stupid not to have found the photograph." Maudy arched an eyebrow as if to suggest that the Metropolitan Police could indeed be that stupid but she relented and conceded the point.

"If they know who she is, and it is reasonable to assume that they do, then they know they have to find her."

"But how does that help us?"

"Thomas thinks that the officer who was leading the team that came to the flat was the same one he followed back to Scotland Yard earlier. Thomas says his face is engrained in his memory."
Maudy thought for a moment.

"I like the irony, I mean of us spying on them, following them. But how? There's CCTV everywhere."

"Sure, but Victoria embankment is a bun fight. Every journalist and television crew in London is there. We can hide in plain sight."

"What will you do if they lead you to her?"

"We will have to intervene, in a meaningful way. The most meaningful way, if necessary."

"And are you prepared for that Fin?"
There was a thoughtful silence as both reflected on Fin's commitment. Maudy had known Fin for many years. He was an intellectual, an historian, a chronicler of the republican cause. There was no doubt about his political conviction, but his preparedness to act, this cast him in a new light. Fin leant forward.

"There's nothing but our own red blood

Can make a right Rose Tree."

He sat back, Yeats with his Maud.

"My mother used to read that to me when I was a little girl" Maud said. They lapsed into meaningful silence before Fin changed the mood.

"What?"

"We could try the woman at the embassy in Marylebone."

"How could she help?"

"I am sure she was lying to us."

"Why would she do that?"

"Put us off the scent. She was desperate to convince us that Mary's disappearance had nothing to do with the security services. But I think she may know who has Mary and where she might be."

"She said she didn't know."

"She was too sure. There are ties that bind: she was doing what she was asked to do."

"By whom?"

"That we don't know. And they don't want us to know."

Maudy thought about it for a moment. Fin could be right and there was nothing to lose by putting pressure on Elmira.

"Leave her to me" said Maudy. "Tell me where to find her."

Fin thought about it for a minute. Not for the first time in their lives, Maudy had taken him by surprise. But the more he thought about it, the more the idea made sense. Elmira would not suspect Maudy.

"Are you sure?"

"How will I know her?"

"You will know her when you see her" he said, texting Maudy the address of the embassy.

"I see" said Maudy, "she is like that is she?" The glimmer of a knowing smile formed at the side of her mouth. She suppressed the evidence by polishing off her latte. Fin stood to leave.

"Keep in touch, every hour: use your Nokia."
Maudy nodded, followed Fin out of the café, and turned away to the left without a word or even a glance.

Chapter 39

Paul reached the Assistant Commissioner's office just as the door opened to allow the room to exhale a draft of warm, fetid air. Behind it a wave of junior ministers and senior civil servants brushed past, making for the lifts. Paul waited impatiently for Rob, who took a while to gather his papers.

"Rob, come and look at this."

Paul half-jogged over the hallway to summon the lift.

"More haste, less speed."

"What's the difference between haste and speed?" asked Paul slowing to Rob's pace.

"I don't know. The deputy headmistress at my primary school used to say it every time she caught a pupil running in the corridor. I think it is a proverb. Way too subtle for seven-year-olds. But it has stuck with me."

In Paul's office Louise was hovering over her desk, waiting for his return. As soon as she saw that Paul had brought Rob with him, Louise launched into an excited explanation of how she had created the two similar images which were now on her screen. Rob took in the images and understood their significance.

"Your doppelganger theory was right then?"

"Show Rob where the second image comes from Louise."

Louise clicked away until her screen was filled by the photograph of the young communicant in front of the church, an image which until a couple of hours ago, nestled contentedly inside the pages of the "The Castles of County Clare" on Lorraine's bookcase.

"I used some software to age her image to roughly the same age as Lorraine." Rob turned to Paul.

"That's Saint Mary's, Feakle."

"It is."

Rob was piecing together the events of the last twenty-four hours.

"Where did you find the photograph?"

"In Lorraine's flat. Inside a book on her bookshelves. A book about County Clare."

"Anything else?"

"There were some novels, all about young girls growing up in Ireland." It only took a fraction of a second for Rob to make the connection that Paul had already made.

"Do you think this is the young Lorraine?"

"It looks very like her; look at the line of the jaw and the eyes."

"Have you ruled out every other possibility?"

"The photograph is dated 1976. First Communion is usually taken at seven, so the girl depicted here was born in 1969. She would have been five in 1974."

"But there would have been any number of girls from the surrounding villages taking their first communion? And they might have looked similar: perhaps there were cousins, sisters even. Are you sure this is the young Lorraine?"

"There is no other plausible explanation. The photograph was in Lorraine's flat amongst books about growing up in Ireland. This is a picture of her as a young girl." Rob looked at the two images on the screen again.

"I am sure that they are images of the same person" insisted Paul, slightly irritated that Rob was taking so long to be convinced. Having peered at the screen for another full minute Rob curled himself upright. He was crestfallen.

"Bugger. We missed it. The old man told us she was sent away to school in Dublin and was never heard of again. We thought she might be in America. But she came to England with a new identity. Mary Maloney became Lorraine."

"How do you know she is called Mary?"
Having taken so long to come alongside Paul, Rob now seemed to have gone a step ahead.

"It is pretty much the most common girls name in Ireland. It is the name of the saint to whom the local church is dedicated: it is plausible that her baptismal name, and her saint's name are one and the same. Often is the case."

"That's a bit of as leap of faith, isn't it?" said Paul.

"Well, if it is, you cannot deny me points one and two, and two out of three ain't bad." Paul wondered if Rob was deliberately quoting Meatloaf. If he was, Paul had to make a further adjustment to his understanding of him.

"Fifty pounds says I am right" challenged Rob. Paul declined the bet: Rob was right too often for him to take the risk.

"It will take only a few seconds to find out sir" offered Louise, who had already typed 'The General Register Office of Ireland' into Google.

"The Irish government archives births, marriages, and deaths by parish. So, if we look up the records for the parish of Feakle for 1969 we should find the registration of the birth of a daughter to Mr. and Mrs. Maloney. Assuming she was born in the parish."

A few keystrokes later and the entry appeared on Louise's screen. The entry was a digital photocopy of the original record written in the careful longhand of the authorized officer. Louise read out the details.

"Sixteenth February 1969. Female. Mary. Name and dwelling place of father: Patrick Maloney, Feakle. Name and surname and maiden name of mother: Ellen Maloney, formerly Hayes." All three stood in silence.

Good job I didn't take the bet, thought Paul. Rob was not about to gloat. Something bothered him.

"Paul, where exactly did you find the photograph?"

"It was in the pages of a coffee table book called "The Castles of County Clare" which was lying across the top of the bookshelves."

"It wasn't in a photo album?"

"No. It was on its own."

"And it was easy to find?"

"I suppose so. Quite easy." Rob studied Paul's face to see if there was a moment of recognition.

"Someone wanted you to find it."

Paul shuddered slightly. It was nearly three in the morning and he had been up for twenty-four hours. But his shiver was caused neither by exhaustion nor a sudden chill.

"Come with me." He led Paul across the narrow corridor to his office where he picked up his cooling coffee and took a cautious draft.

"Tepid" he said, "but still good. Whoever took Lorraine from Baker Street station has been watching our every move. He, or she, or they, led us to the photograph just as surely as they led us to Hounslow and to Stevenage. It was planted there for you to find, just like the white envelopes. They want us to know who Lorraine really is. We should have worked it out when we were in Feakle. It is why we were there. And we missed it. Or rather I missed it.

"I missed it too" said Paul as if trying to console Rob.

"But I should have known. I should have thought about what the old man told us. Should have asked more questions. We gave up too easily. And it all makes perfect sense now. If Lorraine is Mary Maloney, we need to find her."

"Someone has beaten us to that Rob."

"Yes, but whoever that is, they clearly want to lead us to her. And we must be led."

"Why?"

"We have no choice. We cannot play any other move. White is offering us his queen." Rob gestured to Paul to sit down and make himself comfortable.

"Chess is a logical game. The opening moves determine those that follow. Lorraine Watson was snatched from Baker Street station. Why?"

"Because she is Mary Maloney?"

"Because somebody knows she is Mary Maloney. Exactly. But whoever took her sent us a message from Stevenage station designed to let us know that she was in safe hands. Out of danger. He was also at pains to make sure that we understood who she was. It has taken us longer than it should have done, which meant that he had to make some obvious moves. Hence the photograph."

"The photograph."

"The photograph, which brings the white queen out into the open. He is offering her to us."

"But why did he abduct her in the first place?"

"He must think that she is in danger."

"You mean someone else knows who she is?"

"Or was close to finding out, yes. Which is why we have to go after her."

"Before anyone else finds her?"

"The existence of Mary Maloney represents a threat to everyone who has conspired to maintain silence on the events of 1974/5."

"Makes me nervous" said Paul. Rob nodded; despite his apparent sangfroid, he too was anxious.

"It could go horribly wrong."

"It could."

"So, what do we do now?"

"We wait. It is white's move. He will show us where the white queen is."

"Surely there is something we can do?"

"Look around Paul. The whole building is in disarray. No one knows what to do. The Counter terrorism team were completely taken by surprise by this morning's bomb. The whole department has spent five years looking for threats from the east, or more specifically the middle east. All their resources were focused on the threat of Jihad. Now they are desperately ringing around trying to re-hire IRA specialists, nearly all of whom retired some years ago. All we can do is wait for white's next move. He will place the queen where we can secure her. But in the mean-time there is something that you could usefully do. Bring us some fresh coffees."

Anthony was breakfasting early, on banana, coconut, almond and flaxseed cake. His mother insisted that "Food is our doctor" and always encouraged him to eat healthily. Anthony and his sister were brought up on a nourishing diet of pumpkin stews and kidney bean loaves, sweet potatoes, kale, spinach and peppers. These dishes she liberally spiced with nutmeg and lemongrass. No processed foods were tolerated in his mother's kitchen. Anthony loved his mother's cooking but did not know that it was what is now known as a vegan diet. In fact, he had not come across the word until he went up to St Mary's, Cambridge to read Social and Political Science. He was one of only a handful of black British students at Cambridge at that time. That did not especially concern him as he knew that he would be in a tiny minority and he was not daunted by it. He knew he was there on merit. Cambridge surprised him: it had numerous wholefood shops, particularly in the streets beyond the university cricket ground. Venturing across Parker's Piece was like passing through the back of the wardrobe to Narnia: on the other side, down Mill Road, lay another Cambridge. He found this alternative Cambridge by accident. One Friday evening Anthony set off to find a pub that he had been told was well known for its reggae nights. His informant, a postgraduate who had rooms somewhere near the railway station, did not know the exact location but said that he could hear the music on a clear evening, so it must be in one of the streets nearby. Cycling along Mill Road, Anthony found himself lured by the distinctive thumping bass to a pub called the 'Midland Tavern'. It was home to Cambridge's Caribbean diaspora and to Anthony it felt like a home from home. He quickly discovered that the landlord had come over from Jamaica at around the same time as his mother: they had much in common. Anthony made his way there every Friday night. As he picked up the last crumbs of his morning cake with a moist finger, he remembered the smell of the freshly baked, dense loaves in 'Arjuna', the yellow fronted wholefood store just past Fenner's, the university cricket ground.

In front of him on the table was the white envelope that was, as DCI or Dr Rob Martin anticipated, white's next move. Anthony dressed himself against the steely cold, before-dawn air and set out. His route took him past a brightly lit St. Thomas' Hospital and then across the Thames. Although it was only five o'clock, London was wide awake: buses, taxis and delivery vans jostled for position in the road. Lycra-clad cyclists with Go-Pros sticking up from their helmets like a child's drawing of an alien, swore angrily at every hindrance to their urgent progress. Anthony moved effortlessly along the empty pavements. The vehicles snarled and coughed their way across London. As Anthony approached Victoria Embankment, he could see the halogen lights of the many satellite television stations whose crews were mounting an all-night vigil outside New Scotland Yard.

He made his way through the throng of people milling around behind the yellow and black tape that was meant to mark the boundary line for the press corps. It fluttered and twisted pointlessly in the wind as the anarchic journalists crossed and recrossed it to thrust phones into the chests of anyone who looked vaguely official coming out of the foyer. Anthony made his way past one of those retro-designed mobile coffee carts apparently modelled upon Chico and Harpo's peanut dispenser; it was doing a much better trade than the hapless brothers. Anthony slipped between the knee-high bollards alongside the caravan of Transits, each bearing the logo of the media outlet which broadcast from within its cramped space. He passed through the atrium's outer door unhindered and approached the security guard. Anthony tapped the courier style satchel at his hip.

The security guard buzzed him through without a word and Anthony made his way to the reception desk. As he walked, he extracted the large envelope from its folder. At the counter he placed it on the desk as casually as a departing hotel guest returns a room-key he no longer needs. He caught the receptionist's eye to make sure she had seen his deposit; she nodded her acknowledgement. Anthony returned by way of the same security guard who had already lifted the barrier in anticipation of his exit, and regained the fresh night air. Endgame, he thought.

Chapter 40

Grantchester slept under a thick blanket of winter morning. The darkness was enfolding and voluptuous like the embrace of a fur coat. A hedgehog breathed noisily in the undergrowth. The murmur of running water carried across the meadows. Cold air dampened the grass. Tom sat at Professor Needham's kitchen table. He was freshly showered and shaved. An aluminium stove-top coffee maker whooshed like a small geyser as the hot water percolated upwards. A pan of milk hissed to the boil. Tom leapt up and caught the foaming milk as it rose, lifted it away from the heat and allowed it to settle. He poured out the contents of the Bialetti then skimmed the froth from the milk so that it floated on top to make a perfect macchiato. His phone shivered briefly. Tom did not really need to look at it: he knew it would be a text from Anthony confirming the delivery of the envelope, but he checked anyway. Tom smiled and took a sip of his macchiato.

As of this morning Lorraine Watson would no longer exist. There was no time to mourn her passing and Mary was not much inclined to do so in any case as she had become bored being Lorraine. Lorraine was always aware of Mary, of the girl she once was and the woman she might have been, had she not become Lorraine. She was fully aware of her dual personality. Could she untangle that which was Lorraine and that which was Mary? Maybe she could to go back to Ireland, immerse herself in her past, to create a present for Mary. Perhaps that would allow the suppressed memories to come back? Give me the child until he is seven. If the Jesuits were right, then Mary at fifty, now, here in Grantchester, would be the same essential person as Mary was at seven. Reconnecting with her would not be so difficult. But being Mary is problematic for she is burdened with original sin, having eaten the fruit of the forbidden tree of knowledge. Mary reflected that her uncle had been right: it was easier living as Lorraine than as Mary. Lorraine was a blank slate. Her uncle had understood that what Mary knew would affect the rest of her life. Lorraine would help her forget. But now Mary wanted to remember.

As the first glimmerings of light appeared around the edges of the curtains Mary showered and dressed. She went down to the kitchen where she was relieved to find Tom already up.

"Coffee?"

"Yes please."

"Tom, you never did tell me your real name." She wondered if he too had an alter ego and wanted to know how he lived as two people.

"It isn't important."

"No perhaps not."

"It is possible that Tom is my real name." Tom busied himself with the coffee and invited Mary to sit down. Mary's mind was full of thoughts about being Mary. 'Pray for us sinners now' she thought, as she sat down at the kitchen table.

"It is quite a burden to be named after the Mother of God. Girls called Mary are meant to be good girls. Exemplary mothers. Full of grace. Blessed among women. That sort of thing. No one expects anything much of a Lorraine. It was far easier being Lorraine."

"Mary?"

She drank carefully from her cup before asking the question that was really on her mind. She looked up at Tom imploringly.

"Is there any way out of all this Tom?"

"There may be. We need to go now."

Rob sipped at his tepid coffee. The shrill phone disturbed him.

"There's an envelope for you here sir."

"Thanks very much. I'll be right down." White's next move, he thought. He stood at the door of Paul's office from where he could see that Paul was asleep in his chair. His head had fallen back over the headrest, arching his neck, and his mouth was wide open. He looked uncomfortable, but Rob decided not to wake him and to go and retrieve the envelope by himself. He ran through the possibilities as he made his way to the desk. When the receptionist placed the envelope in his hand, he felt that he was back at school and that the envelope contained his A level results. He was impatient to open it but that would be unfair on Paul. They were in this together. Rosencrantz and Guildenstern, Vladimir and Estragon. The waiting was over. The envelope would reveal their fate. By the time he reached his office, Paul was sitting in his usual seat at Rob's desk, rubbing the back of his neck with his hand, clearly regretting having fallen asleep at his desk. Rob showed the envelope to him. It was marked, as before, in the familiar italic script "For the Attention of Dr. Robert Martin. Metropolitan Police. Unsolved Historic Crimes Division."

"White's next move then."

"Do you remember A level results day Paul?"

"Sadly, only too vividly." Paul was still massaging the numbness from his neck.

"Do you remember how you felt?"

"Yes. I was nervous because I knew that the next thirty seconds would affect the rest of my life."

"But it wasn't the thirty seconds that it took to open the envelope that affected the rest of our lives: it was the two years that preceded it. The envelope's contents simply confirmed what we already knew. The letters printed alongside the names of the subjects we had taken were the ones we knew would be there."

"That's because you knew that you would have a clean sweep of A grades. For some of us there were still an element of doubt, of either/or."

In fact, Paul got the grades his teachers and parents had been expecting. ABB was enough to secure a place at King's College, London. At eighteen his main aim had been to study somewhere in London. He didn't mind where, so long as he could go to all of the venues where stand-up comedy was performed. For Paul, King's College was perfect and in his first year he had rooms in Southwark. He cris-crossed London as many as four nights a week. In his three undergraduate years he had seen them all: he had seen those who were already famous, those who later became famous and those upon whom Dame Fortune did not smile, whose names were never heard again. He had even seen "Guns n' Moses," the Jewish parody heavy metal band, whose lead singer Dave Cohen famously announced that comedy was the new rock n' roll. When he graduated, Paul applied to join the Metropolitan Police because it was one of the only jobs that guaranteed that he could continue to live and work in central London.

"So, this envelope will tell us nothing that we don't already know?"

"Or suspect, yes."

"Will it tell us where to find the white queen?" asked Paul.

"Unless we are hopelessly wrong and have misunderstood."

Rob picked up the envelope and reached for his letter opener. He withdrew the single white sheet of A4. This time there was no code, no sequence of letters and numbers. Instead, there was a single phrase, a quotation, of what seemed to be an incomplete line of poetry. It read,

"The day was breaking……with a kind of valediction"

Underneath was written, in the same italic script, the single word, "Litotes."

"Blimey" said Paul. "Is that what you were expecting?"

"Not exactly."

"Bit underwhelming, isn't it?"

"It does indeed announce itself as an understatement. That's what litotes means. The opposite of hyperbole."

Paul was in fact, familiar with both terms. He had read enough about how comedic effects work on the audience to have come across the terms many times. Exaggeration and understatement.

"But how on earth does that tell us the location of the white queen?"

"I am not exactly sure. But I am sure it does tell us. Or it will. We just need to decipher it."

Paul's neck was painfully stiff. "Is it another riddle?"

"Could well be. It is in inverted commas so it almost certainly a quotation, probably a literary quotation. Perhaps the missing words are the words we need. Does that make sense Paul?" Rob was conscious that he was extemporizing.

"We need to identify the author."

"Most quotations are accompanied by the name of the author, aren't they?"

"Not necessarily. Many famous quotations are anonymous. And many are from the Bible and from Shakespeare." Rob read it out again. "Doesn't sound like the Bible. And it isn't in pentameter, so perhaps we can rule out Shakespeare."

"Why do you think it says 'Litotes' after the quotation?"

"Because the phrase is a kind of….."

"But, isn't it in the place where the name of the author would normally be?" interrupted Paul. Doctor Watson had asked the simple question and, in that moment, Holmes had made a deduction.

"How could I be so stupid?"

Paul was lost.

"I should have spotted it straight away."

"What?" Paul didn't have to affect Watson's plainness: he was miles behind Rob.

'Understated, confused author, seven letters.'

"I am lost" Paul confessed.

"The clue is, 'Understated, confused author, seven letters.'"

"I am still lost. Saying it again doesn't help."
Rob couldn't think what else to do so he said it again, slowly, to see if that helped Paul.

"Understated, confused author, seven letters."

"Litotes?"

"Yes. But the confused bit in the clue means that the letters are mixed up. In other words, it is an anagram of litotes, the word for an understatement."

"Litotes is an anagram?" Paul was catching up slowly.

"Yes. Of TS Eliot. The line must be from TS Eliot. Tom Eliot to his friends."

Paul sat up and immediately regretted moving so quickly. But he knew he had heard that name somewhere before. And not in the context of English poetry. He crossed the corridor.

"Louise. Louise. Wake up." Sergeant Tindall lifted her head from her desk and patted the loose strands of her hair back into their rightful place.

"Can you find me Nixon's report on his trip to the garage in Hounslow?"

"Yes, yes." Louise quickly came to her senses.

"Nixon is thorough with paperwork so it should be on the system already." Paul hovered impatiently over her shoulder as she searched for the document.

"Here it is." Paul's eyes devoured it hungrily, scanning down the page until he hit upon the name.

"There it is. I knew it. Tom Eliot." As he ran out of the room he called back to Louise.

"Thanks Louise."

She waved her left hand vaguely in his direction and then reached into the drawer of her desk for her compact. Paul steadied himself in front of Rob.

"Tom Eliot was the name used by the person at the garage in Hounslow. The man who bought two Hondas. I knew I recognized the name."

"Then it is definitely him. Our correspondent. And he shares his name with one of the greatest writers of the twentieth century." Rob read the note again.

"The Day was breaking…with a kind of valediction."

"Where would Eliot use a word like valediction? The act of bidding farewell."

Paul could not contribute anything useful: his knowledge of Eliot was confined to "Cats." Rob scanned the shelves behind him and lifted down the slim light blue volume of a Faber paperback and began reading.

"What are you reading?"

'The Four Quartets.'

"Isn't that a very long poem?" asked Paul worried that he might be left standing there for some time.

"Not compared to 'Paradise Lost'. And in any case, it will be from somewhere near the end."

"How do you know that?"

"Eschatology. The doctrine of the last things. The act of bidding farewell."

Beyond me, thought Paul, who wondered whether he should leave and come back when Rob had finished reading the poems.

"We are approaching the end."

"Like the endgame in a game of chess?"

"Yes. Let's hope it's not a sham sacrifice."

"What?"

"Never mind." He continued reading quietly until he reached the lines he was looking for. Rob read aloud.

"In the uncertain hour before the morning…"

"That's the title of an episode of 'Vikings'" said Paul excitedly. "I watched it the other night. Season Four."

"Is it? I suspect the writer was quoting from TS Eliot. It's from 'Little Gidding', the last of the 'Four Quartets'. It's about the doctrine of last things."

"That makes sense" enthused Paul. "The 'Vikings' episode is all about the last days of Ragnar. And how Ragnar might die."

Rob looked down and began reading again.

"In the uncertain hour before the morning
Near the ending of interminable night"

Paul was thinking about Ragnar and Ecbert in their prison cell, as Rob read on quietly to himself.

"Here we are. Listen to this" He read carefully, clearly.

"The day was breaking. In the disfigured street
He left me, with a kind of valediction
And faded on the blowing of the horn."

So, the missing words are "in the disfigured street he left me."

That's it. That's where we will find the white queen. That is where he, Tom Eliot, will leave Mary Maloney. In the disfigured street."

"But where on earth is 'the disfigured street'?" Paul had no idea.

"I think I may know" said Rob.

Chapter 41

At first light, Maudy made her way to Crawford Street. She placed herself at a table near the window of a Café on Baker Street. From here she would be able to see Elmira making her way to or from the Embassy. It was a crisp, clear morning and the windows had misted up. From time to time, Maudy wiped away the condensation to create a porthole to spy on the passers-by. She had no idea what Elmira looked like: all she had to go on was Fin's assurance that she would know Elmira as soon as she set eyes on her. She could only really see legs and feet from where she was sitting but she thought Elmira's would be distinctive enough. She was on the lookout for something unusual but, so far, the morning commuters formed a procession of unremarkable trainers, sensibly flat-heeled slip-ons, brogues and loafers. But then, as distinct as the sudden fire of a diving kingfisher, a burst of scarlet caught her eye. It came from a pair of Christian Laboutin Pigalle patent leather pumps with red lacquered soles. Maudy guessed that this was what Fin meant and that these shoes belonged to Elmira. She finished her latte, wiped the foamy residue from her upper lip and left the café. She followed Elmira at a discrete distance, and called Fin.

"I think I have found Elmira."

"I knew you would."

"It was the shoes."

"Ah. Where are you?"

"Baker Street. I think she is heading for the Embassy."

"Can you follow her?"

"I am following her. Where are you, Fin?"

"On Victoria Embankment."

"Anything going on?"

"Not yet. It's busy though. People everywhere. Mostly media."

"Ok. Let me know if anything happens."

Maudy rang off. Fin had inveigled himself into the crowds of journalists and television crews standing around flapping their arms and transferring their weight from foot to foot like so many penguins. Their warm breath swirled and hovered above the huddle, lifting and dying on the occasional breeze. Fin's experienced eyes simultaneously scanned the faces in the foreground and surveyed the middle distance. Thomas was positioned to the left with a clear view of the atrium. His hands were thrust deep into his pockets: in his right pocket he felt the reassuring presence of the handgun which he had remembered to remove from the glovebox of the faithful old Peugeot before handing it over to be crushed. On the other side of the road, under the shadow of a tall tree, Anthony had a clear view of both men.

Having gathered up their few possessions, Tom led Mary through an arched door in Professor Needham's walled garden. Despite having spent much of the previous day idly contemplating the garden she had not seen the oak door which was partly obscured by a rambling rose. The door gave onto a narrow path wide enough only for single file. Mary assumed Tom would turn either left or right onto the path which was overcanopied with tightly knit branches from the trees rising steeply above. To her surprise Tom stepped straight across the path to another half hidden arched doorway. Following Tom, Mary expected to find herself in another walled garden, perhaps belonging to a neighbour, but instead found herself inside a draughty barn. It was as dark as the grave but she detected a faint smell of petrol and leather. Tom switched on the dim light, a single forlorn low wattage bulb hanging at the end of a string limply descending from the central rafter. In the grey faint, light she could make out the shape of two cars. The one on the left, and from which the heady leathery, petrol odour emanated, was covered over with blankets. Next to it was a plain red Volkswagen Polo.

"What's under there Tom?"

"A 1967 Bristol 409. British Racing Green. It used to live in the Fellows car park at the back of St Mary's but these days Doc Needham only uses it for his annual burble down to the vineyards of Bordeaux. But he has very kindly given us the use of Kitty."

"Kitty?"

"Yes. All cars have names. Like boats."

"Why Kitty?"

"As in Kitty Pakenham, better known as the Duchess of Wellington. The Bristol is called Arthur. As in Arthur Wellesley, Duke of Wellington. Appropriate names don't you think?"

Tom had moved nimbly around to the driver's side of Kitty and beckoned Mary to get in. No sooner had she climbed in than the automated garage door began to furl upwards revealing the dreary mist of early morning.

"Am I allowed to ask where we are going Tom?"

"We have a rendezvous with a colleague of mine."

"A colleague?"

"Yes."

Mary looked a little anxious.

"Don't worry, you will like her."

Mary thought that she might very well like her, especially if she was a trusted friend of Tom's, but she could not conceal her sense of disappointment that this prosaic journey in a simple red Polo would be their last ride together, that this would signal the end. She knew that at some point they would have to part. She knew that she could not keep Tom for herself. But the notion of being joined by another person felt like an intrusion into their intimacy. It was like the end of an affair.

Tom sensed from her silence that Mary's mind had wandered. He remembered thinking as he left Marylebone station just dawns ago, that he would have to keep so much from Mary. There was so much that he could not tell her. But as they set out on this last journey, he wanted to be able to tell her more. Talk of a 'colleague' seemed churlish and impersonal. He had grown to admire Mary. He liked her. He knew all about Mary before he met her, but he had not glimpsed into her soul until yesterday. He was moved by what he saw there. He wished he could tell Mary more, but his priority was to deliver her into safe hands. And the less she knew, the less could go wrong. He felt a pang of guilty conscience about the way he had treated her. He told himself it was impossible for it to be any other way, but he felt for her. He had been impressed by how long she had lived as Lorraine, living a life that was not really hers. How she had kept Mary at bay. He wanted to treat her as a friend, but he knew he could not.

Tom accepted Mary's protestation of innocence; she had been undone by unhappy accident, the accident of walking into a pub in Kilburn on the same evening that Sinn Fein and the IRA's Active Service Units were gathered there. She had gone in search of herself, of her past, prompted by a yearning for the life that had been taken from her. That was understandable. And he believed her when she said that in doing so, she had no idea that she was risking discovery. And in walking into that pub, on that day and at that moment, time past in Feakle and time present in Kilburn, coalesced and were simultaneously present. The girl and the woman stood together. Mary's uncle had sensed the danger that this might happen and had taken steps to prevent it; but one evening in Kilburn, Mary's past caught up with her. As a girl, she had overhead voices in the darkness, and her memory was her tragic flaw. Time future was contained in time past: that night in Kilburn was contained in the night in Smyth's hotel. The two unhappy accidents of her life were dependent upon one another. Time past and time future pointed to one end. She had carried the burden without complaint; Tom felt that she was aptly named: Mary was blessed among women.

Staring out of her window, Mary saw the flatlands of South Cambridgeshire stretching away on either side: in the semi darkness it was difficult to distinguish the earth from the sky. They passed a sign for Stansted Airport confirming Mary's suspicion that they were heading south on the M11.

Maudy was transfixed by the alternating scarlet flashes of Elmira's shoes. She was like a driver on a country lane hypnotically following the brake lights of the car in front. The shoes were her sole focus, she joked to herself. She disapproved thoroughly: what could be more decadent, more redolent of capitalist excess, than purposelessly showy shoes? Maudy looked down at her own footwear, Goldstar sneakers, calling card of the Maoist guerilla. As she burnished the halo of her own righteousness, she saw that Elmira had made her way into the Embassy building. Maudy decided that she would wait for half an hour and if Elmira did not reappear, she would have to assume it was just a regular day at the office and Fin was wrong about her. She waited for about twenty minutes and was about to conclude that Fin was indeed wrong about Elmira, when a hooded figure emerged from the doorway. This figure was wearing training shoes and leggings but was the same shape and profile as the figure who had entered earlier. It had to be her. This dressed down version of

Elmira looked as if she meant business, and Maudy struggled to keep up with her.

Chapter 42

In a briefing room high above the Thames, the Assistant Commissioner was listening attentively to the various situation updates. A dozen or so senior officers were gathered in a tight huddle: in years gone by the room would have been all male and shrouded in cigarette smoke. Today bottles of water replaced ash trays on the tables and a strong female presence bore witness to the march of history. In the clean, clear air colleagues listened respectfully. The truth was plainly spoken. The explosion was the work of a highly skilled team with expertise in explosives. The existence of an IRA cell in London had taken them all by surprise although Mi5 had been monitoring "persons of interest" in the Kilburn area. These included Maud Byrne, who was the source of a steady stream of strident Republican views posted on social media. But Mi5 concluded that there was nothing of immediate concern in her activities. The Head of Counter Terrorism reported that his team would be able to establish the nature and type of the bomb used, the provenance of the van and other key details from the scene, but he agreed with the Assistant Commissioner's observation that they were many, many steps away from identifying any suspects. This was DCI Martin's cue and he raised his finger to the Assistant Commissioner to indicate that he would like to speak next.

"Yes, Rob. You have the floor."

Paul could not quite get used to this brave new world of distributed leadership and shared responsibility. He was used to hierarchy, to chains of command and he was not convinced that the new world was an improvement on the old one. Still, in the old world he and Rob would not have been given houseroom let alone a place at the top table.

"We may know more than we think" began Rob.
The room was expectant and attentive. The Assistant Commissioner leant forward in anticipation of hearing something thought provoking and interesting. Others followed suit. Rob glanced across at Paul who nodded his approval.

"Let's start with what Donald Rumsfeld called the 'known knowns.' We know that the explosion was targeted at the heart of the judicial system. In fact, it was even more specific than that: it was targeted at the chambers of Lord Justice Lloyd, who has been tasked with carrying out the review of the Guildford pub bombings. We also know that there were no casualties."

The senior officer in charge at the scene confirmed with a nod that these were indeed the known knowns. Rob sipped from his Styrofoam cup of almost cold coffee.

"Therefore, we can conclude that we are dealing with a group able to strike at the heart of one of the most secure cities in the world. They could, had they so wished, have injured, maimed, and possibly even killed dozens. But they did not. Why?"

"Because it wasn't their aim" answered the Head of Counter Terrorism. "In recent years we have become accustomed to the methodology of the Jihadi whose main aim is to bring death to the infidel and create martyrs of the faithful. But we must think differently about Republicanism: its ends are always political, whatever its means."

"Exactly" continued Rob, who wondered if the Head of Counter Terrorism had memorized these platitudes from some sort of Police issue "Beginner's Guide to Terrorism."

"The purpose of the explosion was indeed purely political. It was no accident that there were no casualties. The aim was not to create mayhem but to send a warning to the British government."

"About the upcoming judicial review? "asked the Deputy Assistant Commissioner.

"Yes."

"Why?"

"Because the review was originally given quite clear parameters: it was to be a "ways and means" review of how the bombings came about and an examination of the responses of the emergency services. But then the representatives of the victims campaigned for a widening of the remit to include an attempt to identify those responsible. And no one in government or in the republican movement wants that."

"Hence the bomb" said the Assistant Commissioner decisively. "Let me see if the Commissioner is free. She is dealing with the media, but I think she needs to hear this, especially if I think I know where you are heading with this Rob."

There was a comfort break as the Assistant Commissioner went to see if he could pull rank on the media team who were controlling the Commissioner's time. In the lull, some drank from their water bottles. A couple of others stretched their legs and looked out across the grey expanse of the sluggish Thames below. The Assistant Commissioner returned triumphant.

"She will be here instantly." The Commissioner was indeed almost immediately present and a chair was provided for her to join the throng.

"I understand the gist of the argument so far Rob, so please feel free to continue without the need to recap" she said settling into her seat. Paul marveled. Here was a room full of the most senior policemen and women in England. They spoke to one another with polite respect, with interest in what each other had to say, and using their first names.

"It is completely understandable that the victims' families and the survivors want the outcome to be cathartic, and only the naming of those they consider no better than murderers can assuage them. But the political reality is that nobody in government on either side can allow the investigation to take that revelatory turn."

"If both sides know that neither side can afford for the truth to come out, why the bomb?"

"The explosion was, from the point of view of the IRA, logical and necessary" explained Rob calmly. People stirred nervously in their seats and looked at one another. Concerned looks were exchanged as if to acknowledge that the water was now becoming very murky. Rob allowed the room to recover its composure.

"Surely you don't mean to suggest that the bomb was somehow justifiable?"

"No of course I don't mean to imply that, but I do mean to imply that from their point of view it was timely, to remind the British government of its obligations under the terms of the 'Good Friday Agreement'. From their standpoint, and in the absence of any clear statement to the contrary, it looked as if the Inquiry was about to break faith with historic agreements."

"It would have been better if the PM had not agreed to the review in the first place" remarked an agitated Head of Counter Terrorism.

"Politically impossible, as well you know" purred the Commissioner.

"It creates many more problems than it solves though" continued the Head of Counter Terrorism.

"We are where we are." She invited Rob to continue with a raised eyebrow and a half smile.

"Thank you, ma'am. There is a further complication with respect to the Inquiry."

"What sort of complication?"

"It's a long story ma'am. But if you are prepared to hear it, it will help everyone understand."

"OK. Let's hear it."

"Four days ago, there was a fire on the forecourt of Marylebone station." There were audible sighs and expressions of disappointment around the table. Faces were creased into perplexity.

"I think you might be trying our collective patience Rob" warned the Head of Counter Terrorism.

"Bear with me. It matters."

"This had better be good" rumbled the Head of Counter Terrorism.

"A fire?" The Commissioner calmed everyone's nerves by showing her commitment to Rob's unpromising beginning.

"Yes. It was not a particularly serious fire, although it was fuelled by kerosene and burnt very hot and very fast." Looks around the table suggested that minds were yet to be convinced.

"But the point of the fire was not the fire itself. It was designed to cause a distraction. As Marylebone station was closed, passengers on the incoming Bakerloo line trains had to exit at other stations."

"No shit Sherlock" whispered the Senior Officer. Paul smiled, knowing that his Sherlock was only just beginning to unveil his powers of deduction.

"The significance will become clear in the next few minutes. It was DCI Wilson who brought it to my attention so I will hand over to him to continue the story." All eyes turned to Paul who had not been expecting to be thrust into the spotlight like this.

"Yes, yes" he stumbled.

He sat up like a naughty schoolboy who has just been reprimanded for not paying attention and like that same schoolboy his concentration smartened instantly.

"Shortly after the closure of Marylebone station we received a call from Paddington Green station to say that they had taken a call from the Nightingale hospital. One of their most experienced nurses, had not arrived for work."

The Head of Counter Terrorism threw his pencil down onto the table in disgust and looked for confirmation of his disgust in the faces of his colleagues. "What's this got to do with anything?"

"Now, now" warned the Commissioner. "Carry on, please."

"Her name was Lorraine Watson. She was habitually punctual and rarely missed a day, so the Nightingale were concerned and asked us to categorize her as a missing person. We discovered that she had used her Oyster card at the barrier at Elephant and Castle at about 7.20 am to go onto the Bakerloo line heading for Marylebone, as she did every morning. But she never arrived. She disappeared: there was no mobile phone trace, no digital imprint of any kind. CCTV images showed that she was last seen exiting Baker Street station at 8.05."

"And?" The Commissioner was enjoying the story now.

"No trace of her at all. But we did find images of the arsonist. He might as well have been waving and smiling for the cameras as if he wanted to be seen but he was clever enough to conceal his face. He was riding a Honda motorcycle which he then abandoned in a carpark. Wiped clean of course. Professional job. And that was what got us thinking."

"Did you trace it?"

"To a garage in Hounslow. Insurance write-off. But the garage had an address for the purchaser, a Mr. Eliot, who had also purchased a car, a Honda Jazz. We traced him to an address in the Earlsfield Road area of Merton.

Nothing. An unoccupied flat. Not even so much as a fridge. Completely empty. Except that on the kitchen table there was an envelope addressed to Dr. Robert Martin, Historic Unsolved Crimes Division."

There was an audible sharp intake of breath around the room, followed by an uneasy silence. The Commissioner broke the silence with the obvious question,

"What was in the envelope?"

"A seven-digit code. Just that. Nothing else. We still had nothing on Lorraine Watson. The usual methods had drawn a blank. But then one of my team, who had been trawling meticulously through hundreds of CCTV images found the Honda Jazz parked on Cosway Street, between Baker Street and Marylebone, earlier in the morning."

"I really don't see the significance of this" piped up one of two Commanders around the table.

"Nor did we at first" replied Paul slightly altering the truth to flatter his superior. "But then we worked out that the owner of the Honda Grom motorcycle, who set the fire at Marylebone, was also the owner of the Honda Jazz and might have also been responsible for the disappearance of Lorraine Watson from Baker Street. The Honda was last seen heading into Stevenage, entering a multi-storey car park, where it had been abandoned. The car was empty apart from an envelope on the front passenger seat."

"Addressed to Rob?" asked the Commissioner

"Addressed exactly as before and containing another seven-digit code. The Honda was set ablaze and destroyed."

"I still don't see how and why this is relevant" harrumphed the Head of Counter Terrorism.

At this point Rob decided it would be prudent for him to take back the narrative. He thought that Paul might be going into too much detail, but on the other hand this was a room full of people schooled in procedure and some seemed to be hanging on every detail. The Commissioner indicated that Rob should continue.

"We were faced with two problems. Firstly, we had to crack the codes and secondly, we had to work out why Lorraine Watson had been snatched from Baker Street station by the person who had given us the codes. As the Commissioner knows, I had been tasked by the Home and Foreign Secretaries to undertake a review of the classified material held by the security services dating from 1974 and 1975. In one note, written by an Mi6 officer, I found an identically set out seven-digit code. It was the grid reference for Feakle, where talks took place in December 1974. I mapped the other codes as grid references: they were the birthplaces of two of the Balcombe Street gang. Feakle was the birthplace of a third member."

A heavy silence descended on the room.

"The Balcombe Street Gang were members of an IRA cell who carried out a series of atrocities on the mainland. They were tried and given multiple life sentences. They were released under the terms of 'The Good Friday Agreement'" explained the Commissioner.

"Quite so, Ma'am."

There were exchanges of knowing looks around the table as the truth settled like dust. Even the sceptics and the doubting Thomas's around the table were compelled by Rob's narrative now.

"Go on, please."

"A third envelope, addressed exactly as before, arrived here at Reception. Again, it contained a single seven-digit code, the birthplace of the fourth member of the gang. But what is really disturbing about all this is that the three envelopes with the grid references for Kilkee, Limerick and Carrigart only made a sequence because I already had, on my desk, in highly classified papers, the grid reference for Feakle. Someone knew that I already had one of the clues."

"That is sinister" agreed the Commissioner.

"But who could possibly have known that?" asked a Commander.

"Who indeed. Someone who had taken Lorraine and who knew that Lorraine was something to do with all this."

"And has she something to do with all this?" asked the Deputy Commissioner

"Most assuredly, yes. And it makes things even more complicated."

"Everything you have said so far Rob was leading me to that conclusion" sighed the Commissioner.

"We discovered that Lorraine Watson is an assumed identity. She was born Mary Maloney. And she, Mary, is the key to all of this."

"But who on earth is Mary Maloney?" This was the Commander again, who was nothing if not obtuse, so much so that Paul had never understood how he had risen to such a high position. Due deference to one's superiors and a blemish free tenure of some mundane administrative roles could all too easily smooth the way to the top, he thought.

"Mary Maloney is the daughter of the landlord of Smyth's hotel in Feakle. She was sent away to a boarding school in Dublin and then spirited away to a new life in England where she has lived and worked in London ever since."

"Why was she sent to England?"

"Mary was at home in the hotel on the night of December 12th 1974. Although she was only five, she may be the only surviving witness who can identify who was present at that meeting, including the IRA members who made their escape before the Gardai arrived. When

Mary's mother died, her uncle paid for her school fees in Dublin and then arranged for her removal to England, so he clearly thought she was at risk."

The Commissioner understood the significance of this brief account of Mary's life straight away. "Do you think the IRA know who she is? I mean do you think they know that she has been living in London?"

"That, Ma'am, is what Rumsfeld would call a known unknown. That is, we know that we don't know the answer."

"Worst case scenario?"

"Worst case is that they do know and that they are after her. And because of what she may know, they will need to guarantee her silence."

If they had not done so before, everyone around the table now grasped the significance of Rob's story, long and complicated though it was.

"Realistically, what are the chances of her being able to name names? After all, you said she was only five, and it is over forty-five years ago?" asked the Head of Counter Terrorism.

"Many of those present were regulars in Smyth's. She would have seen them, and heard their voices, often."

"Why else was she abducted?" asked Paul of the room "The assumption must be that she could name names."

"Bloody hell." The Commissioner was not usually given to swearing but she could see that they were caught between a rock and a hard place. "In which case we have to find her. Any ideas anyone?" asked the Commissioner.

"I have an idea. The person who has taken her, as I have explained, has been sending us a series of cryptic messages. If I have understood his latest communication correctly I think I know where we might find her." All eyes turned to Rob.

"Where?"

"In Marylebone."

"How long have we got?"

"Hours. But no more than that."

"Do you think the IRA know too?"

"We should act as if they do."

"Right, we need to seal off the entire area around Marylebone" said the Assistant Commissioner decisively.

"I am not so sure" cautioned Rob.

"It is standard procedure in a case like this. Hermetically seal off the area and put marksmen on the rooftops."

"But as Rumsfeld pointed out, it is the things that we don't know, and the things that we don't yet know that we don't know, which define the nature of risk. And there are too many things we don't know."

"If we don't know them, we can't do anything about them, can we?" said an irritated Assistant Commissioner.

"No, but we do need to proceed with caution. A full-on siege might lead the IRA straight to her. We have to assume that they are watching our every move."

"Rob's right" confirmed The Commissioner. "Ok. Let's take a break, digest all that Rob has told us, and reconvene in thirty minutes. I want everyone to come back with a plan."

Chapter 43

Elmira walked briskly. In Wyndham Place she passed the Gothic Revivalist church of St Mary's. Elmira thought it looked absurd, like a rocket sitting on top of a wedding cake, but she always looked up at it largely because it reminded her of the steepling minarets of the Bishkek Central Mosque. Maudy scurried along some hundred yards or so behind. She was relieved when Elmira headed up Harewood Avenue because it was a straight road and she could hang back without losing sight of her prey; in the smudgy Turneresque light of winter dawn, Maudy thought that if Elmira turned around, she would see only indistinct shadows. Maudy's gaze was fixed on Elmira's back; she did not notice the raised paving stone which tripped her. She stumbled briefly. In the few seconds that it took her to regain her composure she had lost sight of Elmira. Panicked, Maudy ran until, slightly out of breath, she reached Melcombe Place; she was relieved to catch a glimpse of the hooded figure making for Marylebone Underground station. Good, she thought, slowing to a walk. Only one line; north or south, a binary choice. But still a gamble. She gambled on south as there were more stations that way. To catch up with Elmira she had to risk running down the long, steep escalator. As she edged her way onto the Southbound platform, she saw Elmira stepping into the red, grey, and blue liveried carriage of the Bakerloo line train. Maudy launched herself through the closing doors. She realized that she was several carriages away from Elmira and could not see her; she decided she would have to step off the train at every station and scan the platform to check whether Elmira had alighted. She looked up at the linear map and counted eight stops to

Elephant and Castle. Shouldn't be too difficult she thought. Maudy refined the manoeuvre at each station. At Piccadilly Circus she leaned out of the open door and saw Elmira step onto the platform. She did likewise. Elmira lingered briefly at the entrance of the tunnel that led away from the platform, where she pretended to listen to a cross legged saxophonist playing "Smooth Operator." Elmira tossed a coin into his open case. When she heard the robotic voice announce "doors closing," she raced back to the train and leapt in, narrowly avoiding being wedged between the closing doors, whose stiff rubber flanges brushed uncomfortably against her back. Maudy was left standing on the platform scanning the thinning crowds. She decided that Elmira must have headed down the tunnel that led to the Piccadilly line. By the time Maudy reached the tunnel, Elmira was almost at Charing Cross. Maudy had lost her. She took the escalator to the exit. She tried to call Fin but there was no signal. She exited the station into the gaudy neon carnival of Piccadilly Circus and tried again.

"Fin, I lost her, At Piccadilly Circus. One minute she was there on the platform, the next, vanished."

Fin was not surprised; he suspected Elmira was capable of anything.

"Never mind. It was a longshot in any case."

"What shall I do now?"

"Head back to Kilburn and make sure that everything is ready."

"What are you doing?"

"Still outside Scotland Yard. Watching."

"Ok. Speak later."

Fin was right: Elmira was too experienced for Maudy to have had a chance. In fact, Elmira sensed Maudy's presence behind her as soon as she left the café. She knew that she had been followed from the embassy and knew how to lose her. It was easier than she thought it would be. Elmira concluded that Maudy was an amateur and nothing to worry about. Now freed from the need to be as vigilant, Elmira calmly changed onto the Circle and District Line at Embankment, and headed east.

"Tom?"

Tom didn't reply but inclined his head slightly as if to grant Mary permission to speak.

"What's her name?"

"Who?"

"Your colleague. The one we are on our way to meet."

"Her name is Elmira."

"Not English then?"

"What?"

"I mean she's not English. Not with a name like Elmira."

"It comes from Arabic" said Tom indirectly answering the question. "It means princess or aristocratic lady, noblewoman."

"And is she?"

"What?"

"Either Arabic or a princess?"

Tom laughed. "I don't think that she is either."

"But you said that I would like her."

"Yes." Tom glanced at his phone which was rather precariously wedged into a cup holder.

"Where are we now?"

"We are in Essex. Chigwell is on our left."

"Chigwell? As in Windy Miller?"

"That was 'Camberwick Green'. And you are thinking of Chigley, not Chigwell."

"Oh yes."

There was a pause. Tom started to laugh.

"Don't laugh at me Tom. I mean Chigwell, Chigley. An easy mistake."

"I wasn't laughing at you. I was running through Captain Flack's roll call of the Trumpton Fire Brigade. You know, Pugh, Pugh, Barney McGrew, Cuthbert, Dibble and Grubb. Did you know that Brian Cant had trials with Ipswich Town?"

"Tom, how on earth do you know so much?"

"I don't know that much. I'm just curious."

"Well, I am quite curious too. Right now I am curious about where we are going and what is going to happen when we get there. Tea with Elmira?"

Tom felt considerable sympathy for Mary and immediately forgave her slightly peevish tone.

"No, I doubt that there will be time for such niceties."

"And who is Elmira anyway?"

"A colleague."

"You said that before. And I understood." Mary was almost becoming feisty now, but Tom understood her frustration and simply said,

"A colleague and a good friend."

Mary smiled. "Tell me more. How good a friend?"

"You'll see."

"Where are we meeting?"

"In the City of London. The square mile. The land of the giants, the Gherkin, the Walkie-Talkie, and the Cheesegrater. Among other things."

"More sights to see than in Stevenage then?"

"Did you not enjoy our daytrip to Stevenage?"

"I have to say I preferred Cambridge."

"Me too."

They were less than thirty minutes from their destination; shortly after that, he would be handing Mary over to Elmira and in all probability, he would never see her again. He would have liked to have said more, much more, but he left it.

Thomas was on the move, phone pressed to his ear.

"Fin"

"Yes"

"What are the chances of them idly walking out through the front entrance?"

"Why, what are you thinking?"

"That they will take an armed convoy out of the back, into Parliament Street. It won't be a covert operation. Not after Lincoln's Inn. They know that was us. They will be tooled up. They will be expecting us. It will be marksmen on every rooftop, unmarked cars in every street."

Fin thought. "I am not so sure Thomas. They won't want to attract attention."

"None the less I think one of us should go around the side and keep a watch on the back."

Fin saw no harm in having Thomas positioned round the side.

"Ok. Go now. Joe and Conor are waiting in the car in Vauxhall. Call them in as soon as you need them. I am going to stay here. Make your way to the Red Lion."

"Ok, Fin."

At that very moment, in a briefing room above, Rob was, in fact, counselling caution. Had the Commissioner not been persuaded by Rob's argument that the IRA would be watching them closely and that they must not give Mary's whereabouts away, then Thomas would have been right, for the Head of Counter Terrorism was all for going to Marylebone fully "tooled up" as Thomas put it. The Commissioner was considering all possible options, with the Home Secretary listening in on speakerphone. The Commissioner asked the Home Secretary for his view.

"I am very much of the view that we politicians are best advised to leave it to the professionals. Take whatever course of action you deem fit and I will support you."

Those in the room were flattered by this vote of confidence in their abilities but the Commissioner was still a bit taken aback when the line clicked dead and the Home Secretary left the call. The Head of Counter Intelligence spoke next.

"I agree with Rob, Ma'am. We have a chance here to recover the target and at the same time flush out the enemy. They will be watching out for us and will disappear at the first sign of an ambush. We have to tread lightly."

After twenty minutes further deliberation an operational plan was agreed. The Commissioner put her Assistant Commissioner, Specialist Operations, in overall command, but detailed DCIs Martin and Wilson to take charge of the Marylebone rendezvous. She wished everyone good luck and returned to the task of preparing another deliberately bland media briefing.

Tom and Mary continued their journey in awkward silence for a while until Mary pushed a button on the radio and filled the Polo with the rise and fall of the opening of a Brahms' Symphony

"Professor Needham is something of an authority on late Brahms" Tom explained, unnecessarily.

"Well, I didn't think he would be a fan of Radio 2" Mary replied tartly, reminding herself that Zoe Ball's voice was the last thing that she heard before she left her flat four mornings ago. It was less than a week but it seemed a lifetime ago. In a way, it was a lifetime ago, she thought, Lorraine's life. And it was Lorraine's flat, not hers, and Lorraine didn't exist anymore, so it didn't really matter if she never saw the inside again. But equally she knew that she could not return to County Clare. Mary was at the mercy of whoever it was Tom was taking her to. Her life was in the hands of others, as it had been ever since her uncle sent her away to school in Dublin. He knew that her life had changed forever, but Mary had not realized the full ramifications until, when she finished school, her uncle sent her to England. And now her destiny was about to be reshaped for a second time. She had no choice but to accept her fate. 'Be it unto me according to thy word' she thought. It is the burden of being Mary.

Tom turned off the South Circular and negotiated the gradually thickening traffic through Barking before parking in the station car park.

"Here we are."

"Here?"

"Yes here."

"Barking?"

"Briefly, yes. We have a train to catch. Come on." Mary collected herself. "So, this was how it ends, not with a bang but a whimper."

"It hasn't ended Mary."

"Where are we going now?"

"Not far." He led her to platform five, where a train was waiting.

"Eighteen minutes to Fenchurch Street" said Tom cheerily.

It was still early enough for the train to have some standing room. Tom and Mary wedged themselves into the available space between the pin stripes and colourful ties of the office bound brokers, dealers and fund managers travelling in from Leigh-on-sea and Shoeburyness.

At Fenchurch Street Tom ushered Mary slowly through the ticket barriers so that the closed-circuit television had a clear view of Mary's face. He knew that in the immediate aftermath of the blast, every camera on every major route in and out of the capital was being carefully monitored and he needed the black knights to know the white queen's next move. He trusted that Mary's image would be picked out immediately and her arrival in Marylebone calculated to within a matter of minutes. At the exit onto Fenchurch Place, he led her to Hart Street and stopped abruptly at the jail-like wrought iron gateway of St Olave's church.

"Look there Mary."

Tom was pointing at the skull and crossbones carved in its tympanum. "Dickens called it 'Saint Ghastly Grim.'"

"I'm not surprised" said Mary.

"It's one of the few medieval churches that survived the Great Fire."

They entered under the gateway.

"Who was Saint Olave?"

"King of Norway. Eleventh Century. Helped Ethelred the Unready defeat the Danes."

"Was he canonized for that?"

"Maybe. But he is also thought to have Christianised Norway. The main cathedral in Oslo is named after him."

"Why are we here Tom?"

"Come on. You will find out inside."

Why here? What was it about this church? wondered Mary.

"Although the interior of the church had to be rebuilt in the 1950s, it retains the intimacy of a medieval space" explained Tom walking slowly down the nave.

"I didn't know you moonlighted as a tour guide Tom." Mary was still tart. It was the fear of the unknown. Tom was scanning the aisles.

"Looking for something?"

"Over here." Tom was pointing at the bust of a round faced woman in a headdress with curls hanging either side of a long slender neck.

"She was only twenty-nine."

"Who was she?"

"Elizabeth Pepys. Wife of Samuel. He is here too. Well at least he is buried here. There was a monument to him, which he designed himself, but it's lost. Instead, he got that slightly insignificant nineteenth century bust up there." As they stared up at Mrs. Pepys, they felt the presence of a third walking beside them.

"You were here all along?"

"Yes. I was down in the crypt."

"Mary, this is Elmira. Elmira, this is Mary."

"Of course." Mary instinctively reached out to take Elmira's hand, transfixed by her dark eyes.

"Mary, Elmira will look after you from here."
He leaned towards Elmira and bestowed the softest of kisses on each cheek. Elmira closed her eyes and breathed in deeply. Their fingers interlocked briefly. Tom departed without another word. Mary had never seen such a clear complexion as Elmira's. Each kiss left the impression of a poinsettia leaf on Elmira's cheeks, mimicking the contours of Tom's lips. There was so much Mary wanted to ask her.

"Come" said Elmira, taking Mary by the elbow. "We have to go." When they stepped into the daylight Tom was nowhere to be seen.

Chapter 44

Since he was the one who found the CCTV images of Mary previously, Nick Booth had been tasked with searching for her again. Nick had enlisted half a dozen colleagues and they were huddled together in the control room whose screens flickered with grainy images of London. Some of them stared at images from Heathrow and Gatwick; others squinted at images from the arterial roads. Nick had given himself the task of looking at images from main railway stations. Because he thought that lightning may very well strike twice, he selected Marylebone station. Then he decided to look at images from the other three stations on a Monopoly board for no other reason than that.

"Why not?" remarked Paul when Nick ran the idea past him. In fact, Paul thought it was a cleverer idea than Nick could possibly know. After all they were being led by someone who played games with them: maybe he was as keen on Monopoly as chess. Suddenly Paul was aware of Nick's frame in the doorway of his office.

"I've found her."

"Already?"

"Fenchurch Street Station. About half an hour ago." Paul pushed himself back in his chair and ran after Nick. There was no doubt. It was her. Paul leapt across the corridor into Rob's room.

"Mary is at Fenchurch Street station. Or at least she was about half an hour ago."

"Then we have less than an hour. This is the endgame, Paul. When white surrenders her queen."

Within seconds the corridors, lifts, the atrium and car park were a blur of activity. The assembled media crews sensed a step change and moved forward: some of the more brazen journalists stepped over the tape that was meant to hold them back. Fin moved forward with them but stopped at the tape: he could not afford to be visible. Anthony, whose eyes were fixed on Fin, felt his phone vibrate. Once he was sure that Fin was essentially trapped, at least for a few seconds, he took out his phone and looked at the screen. It was a text from Tom.

'ETA Marylebone one hour.'

That would explain the heightened activity, thought Anthony. He decided to leave Fin to his fate and made sure that he could still see Thomas, who had taken up the perfect surveillance position near the 'Red Lion'. Two unmarked cars appeared: the first, driven by Sergeant Nixon, carried Rob and Paul. Positioned as Thomas was, he had a good view of the passengers. He recognized Wilson.

"Conor?"

"Yes."

"They are on the move."

Conor threw the phone onto Joe's lap and pressed his right foot as hard as he could into the fraying carpet. The Vectra howled: Joe clung to his seat. Conor had been driving around on the south side of the river and was just passing the Park Plaza when Thomas called. He was across Westminster Bridge in seconds. Thomas ran down from the Red Lion and leapt into the back of the Vectra.

"Which way?"

"Victoria Street."

Thomas reached for his phone again.

"Fin"

"Yeah"

"We are tailing them. Victoria Street. I will let you know where they are heading."

As Fin pocketed his phone, he could see the Commissioner and her entourage coming out to address the assembled media. The journalist and film crews surged forward, thrusting their microphones, like so many lollipops, towards her. Fin was just about able to carve a passage through the crowd, back onto Victoria embankment. As he did so, he caught sight of the convoy of half a dozen unmarked Range Rovers.

Elmira and Mary were now only a short distance away. At Embankment they changed onto the Bakerloo line, having made the short journey from Tower Hill. They were invisible to the madding crowds. Elmira had her hoodie pulled forward and Mary's features were concealed by a generous scarf and a pair of sunglasses, which Elmira had provided for the purpose. They sat together, their knees and thighs touching. Mary wanted to be close to Elmira.

"Why did Tom hand me over to you in that church? I mean, why there of all places?" She spoke softly.

"It's a Pepys thing," replied Elmira with a smile.

"Pepys?"

"Yes."

"Why?"

"It is to do with the circumstances of our first meeting."

"What there in that church?"

"No. We first met on the lawn in front of the Pepys Library."

Mary thought carefully about her next question. She wasn't sure what to say, so simply said,

"Were you at St Mary's College too?"

"I studied Persian."

Mary thought it made perfect sense. Tom and Elmira were as beautiful as each other. Mary was satisfied and left it at that.

Thomas called Fin again.

"Park Lane, heading for Marble Arch."

"On my way." Fin flagged down a black cab.

"Marble Arch please."

Anthony flagged down the next available black cab.

"Dorset Square Gardens, please."

Once clear of Oxford Street the two unmarked police cars had a clear run up Portman Street and across Marylebone Road.

"You never did say where, exactly, in Marylebone, the white queen will be."

Rob looked at Paul.

"Remember the line from 'Little Gidding'? 'In the disfigured street he left me'"

"Yes. The Four Quartets."

"We received four clues, a quartet of clues."

"And?"

"Each clue was the birthplace of the four men who were arrested following the siege at 22b Balcombe Street. Balcombe Street is the disfigured street: their figures were removed from there; in that sense Balcombe Street was dis-figured."

Brilliant, muttered Paul sotto voce, and then aloud,

"The white queen will be in Balcombe Street then. But where?"

"I am not completely sure but it will be as near as possible to 22b."

With perfect timing Nixon turned left into Balcombe Street and as Rob had requested brought the car to rest in a parking bay just beyond the pub. The second unmarked car drifted quietly to rest a hundred yards behind them. In the Vectra, Conor had just turned left into Balcombe Street from Taunton Place. He could see the two unmarked cars a couple of hundred yards ahead and was nervous about getting any closer.

"You know where this is, don't you?" asked Conor.

"I do. How could I not know?"

"I don't like it" said Joe.

"Lightning doesn't strike twice" said Thomas confidently.

"No?" Joe was worried that it might very well do precisely that.

"Why here then, Thomas?

"I don't know do I?" he replied petulantly.

"It could be a trap". Conor switched the engine off.

"Any movement in the cars up ahead?"

Conor took the binoculars from the glove compartment and trained his view straight down Balcombe Street. The morning had broken free of the early dense mist which had shrouded Mary and Tom as they left Grantchester a couple of hours earlier; the sun had burned off the smudgy grey cloud in which Maudy first lost sight of Elmira, and its low heat had warmed the breath of the journalists stomping their cold feet outside Scotland Yard.

"No. They are sitting still."

In the roads around Marylebone station armed officers decanted silently from Range Rovers, moving stealthily into position. A couple of them, machine guns held diagonally across their chests, sauntered casually around the forecourt of the station where no-one batted an eyelid at their presence. Thomas called Fin.

"Balcombe Street, Fin, we are in Balcombe Street."

"What? Are you kidding?"

"I am not."

"Why there?"

"I don't know, but it is making me nervous."

"Can you see anything?"

"The police are parked further down the road, towards the station."

"Any sign of Mary?"

“No.”

“Well sit tight. I am on my way.” Fin leaned forward to give the driver new instructions.

“How long will it take?”

“Less than five mins guv. Straight up Gloucester Place.”

Chapter 45

In the strategy briefing in New Scotland Yard the Assistant Commissioner had instructed every member of the quickly convened 'Operation Mary' team to be on the lookout for a male and female travelling together. Pictures of Mary had been distributed to everyone, but as Tom had been so careful as to avoid every camera there was no image of him. But all units were on the lookout for Mary and a male companion. So it was that Elmira and Mary emerged from Marylebone station and were able to walk straight past the armed officers who did not give the two women walking arm in arm a second glance. They strolled leisurely and undetected past the police Range Rovers parked in Melcombe Place and Dorset Square. Two women, effectively invisible, at least until they reached Balcombe Street. Paul Wilson had studied Mary's face so carefully that, even though she was partially obscured by the headscarf and sunglasses, he recognized her immediately.

"Look. The two women coming towards us. I am sure that's Mary on the left." He reached forward for the radio. "All units. Target sighted in Balcombe Street. Standby." In the Vectra, Thomas was becoming agitated.

"Conor, you stay here. Joe, you come with me." Thomas reached into the hold-all shoved under his seat and took out two revolvers and two balaclavas.

"Here, pocket these." Thomas, who had a gun in one pocket, felt much more confident with one in each.

"Don't put the hood on until I say. And keep your gun hidden. Get out of the car and walk slowly down the road as if we were regular pedestrians. Conor, pick us up as soon as you see anything. OK?"

"What about Fin?" Conor was not used to talking orders from the younger man and he would have liked confirmation from Fin.

"There's no time: we can't wait for him."

Elmira and Mary crossed Balcombe Street right in front of Rob and Paul's car, to enter the 'Sir John Balcombe'. As soon as the narrow doors closed behind Elmira and Mary, Paul and Rob exchanged a knowing glance.

"Now?"

"Now" confirmed Rob.

"Keep the engine running Nixon" said Paul, half way out of the door.

As Rob and Paul entered the pub, they glimpsed a slight, agile, hooded figure slink through the side door, out onto Taunton Mews. They did not give chase: she did not matter; the white queen was here. Mary was preoccupied with taking off her coat, her sunglasses, and her scarf; she had not even noticed that Elmira had walked straight through the bar and out of the other door.

"Hello Mary. This is DCI Wilson and I am DCI Martin."

"Please. Rob and Paul," said Paul.

"Ah yes. Tom told me that you were the ones he had chosen to find me" smiled Mary.

In the street, Thomas and Joe quickened their pace. As soon as he saw Rob and Paul go into the pub, Thomas put two and two together.

"That's the pick-up. In the pub. Come on. Let's go." Joe and Thomas pulled their balaclavas down to their necks and ran. They would have to try and snatch Mary as she left the pub and bundle her into the car. Through the binoculars Conor had seen Thomas and Joe putting on their balaclavas and recognized his cue for action. He reached for his balaclava, a rugged dark green one with black eyeholes. He made sure it was on firmly, then launched the squealing Vectra down Balcombe Street.

As the three figures stepped onto the pavement from the Sir John Balcombe, Joe launched himself at Paul, rugby tackling him to the ground. Paul crumpled easily, having no time to brace himself. The force of Joe's lunge caused Mary to come loose. Rob instinctively retreated through the door of the pub and hid as best he could. Joe held Paul down, his forearm across Paul's windpipe making it hard for him to breathe. Thomas grabbed Mary and held her in front of him, with one arm across her neck. He surveyed the scene. He saw two officers with their semi-automatic weapons aimed directly at him, one at his head, one at his heart. To his right, two Range rovers had moved to seal off the road. Thomas did the only thing he could do in the circumstances: he produced the revolver from his pocket and held it to Mary's temple.

"Lightning does strike twice" he whispered.
For a few moments nothing and no-one moved, as if they had all stepped outside time. The stillness was broken by the screeching of the Vectra's brakes as Conor pulled up alongside the pub and threw open the front passenger door. The marksmen held fire.

"I thought we were in trouble for a moment there", said Joe, leaving a rasping Paul and opening the back door.

As Joe bent down to climb into the Vectra, Nixon revved his engine to the red limiter, slipped the clutch, and reversed as fast as the laws of physics would allow. He slammed into the Vectra with such force that the suspension crumpled and the car dropped to its haunches with a sigh. The radiator spewed hot water. The engine raced and then died. Conor was shaken. He tried to open the driver's door but it was jammed. The last thing he saw was a dark shape at his window: there was a single muffled shot and from the pavement it looked as if someone inside the car had thrown a pot of red ink against the passenger window. Joe had been jolted backwards with such force that he had broken his standing leg; like a wounded stag, his cries were also ended with a single shot.

Thomas found himself alone. He held Mary hostage but he had nowhere to go. There was no way out. He calculated his chances at nil. He had always been prepared to die for the cause. He moved the gun backwards from Mary's temple to his own. He was not going to be taken alive. A single shot rang out. As Thomas slumped to the ground, Mary found herself standing alone and free. Rob pushed open the door of the pub until it jammed against Thomas' stricken frame. He squeezed through the gap. Paul was brushing the grit and dirt off his bleeding knees.

Rob held a visibly shaking Mary. Incapable of any other reaction Mary merely lowered her head into Rob's chest. The only faint sound was the barely detectable regular drip, drip, drip of liberated engine oil.

After what seemed several minutes, Rob walked Mary slowly to one of the waiting Range Rovers. It's dark, womb-like interior comforted Mary who sat between Rob and Paul. All she could think was that she wished Tom were here beside her. Rob gave the signal to the driver and they sped away down Gloucester Place. They passed a black cab parked on the corner of Dorset Square. Once she was sure they had gone, Elmira came out from the shadows and climbed in next to the waiting Anthony who nodded to the driver to go. The cab pulled away. It was an unremarkable enough scene, or so the driver thought, as he took the measure of the pair in his rearview mirror. Probably sweethearts, he thought, as

Elmira placed her hand on Anthony's. On Melcombe Street, another black cab slowed to a crawl. Its passenger glanced up Balcombe Street where he saw the reflections of a myriad of blue lights pulsing in every window. Fin leant forward again.

"Change of plan. Take me to Kilburn High Road." Without a word, the driver turned left back onto Marylebone Road. Fin looked around and saw through the rear window that the police were sealing off Dorset Square with tape and cones.

Chapter 46

Four days later, Rob Martin stood in front of Number 11, Millbank. He craned his neck so that he could take in Jagger's statues of Britannia and St George flanking the neoclassical arch, overlooking Lambeth Bridge. These Portland stone figures were not familiar to him but he did not think that they bore comparison with Jaggers' Unknown Soldier on platform one of Paddington station. They seemed to resist interpretation, their symbolism recondite and their appearance austere. And they were quite difficult to see properly, even though they had been recently restored. Rob lowered his head and climbed the shallow steps: the left hand of three double doors opened from the inside at his approach. He took the stiff white card from his breast pocket and showed it to the guard.

"This way please sir."

The guard accompanied him to the lifts that accessed the South Block, on the right-hand side of the vestibule.

"Seventh floor sir" he said holding the lift door open for Rob.

"Thank you."

The card was something of a mystery. It had arrived on his desk yesterday morning. The envelope was addressed to Dr. R Martin. The card inside simply read:

Dear Robert,

Please be so good as to come to number 11, Millbank, tomorrow morning at eleven am.

From the Office of the Home Secretary.

Rob naturally assumed the meeting would be a debriefing following Mary Maloney's safe recovery. He had not mentioned it to Paul and as Paul had said nothing to him Rob understood that he was here alone. The lift doors opened and he found himself in a narrow corridor. There was a window to the left offering a view of the tops of trees and sky from which Rob deduced that they were at the top of the building. He turned right and found to his slight surprise that there were only two doors and one of those was clearly a cloakroom; he knocked gently at the other. The sign over the doorway read "The Cammaerts Room" A kindly looking civil servant opened the door.

"Ah. Mr. Martin. How kind of you to come. Would you mind waiting here a moment?"

Rob was clearly in some sort of ante room because there was a further door in front of them and the room that they were in was too small for a meeting. The civil servant pointed him towards the three comfortable looking armchairs. On the low table between them were today's newspapers.

"Do help yourself to tea or coffee. My name is Charles by the way."

"Thank you very much, Charles."

Rob poured himself some coffee and sat down in one of the armchairs. By the time he did so, Charles had disappeared, presumably through the door to a much larger room. Rob felt as nervous as he had done when he sat outside Dr Reynolds' rooms at St Mary's, waiting to be interviewed. He wondered if he might be subject to a similar cross examination today. He picked up 'The Guardian' and lost himself in a story about water companies discharging raw sewage into rivers. Rob found himself agreeing with the comments of an indignant Feargal Sharkey about the derisory nature of the fines meted out to the deliberate polluters, when Charles reappeared at the door.

"Do come in."

Rob struggled to fold the large pages of 'The Guardian' and nearly spilt his coffee as he banged his knee on the table as he stood up. Charles hesitated and smiled, as if to give Rob a few moments to compose himself.

"No rush."

Rob welcomed the opportunity to compose himself. He took three or four breaths, checked the knot of his tie was exactly in the middle of his collar, smoothed his hair with the flat of his hand and then nodded his readiness to the patient Charles.

"All set?"

"Yes, I think so."

"Good. Come on."

Charles opened the simple oak door. Before Rob was a cherry wood Harvard conference table and ten chairs. Eight seats were already occupied: Charles took his seat, the ninth, and indicated to Rob to take the tenth. Rob recognized, to his right, the Chief of the Secret Intelligence service, the Director General of Mi5, the Chair of the Joint Intelligence Committee and the Cabinet Secretary. At the head of the table sat the Home Secretary. One of the four seats, next to the Home Secretary, was taken by Charles; he could not immediately place the other three people on his left. The Home Secretary stood.

"Ladies and Gentlemen. On behalf of his Majesty the King, the Prime Minister wishes to convey to all of you his sincere and heartfelt thanks on the successful completion of 'Operation Mary'. As you know, we launched the operation when it became clear to us that we needed to bring Mary in, for her own safety. We could have acted swiftly and decisively to do just that, but we took the decision to bring about her safe custody in a way that could also honeytrap an IRA cell that we knew to be active. It was a dangerous and risky strategy.

It went to the wire. But Mary is safe, three IRA men are dead, and we have prevented any further bomb attacks disrupting the work of the courts. Each of you played a vital role. Thank you."

The Home Secretary resumed his seat and after a short consultation with Charles he leaned forward, his arms outstretched, his hands clasped conspiratorially. He nodded in the direction of the Director General of Mi5 to indicate that it was his turn to speak. He too drew himself forward to speak, softly, quietly, carefully. He addressed himself directly to Rob who felt the eyes of the room upon him.

"DCI Martin. Robert. We have been following your career with great interest for some time now and we knew that you would be able to help us in the delicate matter of bringing Mary Maloney safely in. We knew you understood the burden of history and its relevance to the present. We knew you had the necessary skills and we had every confidence that you would be able to follow the trail that we set for you, the trail that would lead you to Mary. In the event, you did miss the opportunity to identify Mary conclusively when you were in Feakle."

Rob looked down at his hands, folded in his lap. He felt contrite. He knew he should have pressed the grieving widower for more information. He felt like a naughty schoolboy being reprimanded. The Director sensed Rob's discomfort.

"But that was a small matter and easily remedied within hours. Throughout you were in the hands of our very best covert operations team, who made sure that you recovered quickly from that mis-step. Your conduct in the Endgame was impressive. Well done. Now, let me introduce you to the team with whom you worked so effectively. Firstly, Elmira Kim."

Elmira stood and offered him her hand. Rob knew that he was looking into the eyes of the slender figure he saw leaving the 'Sir John Balcombe' by the side door, the woman who had brought Mary safely in. Later Rob would learn what Fin had suspected, that Elmira was also a double agent working undercover in the embassy of Kyrgyzstan.

"Next, this is Anthony Taylor."

Although Anthony was wearing his plaited hair in a tight bun, Rob recognized that this was the man he had seen when he reviewed the CCTV footage from the cameras in the atrium of New Scotland Yard. This was clearly and obviously the man who delivered the third white envelope to reception. This was the same man that Paul had fruitlessly cross-examined in Wooler Street, and the same man whom Sergeant Tindall had described to Paul in such warm, glowing terms. He could only guess at the full extent of Anthony's role, but he sensed that it might have been considerable; after all he lived next door to Lorraine for some time, presumably as her guardian angel. Rob was still enjoying Anthony's firm handshake when the Director General turned his attention to the third figure.

"And this is the team leader, Tom Eliot."

As Tom stood to greet him, Rob felt something of a shiver run down his spine. Just like Mary, he found Tom's smile compelling. It was the smile of eternal reassurance. As they shook hands Rob took in all that Tom represented to him. He was Jason Bourne to his Pam Landy. He was Godot to his Vladimir and Estragon, Hamlet to his Rozencrantz and Guildenstern, the ghost in his machine. Rob would find out in due course that Tom was Elmira's lover and Anthony's room-mate at St Mary's College. And Tom was, without irony, christened Thomas Eliot. Rob's mind raced as he took in the real presence of the man, the man with whom he had played chess. Introductions completed, all four resumed their seats. The Director General of Mi5 was not quite finished.

"As you can see Robert, we have a place for you around this table, should you wish to join us."

Rob knew what was being asked of him. He was being asked to join the SOE, the Special Operations Executive. Suppressing the lump in his throat, he stood and spoke clearly.

"For King and country."

"For King and country" replied the other nine.

"Excellent. Professor Needham will be absolutely delighted" said the Home Secretary, gathering his papers.

The Professor's name reverberated in Rob's mind, triggering echoes in his memory. Dr Needham and Dr Reynolds. Of course. He looked at the scene before him with renewed understanding.

It had been Professor Needham's idea to re-commission the Special Operations Executive, with much the same mandate as it had under Churchill, to conduct espionage, sabotage and reconnaissance, wherever necessary. Its members, chosen for selection by Professor Needham, were free from the usual chains of command in the security services: the SOE reported directly to the Home Secretary. Rob knew enough about the history of the SOE to know that its members were also known as the Baker Street Irregulars, named after Sherlock Holmes' street urchins, who go everywhere and hear everything. Now, he mused, Rob has become a Baker Street Irregular too. Baker Street. In our end is our beginning.